The River

Everything was slipping from his control. He didn't hear his son's voice until it was shouting in his ear, and still what he heard almost made no sense, although he'd been waiting for it all night. The hand gripped his shoulder, the voice was hysterical. 'Dad, it's going,' Lewis said.

Garvey looked up, and watched part of the bank collapse. It happened slowly at first, and then with increasing speed. First a ten-foot section of the levee's lip began to bulge, and then, in the centre, a spurt of water appeared and trickled down towards where the dozer was. The spurt grew, and as Garvey watched, the entire section gave way, and a small waterfall cascaded towards him. He was dumbstruck. At his side, his wife materialized, screaming. She thrust him forward, as if to wake him up.

'Tom! It's Beth, over there. Beth! Oh get her, get her.'

The River

STEVEN BAUER

Based on a screenstory by **ROBERT DILLON**

SPHERE BOOKS LIMITED
London and Sydney

First published in Great Britain by Sphere Books Ltd 1985
30–32 Gray's Inn Road, London WC1X 8JL

TRADE
MARK

Printed and bound in Great Britain by
Cox & Wyman Ltd, Reading

for my parents

Author's Note

I'd like to express my appreciation to a few people whose contribution was crucial to the completion of this novel.

First, my thanks to my neighbors Harold and Phyllis Sizelove, whose white barn and acres of rolling farmland I saw every day I worked on this book. I called on their expertise concerning farming and I appreciate their generosity. Next, I'd like to thank Mark Winegardner, who read the manuscript practically overnight, and whose careful reading and considered suggestions allowed for a touch more verisimilitude concerning regional slang and professional baseball allegiances. And an enormous debt of gratitude is due Melva Brown, whose patience and unstinting dedication to the preparation of the manuscript allowed the novel's completion.

Finally, I'd like to thank my wife, Elizabeth Arthur: "This, no tomorrow hath, nor yesterday/Running it never runs from us away,/But truly keeps his first, last, everlasting day."

PART ONE

· 1 ·

Tom Garvey lay as still as he could, trying to relax. *Breathe deep,* he thought. *Take a deep breath and hold it*. Mae had told him about this exercise after reading some magazine she'd picked up at the IGA in Millrock, and sometimes it worked, he didn't know why. But tonight it seemed to make him more tense, as though the extra oxygen pumping into his blood carried little messages which said, *Do something!* But there was nothing he could do.

He rolled over and sighed so deeply it sounded like a groan. With his back against the sleeping body of his wife, he tried counting bushels of corn, then remembering the names his daughter had given the recent brood of piglets, but he'd never been good with those fairy tales, and he got stumped after Sleepy and Grumpy. It made sense, of course, after she'd named the mother Snow White, to name the piglets after the dwarves, but damned if he could remember what the names were. And there had been a dozen piglets, so five of them had names faked to sound like the others. Teeny, for Christ's sake. Barney.

Breathe deep, he told himself, *concentrate on Mae's breathing, breathe along with her*. But there was that other sound, steady, insistent, louder than his wife, and try as he might, he couldn't shut it out. Faint as distant thunder, the rain continued.

It was no use. Garvey swung his legs over the bed's edge and tried to ease from between the sheets without disturbing

Mae. She stirred as the sheets rustled, turned toward the space where Tom had lain, and her arm fell gently, as if she'd wanted it there. Had he been in bed it would have fallen on his hip, a reassuring pressure.

He reached up and scratched his shoulder; his muscles ached from misuse. It had been three days now, the rain as constant as his breathing, the sky a sullen grey. This wasn't a storm; this was more like a flood. At least Noah's sons were full grown and had wives, and the whole family could work. The only help he had slept under this roof—Mae beside him, steady as a boulder in the middle of a river; his son Lewis, nearly twelve, becoming a man; and Beth, at six, asleep with her doll Ernie and her dreams of dwarves and piglets and horses.

He tried to remember what his own childhood had been like, but couldn't pin a single memory. No, his life had always been like this—thirty-six years old, married, the father of two children, deeply in debt, ready to farm another season, bushels of corn falling down the chute, and the money it brought him disappearing into the bank's coffers. Usually he didn't mind: it was the life he was born to, and, hell, he *loved* it—the rich smell of the earth as he worked it with the tractor and plow, the pounds of seed, bright as the sun on the lazy summer skin of the river.

Garvey stood, hitched up his boxer shorts, and shivered. It was much too cold for the beginning of May in Tennessee, and the dampness didn't help. He eased himself out of the bedroom, and down the hall. He opened Lewis's door a crack, and peeked in. His son lay on his back, his visible arm flung over his forehead hiding his eyes, and Tom heard the ruffle of his breath, a faint snore. Lewis was getting there, no doubt about it: soon he'd be full grown. But now—this year, the next—Tom would still have to do it pretty much alone.

In the kitchen he found the box of Ohio Blue Tips. The rough patch for striking had worn out long ago; Mae always emptied the new matches into the old box and gave Beth the bright sharp cardboard rectangles to play with. She built towns with them, coloring the sides with crayon stubs, making roofs of newspaper. Tom remembered when Lewis had played like that; in fact, he remembered when he himself had made a copy of the Farmer's Federal Loan and Trust for his own father, carefully drawing the bricks with a pencil and coloring each one that faded orange-red of a small town bank. He smiled wryly; now he understood that the last thing his father had needed was a reminder of the mortgage on these three hundred acres.

Tom struck a match on the porcelain of the gas stove and lit the old kerosene lamp. It stood squatly on the scrubbed oak table, a reminder of simpler times. Kerosene was cheaper than electricity. Besides, he had to admit he liked the light. When the overhead bulb was on, he could see the scratches in the cabinets, the black spots in the sink where the porcelain was worn through to the cast iron, the faded linoleum, so scuffed that both its black and white squares looked grey. In the suffused lamp glow, everything appeared softer, smoother, as though the rich light of minerals pressed for centuries cast Garvey back to a time when farming was the best thing you could do with your life, something everyone respected.

He took a loaf of bread and a big plastic tub of peanut butter from one of the cabinets. He opened the refrigerator door and blinked in the sudden burst of electricity. The shelves were pretty empty. Garvey took the sticky jar of grape jelly from the door and carried it to the table. Then he slathered one piece of bread with peanut butter, coated the other with jelly, and slapped them together, took a bite. At least there was fresh milk. He went back to the refrigerator, and standing in the electric glow, he grabbed the jar from the top shelf and took a big swallow. Ah, there it was: nobody but a farmer knew what it tasted like.

He put everything back and carried the knife and plate to the sink. On his way he stepped in the puddle, and his carefully cultivated mood vanished as though the water had been flung in his face. He reached to the right of the sink and touched the switch. The room sprung to shabby life, and in the glare of the overhead bulb Garvey found the trickle of water running across the floor, and traced it to the kitchen door.

The rain was coming from the west, a long sweeping easy rain. It pummeled the western slant of the roof, ran down the shingles, into the rusted gutters and troughs, overflowing the barrels at the house's four corners. It brimmed over the gutters and ran in sheets down the sides of the house, and now ran through the crack between door and sill Tom hadn't found time to fix. He ripped a hand towel from its bracket, threw it to the floor, and pushed it against the wall with his bare foot. Instantly it was soaked with more than it could hold.

Garvey went to the sink and stared out the window. Its eight panes were smeared with rain; the rectangle of light from the overhead bulb wavered on the rain-soaked ground outside. Straining against the darkness, Garvey tried to see beyond the old pickup standing in the driveway, to the road, and on its other side the rising slant of levee. No, it was all darkness. But he knew what lay beyond that. He listened for its quiet rustling, like the sound the wind made in November weaving like a drunkard through the corn stalks.

He couldn't hear it, not yet. But if this rain kept up, he knew he'd hear it. He knew it would be all he'd hear, waking or sleeping—the river rising, eating away the levee, the quiet authoritative voice of water moving skyward and south at once, pushing the land before it, threatening once again to overflow its banks and turn everything into a still vast lake. Garvey remembered his biology teacher in high school talking about how humans had all been fishes once, how they'd had fins and gills, and had crawled up onto land and lay in the sun. At times like this, he wondered if it had been worth it.

"Tom?" Mae's voice was quiet, tentative, but it startled him so deeply that he swung around, as though she'd caught him doing something shameful.

"God," he said. "You scared me."

She stood in the lightbulb's glare, shading her eyes with

her wrist, her blond hair and freckled skin shockingly washed out, as though all her blood had been drained. "What's the matter?" she said.

"I woke up," he said. "I was hungry. You're gonna have to feed me more at dinner time." He tried to lighten his tone, but Mae pursed her lips to let him know she wasn't fooled.

"You've got to get some sleep. How'll you feel in the morning?"

"Same as now," Tom said, and turned back to the window. "Waiting for this damn rain to stop."

"Honey, staying awake isn't going to make any difference to the weather. Honey?" He swiveled his head to her. She lowered her hand and tightened her cheap brown bathrobe around her throat. "Tom, it's freezing in here, and you're standing there almost naked. You'll catch a cold. Come back to bed now. Do I have to drag you?"

"You know you never have to do more than ask," he said.

She smiled at him suddenly, one of those dazzling smiles he'd first noticed when she walked the halls of Millrock High. "Now that's a lie, Tom Garvey, and you know it. You're stubborn as an elephant."

"I'm stubborn as the river," Tom said.

The grin left Mae's face. "Come back to bed. I don't want to hear any talk about that river."

"All right," Tom said. "But you and I both know ignoring it won't make it go away."

"Who said anything about making it go away? How many years have we been living here? You think I ever forget the shadow of that levee? But let me tell you one thing. Staring out the window never stopped a rainstorm or made a river go down since *I* was born."

"I guess you're right," Garvey said.

She moved to him and hugged him. He could feel her hands move up the knotted muscles of his back until she'd locked them behind his neck and pulled his face down toward her. For a moment, before they kissed, he caught a glimpse of her body in the breech of bathrobe, and he shivered. It *was* cold in the house.

Tom Garvey pulled away. "Okay," he said. "Let's go."

"I said *sleep*."

"I'll do my best," Tom said.

· 2 ·

Four days before, the weather had been glorious, cloudless. Spring had come to Tennessee early this year. The January freeze had been neither long nor deep, and the thaw was gradual. Mae's daffodils and hyacinths were blooming by the beginning of March. The spring rains had come widely spaced, and the ground held a tractor by early April.

Tom had plowed the previous fall, after harvest, so all he had to do was disk and spray to get the seedbed ready for the corn. For once, he had more time than he really needed and as he dragged the disk, he stared at the dogwood bursting on the surrounding hills. He and Lewis, with the six-row planter, got the crop in the ground by the twenty-second, and now the acres of bottom land were studded with thin green spikes. The lilacs Mae loved so much had already bloomed and gone. The river ran smoothly south to the sea. And then the sky clouded over and this rain began.

At first it was the gentle rain that Garvey loved, a quiet mossy rain, the air filled with a grey mist that seemed to soak into the earth. Everything took on an astonishing clarity, the blue paint of the pickup shining in the driveway like a sapphire, and the grass and new leaves a green so deep they reminded Garvey of pictures of Ireland. He took a walk by himself, and came in soaked to the skin and happy.

The third day his happiness turned to suspicion. When he awakened, the sky was darker, and he thought he saw thunderheads building in the west, behind the wind. In that light, everything lost its color, and the grass now looked bruised and muddy. Garvey stalked the levee and stood, staring at the steady pock-marked surface of the river. It still looked tractable, a brown moving highway which might take him where he wanted to go. But as he watched, a painted plank sailed by, giving an indication of the water's speed, and it sent his heart a chill. It seemed to him he could feel the raindrops growing larger, heavier, and the charm he'd felt two days before was gone. This was the grey of steel and lead, and he'd never been fond of metal. On the way back to the farmhouse, he couldn't help notice how the driveway now supported trickles of water, how the county road seemed a liquid sheet.

The trunks of the shagbark hickory grew darker, hunched into themselves, as though shrinking or warping. When he looked at the pickup, he could swear it had sunk partly into the ground. The yellow school bus brought Lewis and Beth home from school, and Lewis's worn corduroys, the clean white socks that Mae had sent Beth off to school in, were spattered with mud. Snow White lumbered in her pen. If Beth had had to name the pig then, she would have chosen something like Dirt Brown.

The pig trough was speckled with raindrops, the new furrows ran with rain in the greening fields, and a small stream dribbled over the lip of the rain barrel and down the sides. It rained all day and all night. By the morning of the fourth day, when Tom and Mae got up for the second time, the telephone began to ring with calls from neighbors—Sally Tessley spoke to Mae for close to half an hour, and from the tone of Mae's voice, Tom knew the other woman was crying.

Neither Beth nor Lewis wanted to go to school. With

Lewis, this wasn't unusual; he'd gotten terrific at faking deadly stomachaches which vanished with the velocity of the slowly accelerating school bus—he'd be like his father, Tom could tell, and he was partly proud to have a son who wanted to be a farmer, and partly itchy, uncomfortable, knowing the days of this kind of life were numbered. But Beth would kick and scream to go to school, even when she was sick. There was something about this sudden onslaught of rain, though, which made both the children quiet, sulky. Beth wanted to stay in her room with Ernie, and Lewis wanted to . . . *Let's get this straight,* Tom said. *You want to read a book?*

Now Tom sat hunched before the radio in the kitchen waiting for updates on the weather, while Mae walked restlessly from room to room, unsure what to do with herself. She splashed to the henhouse to gather eggs; the chickens were dumb enough to be unaffected by the weather, and the wire basket by the stove was piled high. The radio announcer's voice droned on into the afternoon. When Tom stood up from the chair and walked to the sink, the sky was darker, more black than grey, the clouds pressing down on the earth like a large hand. And at four o'clock, after fifteen minutes of the dullest country music he'd ever heard, the announcer came back on to say that tomorrow would be more of the same.

Tom slapped his knee so hard it stung; through the denim he could imagine the imprint of his hand. "Shit!" he said.

Mae was at the counter mixing milk and eggs together in a bowl, making a custard to keep busy. "Shh," she said. "The children are in the next room."

"I didn't say anything they haven't heard before," Tom said.

"I don't care," Mae said. "I don't like it when you lose your temper and yell. Why don't you go out to the barn and wrestle with a bale of hay?"

Her tone made Tom so peeved he stood up, as if about to follow her suggestion. "Tom Garvey," Mae said. "I saw that look on your father's face, and I don't like it any more on yours than I ever did on his. Now cool down."

It wasn't Mae making him antsy. It was the weather. He'd read about this thing called "cabin fever" that people got in Canada in the winter, how the long dark nights and the cold kept people indoors until they went kind of crazy. He guessed that could happen to anyone, if they felt cooped up enough. He wanted to break something; he wanted the satisfying smash of glass against rock, or the sharp crack of a rifle and the thud of a bullet hitting the banked dirt behind the target. Maybe he *would* go out and wrestle a hay bale.

"Sorry," he said. "I could have sworn I saw a break in the clouds earlier. A little light in the west."

"Another day like this and I wouldn't be surprised if you saw angels around the dinner table," Mae said.

"I'm going for a walk," Tom said. "I got to get out."

"Good idea," Mae said. "I'd join you, but if I don't get this custard in the oven, it won't be cool by dessert."

It was just as well, Tom thought. If she'd come, they'd probably have taken the argument outside. The argument? There wasn't an argument. There was just rain.

He let himself out the door and stood in the drive, near the pickup, his face tilted into the slanting rain, taking it like a slap across the cheek, a challenge. Yes, this was better; better to be out here than cooped up like a coward; better to get into the fight than to feel that panic bubbling in your chest.

He started to walk toward the river, and then to run, taking perverse pleasure in splashing through puddles, slipping, almost falling. He climbed the levee slowly. For a while it was like that myth he'd been taught about in high school; he'd no sooner get a couple of feet up when he'd slide back down. But he buried the toes of his boots as deeply as he could, and inched his way up.

He could hear the noise before he reached the top. Not a rustle but a deep-throated roar, a jungle noise. From where he stood, staring at the rolling surface just below him, the water looked like liquid solder. Trees, shrubs, the roof of an outhouse swept by. This must be what it was like when a volcano erupted, and the molten core of the earth overflowed and swept away every insignificant man-made thing in its path. He was scared, but he couldn't help feel the exhilaration, after days of standing still, of having begun the struggle.

He took the flashlight out of his jacket pocket and shone it upstream at the flood pole with its red markings a foot apart. The double band at *9* was just about underwater. Two feet to go before his land flooded; nothing left but to get his family outside. He thought, quickly; he'd already gotten sand for the bags; he'd already checked the dozer's oil and gas and wheeled it into position. Lewis would start the generator as he got the dozer moving. They'd have to rig up some lights. Mae knew where the sandbags were. He took one last look at the river. Was that a cow he saw? Something bloated and poisonous-looking, hung in the crotch of a tree, shot past.

Tom Garvey jumped and landed halfway down the levee, skidding on his heels. At the bottom he resumed his run. He crossed the strip of land to the county road, he splashed across the macadam and up his driveway, past the pickup. Mae was leaning into the rain, silhouetted in the yellow rectangle of kitchen light. We're into it, he thought. This is it.

He felt his name before he properly heard it, shaped in his wife's mouth and flung against the darkness. "Hurry," he heard her yell. "The levee's gone out above Cumminsville. Judy Birkin called. They've started bagging at Millrock. What do we do?"

He caught her around the waist, and water cascaded down his arms, soaking her jeans. She pulled away, even as she waited for him to answer. "We stalled too long already," Tom said. "I can't believe I been waiting for the rain to stop. You know where I keep the bags in the barn. You and Beth start bagging, and Lewis and me will work the tractor. I was just on the levee. It's holding, so far. But we better get to work."

"Where's the river?" Mae asked.

"Just under 9," Tom said. "And rising." Without knowing why, he felt his face break into an enormous grin. "Oh, honey," he said. "We're in for it bad, I think. We don't have a snowball's chance." Mae frowned at him. "You know I love a good fight," Tom said. "And I never found a better fighter than that river. Unless," he added, "it was you."

"Come on," Mae said. "I don't want any of your horse crap now."

· 3 ·

The rain seemed like a thousand separate insults as Garvey sat behind the dozer's controls, straining against the levee, lifting dirt against the river's inexorable rise. In the dim headlights he could hardly see where the levee gave way to black sky, though, faintly, up and down the bank tiny lights glinted where his neighbors worked. He glanced over his shoulder, searching for Lewis, then swung his attention back to the dozer's blade as it hit the bank, hustling him roughly in the seat. His pants were so wet, and his legs so cold, he was amazed he could move his feet from gas to clutch to brake. Dammit, he thought, where was Lewis anyway? He'd set the boy to work on the lights; together they'd buried a couple of poles as deep as they could in the ground, then clamped spots to them. Now Lewis was starting the generator, and soon—but there it was. Garvey blinked in the sudden light. Down the levee his wife and daughter struggled with sandbags. From where he sat, black diesel smoke curling around him like a wreath, the rain pelting down, Mae and Beth were heroic figures like the ones in the WPA frieze on the courthouse in Rosner. They moved as if in slow motion, their backs bending against the sand's weight. Garvey saw Lewis run to the pickup and pull the plastic knob.

All around him now light streamed, illuminating the rain-washed levee. Tom slammed the dozer in reverse, backed up, lowered the blade. The motor churned against the weight of waterlogged earth. Its rough noise rose to his ears, louder than the storm or the roaring of the river. Against the straining engine block, the rain evaporated in a thick steam, hissing as it hit.

Into the peripheral glare of the headlights Lewis ran, looking up at Garvey. "Get away," Garvey yelled. "It's too dangerous." Lewis cocked his head as though he couldn't hear his father's voice—no wonder with the engine's drone and rattle and the incessant pounding of the rain—and moved forward to catch the message. "No!" Garvey yelled again. He could feel the tendons in his neck as he struggled to make himself understood. He wrestled with the controls as the dozer's blade took another bite of land and carried it forward. For an instant he let go of the throttle and motioned furiously with his hand, pushing Lewis away. It seemed to work. The boy took a step backward, and then another. He put his hands on his hips and lifted his shoulders in a large shrug, then turned toward the muddy bank to look for leaks.

Mae stumbled into the light as well; Beth clutched one hand, and in the other Mae dragged the last of the burlap sacks. Their faces streamed with dirt and rain, and Tom could see from the way Mae pushed through the mud that she was operating solely on will. She shook her hand loose, gave Beth a bag, and the two of them stooped together, filling them with whatever came under their hands.

Tom backed up, put the dozer into forward, and charged the levee again. To his right he saw Lewis wildly waving his arms and he groaned, seeing what he feared. Lewis stood in brown ooze to his knees. He had to get the damn dozer over there and pile some dirt on that spot before the whole thing caved in and they were all washed away. If a hole opened up at the bottom, the river would force its way through with the power of water jetting from a firehose. He lowered the blade and went forward cautiously. The sharp metal edge scooped loose mud, a breaking wave like melted chocolate, hunching and streaming toward the place where the water oozed. He watched in dismay as brown water spurted over the dozer's blade.

This was bad; he didn't know how much longer the levee would hold. He eased the throttle and stood, trying to warn Mae and Beth to get back, stay away. The fireflies of light up and down the bank caught his attention for a moment; for miles around, men and women worked as he and his family did, to stem the tide. But his wife and daughter paid him no attention. They looked down at their hands carrying clods of dirt, rocks, anything they could find to fill the bags. Christ, Garvey thought. If they're not worried, what am *I* doing? He backed up again, aimed the dozer, and dug deep.

What was that at the corner of his eye? He thought it was a sweep of darkness, water cresting the levee, and as he swung his gaze in that direction, he misjudged the depth of the blade. The dozer's engine screamed, strained beyond endurance. With a sudden report like a pistol shot, Garvey heard one of the bearings blow on the left track, and his stomach went cold as the metal cleats ground to a halt. Moving on the right track alone, the dozer began to spin crazily, twisting away from the river and levee. Its headlights raked across Lewis, and then across the sodden fields, and as the blade rose and the dozer began to climb a small incline, the light shot upwards against the sky. Hundreds of thousands of dark dots, like a hail of locusts descending, sped through the light.

Headed in a new direction, his face streaming rain, Garvey struggled with the controls. Lewis suddenly appeared, his mouth wide open. It made Garvey wild. Rising from the saddle of the bucking dozer, Garvey tried to balance, screaming, "Lewis, get back." He seemed to have gotten through. The boy stepped away, slipped, twisted on one hand, and scrambled like a lopsided crab. If only the dozer were so agile. He had to bring it under control before something even more disastrous happened. Now it was tilting, spinning again, moving in its slow and stupid circle back toward the levee. The earth shifted, the lights bumped against the levee's crest, and what Garvey most feared happened. One end of the blade dug into the ground. The machine jerked forward and the coupling snapped. Suddenly, as the machine twisted yet again, Mae appeared in the headlights and threw herself out of the way, gathering up Beth and stumbling into Lewis, who fell, jumped, just escaped the blade's wild edge. Up there alone, Garvey found a new fight—his main concern was no longer the rain, the earth, the river, but this machine with a mind of its own.

He finally brought it to a halt, leapt down from the contoured seat, and struggled with the broken coupling, frantic to fix it. Everything was slipping from his control. He didn't hear his son's voice until it was shouting in his ear, and still what he heard almost made no sense, although he'd been waiting for it all night. The hand gripped his shoulder, the voice was hysterical. "Dad, it's going," Lewis said.

Garvey looked up, and watched part of the bank collapse. It happened slowly at first, and then with increasing speed. First a ten-foot section of the levee's lip began to bulge, and then, in the center, a spurt of water appeared and trickled down toward where the dozer was. The spurt grew, and as Garvey watched, the entire section gave way, and a small waterfall cascaded toward him. He was dumbstruck. At his side, his wife materialized, screaming. She thrust him forward, as if to wake him up. "Tom! It's Beth, over there. Beth! Oh get her, get her."

Tom leapt forward, racing with the water. He reached his daughter and scooped her into his arms even as the muddy stream knocked her off her feet. He felt the water rise over his ankles to his thighs, his knees, with astonishing speed. It had the solidity, the sheer weight of cement, and he felt rooted to the spot, hugging his daughter's breath right out of her, as he watched his wife and son engulfed by the water. He saw a head, a leg thrust above the turbulent surface. He whirled and watched the rest of the levee holding, miraculously. And then he saw the dozer begin to tumble, the huge yellow machine rolling toward him as if it were toy. He struggled out of his cement imprisonment, toward the slight rise of land the dozer had ridden before.

Mae and Lewis had regained their footing. By the dim glare of the lights he reached his wife, hugged her around the waist and lowered Beth into the water. Then he pulled Lewis close. Into his son's ear he yelled "Grab her hand" and thrust Beth's wrist between the boy's fingers. "Don't let go, whatever you do. Now come on, all of you. Let's get out of here. My feet are wet."

Mae looked dazed, but his joke brought the thinnest of smiles to her face. "It's going to reach the house, you know," she said.

"I know," Garvey said. "Come on. All of you. Beth, you obey your brother, now. Lewis, go to the barn; I'll get the cattle. We got to loose the animals."

· 4 ·

With his sister firmly locked in his grip, Lewis Garvey started for the barn. Where the land dipped, the water almost reached his waist. It was dark, and cold, and desolate: all that kept him going were the dim lights burning in the kitchen of the farmhouse and the struggling figures of his parents ahead of him. Why hadn't one of them taken Beth? They could have carried her. But here he was, practically dragging her as she whined and cried.

"Lewis," Beth said. "Do we have to go so fast?"

"Don't you want to rescue the lambs? How do you think they feel locked up in their pens with water all around?"

Beth quieted down and clung more tightly to his hand. "What about Snow White?" she asked.

"What about her?"

"Can hogs swim?"

"I don't know," Lewis said. "That's why we have to get them out. Then they can find a safe place until the water goes away."

"How long will that be?" Beth asked.

"I don't know," Lewis said.

By the time they reached the barn, it was already flooding. Lewis could hear the frantic high-pitched barking of Lady, their border collie, above the somber lowing of the cows, the squeals of the pigs. He was sure Snow White would be fine: but he wasn't sure about the piglets. Although a hog was heavy—heavier than a ton of lead, his father had once remarked, which always made Lewis think that a full grown hog weighed two thousand pounds—he was sure she would float, like an enormous cake of soap. But the piglets hadn't managed yet to coat their bones with layers and layers of lard.

He pushed his shoulder against the door and squeezed inside, pulling Beth after him. They gasped and held their breath. It was darker inside than out, and the air was thick with the fetid odor of fear. Manure mixed with water and straw floated at their ankles.

"Lady!" he yelled, letting go of Beth's hand. He hunkered down and clapped his hands and the border collie darted toward him, then back to the gate restraining the lambs and sheep. Lewis unlatched the gate and pushed it open against the rising water. Instantly Lady was inside the pen, barking and nipping at the sheep's back legs. "Out!" Lewis yelled, "Come on! Out of there! Lady, flush 'em!" Lady cut into the flock and separated a sheep from the others. Its eyes were wide, terrified, and it bleated piteously, almost like a honk. At another time Lewis might have laughed, but the animal could barely stand on its quaking legs. Finally Lady managed to push it out the gate, and the others followed, out of the pen and through the widening barn door. Lewis tumbled after them into the storm again, followed by Beth. In front of him, Lady barked hysterically and the sheep moiled together, a white blot amid black water.

Across the yard he could see his mother running for the farmhouse, and before he could stop her, Beth was running too. He had to free the rest of the animals, but his father had told him *Don't let go of Beth!* Lewis yelled at his sister, hanging onto the barn door, swept toward her and back inside at once.

She stopped and yelled back, "I have to save Ernie."

"Beth," Lewis yelled. "Daddy said for you to stay with me. He's just a stupid doll."

"He is not stupid," Beth said. He stood and watched as she splashed across the yard, and then he turned back to the cows and pigs.

· 5 ·

Beyond the barn Tom Garvey wrestled with the gate to the cattle pen. The cows had been sequestered in the barn, but the Brahma bull raged in the pen, pushing against the wooden slats, now and then lowering his horns and charging. Given enough time, the bull would get out by himself, but Tom didn't relish the task of repairing the pen. He'd have plenty to do when the flood was over, and that was one job he thought he'd save himself. He reached over the gate and bashed the animal on the head with his fist, as hard as he could. Momentarily dazed, the bull backed off a bit and stood his ground. Tom cleared a couple of feet of space with the gate, not enough to let the bull through, only enough, in fact, should the bull charge, to rattle Tom's teeth loose from his skull. Reaching as far as he could, he bashed the bull on the head again. The animal kept his ground, and grunting in exhaustion, Garvey managed to push the gate open and climb the rungs. He waved his free arm in front of the bull's contorted face. "Yow Bram," he screamed. "Yow."

The Brahma raged through the water, snorting, his eyes flecked with fear, and, at the last minute, turned to charge at Tom. Tom stuck out a booted foot to smash him between the eyes, and with both hands reached over and grabbed the top of the siding. He managed to dodge the terrified bull, who splashed through the gate, out of the pen, into the rising flood.

Garvey hoisted himself up on the siding and tried to catch his breath. Everything was chaos. As he watched, the one brightness, the light in the kitchen window, went out. The yard between the house and barn was filled with terrified bleating sheep and a crazed barking dog. He thought he could see his daughter run through the water toward the house where Mae was. He shook his head in weariness and wonder; hard to believe his land had flooded again.

· 6 ·

Mae Garvey started when the electricity went out, though she'd been ready for that. She carried the lit kerosene lamp and put it on top of the old oak hutch which had been her grandmother's, and her grandmother's mother's before her, and bent to open the second drawer from the bottom. It wouldn't budge. She tried again, this time pulling with all her strength. It moved a bit and wedged; the moisture of the last week had swelled the wood. She stood, put her hands on her hips and took a deep breath. "Beth," she yelled to her daughter, who, without a word to her, had clattered up the stairs. "You come down here this minute and help me. I need you."

The drawer contained her great-grandmother's wedding quilt, painstakingly made by hand over the twelve months of her engagement. It was so beautifully done, so lovingly stitched and pleated and quilted, it made Mae's chest ache every time she unfolded it and looked at it. Tom didn't feel the same way about it, but then it wasn't his. For Mae, it was the one thing in the house she wanted to save.

In the lamp's glow, she saw her daughter totter uncertainly at the top of the stairs. Beth looked so much younger than six, so vulnerable standing there in her soaked and mud-stained pants, holding Ernie in one hand, the other hand hovering near her mouth as though she were about to suck her thumb.

"Come on, sweetheart," Mae soothed. "Everything's

going to be fine. You come down here now and help me. We've got to get the quilt out."

"What's the matter?" Beth said.

"The drawer's stuck. Come on." When Beth hesitated, Mae lost her patience. "Come on now. Leave your doll. You're a big girl." At first Mae thought Beth was going to cry, and she felt badly for having scolded the child. But then, as often happened, her daughter surprised her, thrust her chin out, and came down. Mae was filled with a fierce pride, more than maternal, that these small creatures she'd had so much to do with should turn out so well; it was like raising a calf and having it win the blue ribbon at the county fair, but better. She struggled with the drawer; then Beth was beside her, and Mae concentrated on the left handle while her daughter pulled the right. They grunted; it moved an inch and stuck again. "Okay, Beth," Mae said. "Now when I say three. Ready? One. Two. Three." They pulled again, grunted, and the drawer leapt another half inch. The front had cleared now, but Mae's hand would have had to be thinner than paper to get in the crack. "We'll have to do better than that. You tired, sweetheart?" Beth nodded, and Mae stroked the back of her head. "Let's just get this quilt out and then we'll look for somewhere to go."

"I'm hungry," Beth said.

"On three. One. Two. Three." They pulled, and at first Mae didn't feel anything happen, but then, slowly, the wood began to slide and suddenly the drawer was open. She smiled and hugged her daughter. Beth had already picked up Ernie.

Mae reached in for the quilt. It was huge, heavy, wrapped in strong plastic. She tucked it under one arm, blew out the kerosene lamp, and, grabbing Beth with the other hand, rushed through the kitchen and stopped in the doorway. She could dimly see Tom as she shooed and sooo-eeed and pushed and gathered. The yard seemed like some crazy painter's version of a barnyard. Who was that painter Joe Wade had shown her? Botch? Bosh? It looked like something he would paint, chickens fluttering above the water, cows lowing and mooing and moving about. What was that sitting on top of Jessica, Beth's favorite cow? Was that a chicken? *And where was Lewis?*

She strained her eyes to make out something else, and when she did, she leaned against the wooden door frame. It was the waterline, moving up from the barn toward where she stood. No doubt about it. The water would reach the house. "Oh Lord," she said.

· 7 ·

Snow White might not weigh a ton, but whatever she weighed Lewis couldn't make her move. He'd done everything he could think of. He'd called her name and stroked her behind the ears. He'd described the leftovers of a sumptuous dinner, the kind of slop that usually made Snow White roll her eyes and follow. He knew she understood English, though he'd never heard her speak it.

And then he'd resorted to brute physical force. He weighed in at eighty-nine, and had the force of human intelligence to boot. Lewis planted his feet in the mud, put his back against Snow White's side, and pushed with all his force. The sow shifted, knocked him off balance, and he landed on his behind. Well, he could understand that, he thought. Right here, it was still a little dry. But the water was coming to this end of the barn too, and he had to get her out. "Okay, Snow White," he said. "You understand what I'm saying so you better listen." The pig had turned to look at him. "Snow White, you're a hog. H-O-G, hog. Now *get*. Now. Sooooeeeee." He made his voice sing out at the end, rising like the water, and, to his amazement it worked. Snow White turned and lumbered out of her pen into the water, a dozen piglets squealing at her side.

· 8 ·

They'd gathered the animals together as best they could, and taking what they could carry—a bag of food from the kitchen, a coffee pot, a kerosene lantern, some blankets—the Garveys trudged away from their farm toward higher ground. Whatever purpose Tom Garvey had felt that afternoon was gone, and his mood had turned to sullen depression. Beside him, Mae tried to keep up a stream of chatter to distract the children, who were cold clear through, and frightened. Beth kept asking about the animals, calling each by name, and Tom had never known that besides the piglets she'd christened the chickens and lambs. She'd collected names from books and TV, names like Grinch and Toto and Eeyore. If he ever had a spare moment again, he'd ask Mae when all that had happened. She probably knew. They'd have an uncomfortable night, and the crop was destroyed. It might be Memorial Day before he got another crop in the ground. He'd have to borrow more money from Simpson to buy the seed. And Wade would be watching, waiting, careful, quiet, insidious as the water.

How long would it be before they got back into the house?

Beside him, Mae shivered. The entire family was silent: even Beth had stopped her questions. "Hey," Tom said. "What's everybody so gloomy about? Beth, what's that song they were teaching you in school?"

Mae looked at him suspiciously; usually he was trying to get Beth to be quiet. "Which one?" Beth asked.

"You know," Tom said. "The one about the mule."

"The mule?" Beth asked.

"He means 'The Erie Canal,'" Mae said.

His daughter's breathy voice broke the stillness, terribly off-key. "I got a mule her name is Sal..."

"Fifteen miles on the Erie Canal," Tom sang.

And then they all were singing, for the moment, with no thought of tomorrow.

· 9 ·

Joe Wade sat behind the controls of the Leutzcorp helicopter, tapping his index finger on the knee of his khaki pants. Beyond the concrete landing pad, the twin towers of the granary rose, their bright yellow and black cylinders like overgrown silos. As soon as the Senator arrived, Wade would pilot a reconnaissance of the flood's devastation in the river valley, and he couldn't help feeling a childish glee. He loved flying; he loved distance and speed. On the ground he floored his new Bronco, and anything was reason enough to take the helicopter up.

With the flood having wiped out the first corn crop, Leutzcorp was in a powerful bargaining position with the farmers: Wade, under his father-in-law's orders, was going to start putting pressure on these small-time operators to sell. Leutzcorp wanted that land; more exactly, Leutzcorp wanted that water. Now that Ed Neiswinder had joined the legislature in Nashville, Leutzcorp had even more leverage; Wade and he had belonged to Sigma Chi at the University of Tennessee, and for reasons Wade couldn't fathom, Edwin Neiswinder believed in that brotherhood stuff.

In the copter's back seat, Howard Simpson and Harve Stanley hunched. Simpson, the chief loan officer at Farmer's Federal Loan and Trust in Millrock, was in on the Leutzcorp plan, and of course Stanley, as Wade's foreman, was behind him with the full force of his limited intelligence. Wade turned and glanced at the two men; Stanley, his head lowered on his thick neck, looked barely conscious. Simpson didn't like flying; even the most casual observer could see he was nervous, queasy.

Joe flared his nostrils in faint dislike; he'd known Simpson for seven years now, since the man had been transferred from the branch in Rosner, and try as he might, he couldn't warm up to him. There was something bloodless about him. Even his golf game reflected it—he went through the motions, and could drive a ball on a fairway, but when it came to shaving strokes, he didn't have the nerve. Now he sat, his shoulders caving in, nodding as if a Muzak arrangement were drifting over his headset.

Through the glass of the small office attached to the hanger, Wade saw Neiswinder talking to someone. Wade flipped the key and the rotors began to turn. Neiswinder raised his hand and held it flatly before him, like every politician in America, pivoted and strode across the tarmac, followed by a Leutzcorp employee Wade remembered pouring water at a banquet, or hanging up coats, a gofer. He raised his voice over the increasing noise of the copter's blades. "You guys got the story straight?" he asked. He turned to see if Stanley and Simpson had heard.

"Right, Joe," Simpson said. Stanley blinked, like an ancient turtle.

Neiswinder walked with his shoulders back, as if he were leading a parade down Lamar Avenue in Memphis. At any moment he would break into a huge smile, step forward and shake the hand of someone in the imaginary crowd. The gofer opened the copter's door and Neiswinder filled the small opening. His self-assurance vanished as he surveyed the copter's interior.

Wade winked, and gave a mock salute. "Hop in, Senator," he said. "Let's take a ride."

"Morning, Joe," Neiswinder said, flashing his teeth. "Where's the pilot?"

"He's not feeling too good, Ed, but don't worry. I'm sure I can figure out how this thing works." Neiswinder smiled again and climbed aboard. Wade could see from the tension at the corners of his mouth that he wasn't completely convinced. "Just strap yourself in now, Ed, there. That's it. Now hold on. Let me see what happens when I . . ."

Okay, he thought. *Here we go.* The rotors picked up speed. Wade watched with satisfaction as the whirling blades sent a wind skittering over the tarmac, pushing a faded candy wrapper and a few dried leaves. Slowly at first, as if the helicopter were gently stuck, the machine left the ground, and Wade expertly pointed it toward the horizon. In no time they'd left behind the granary's twin towers.

To the east, the main street of Millrock seemed desolate in the harsh blaze of late spring sun; a few toy cars dotted its sides. From this height, the entire landscape looked dazed and battered. The silver ribbon of the river wound its way southward, and then exploded to the east as a huge lake spread out where the flooding had occurred.

The men in the copter were silent. Stanley was probably nodding off. If you didn't keep that guy busy, he'd sleep standing up. Simpson drummed his fingers on his hound's tooth trousers. Next to him, Neiswinder was the consummate politician, knitting his brows, holding his hands tightly in his lap, looking out over the watery devastation with sympathy. Wade remembered how Neiswinder had campaigned for student body president at Tennessee, one day appearing with a stalk of straw between his teeth to appeal to the Aggies, the next day dressed in kelly green pants to talk to the Betas.

Wade let the hint of a grin touch his face; if Neiswinder wanted to express concern for his constituents, Wade would give him the opportunity. He nosed the helicopter down slightly; below them a two-lane country road flicked by, the broken white line down its center a kind of erratic punctuation. The macadam acted as a sounding board, reflecting the roar of the chopper's engine and whirling blades. And then the noise changed abruptly as the white line disappeared under water, a brown unruffled surface that spread out around them. Wade stole a glance at Neiswinder. The guy was good. His lips were tightly pressed together and his head shook gently.

The copter sped across the unbroken expanse of water toward a flooded farm. Wade brought the copter lower; with the sun over his left shoulder he now could just catch the sinuous shadow the copter cast on the water. The noise now was muffled, a constant thudding. "What a shame," Neiswinder said, almost under his breath. Wade cut southwest, scudding across the patched roof of a barn and the asphalt-shingled roof of a white farmhouse standing alone in a flooded field, an emblem of desolation. Wade thought the Senator might be moved to an elegiac lyricism, but Neiswinder just shook his head. Wade tried to keep his tone informative and noncommital.

"All this bottom land used to be duck marsh back two hundred years ago. Natural springs all over it. Real fine water."

"How many farms flooded, Joe?" Neiswinder asked.

Over his shoulder, Wade asked Simpson, "What do you figure, Howard?" Howard was good with numbers. He came to life abruptly, like a puppet suddenly picked up by the puppeteer. "Oh, maybe eight, nine, all told. Same as always."

"What do you mean?" Neiswinder asked.

"Every time the river does this, the land floods in about the same spot."

"Seems to me nature's trying to tell them something," Wade said. He turned and looked at Neiswinder blankly, and while he stared he nosed the copter toward the water.

Neiswinder stopped looking concerned and looked vaguely ill. "Don't worry, Senator," Wade said. "I've got everything under control." Below them, a herd of cows clustered on a small piece of ground, a solitary island in the chocolate water. Wade could see their mouths open in soundless bellows. As the copter passed overhead, the herd stampeded into the shallows; the chopper's downdraft whipped the surrounding trees and flustered the water.

"Why not take us up a little, Joe?" Neiswinder said.

"Certainly, Senator," Wade said.

"Drop the *Senator,* Joe," Neiswinder said. "I can do without the sarcasm."

Wade took the copter up, regaining a perspective over the landscape. Every now and then the sun glinted off the water, as if it were a large reflecting pool, changing it in an instant from a rich brown to brilliant gold. About a mile farther on and to the south he could just make out the barn and farmhouse belonging to Tom Garvey. If Wade knew Garvey as he thought he did, the Senator was in for a treat: not just the flooded farm, but the flooded farm family as well. Garvey was one of those guys who just wouldn't quit; knock him down, bloody his lip, punch him in the gut and he came back for more. You'd have to kill him to make him quit. He'd been that way with baseball, and he'd been that way with Mae Stillwell. Back in Millrock High, Tom Garvey had been a *presence;* taciturn, scowly, handsome. He was a farm boy, up in the morning to milk the cows, home after school to take care of the farm. Never did too well gradewise. But when you met him, you knew he was *somebody;* the way he'd knit his brows together and fix you with those dark eyes. There was the barn, the farmhouse, the trees by the bedroom window, the old tire swing hanging by its frayed rope. And there they were.

"Those are the Garveys down there," he said.

Neiswinder's face lit up. He peered at the stricken family with as much intensity as he could muster. "They might qualify for disaster relief."

The sincerity in Neiswinder's voice was unmistakable.

Wade was surprised; it suddenly struck him that Ed Neiswinder might be genuinely concerned. "These men don't want state aid, Senator. They're an independent breed. You know what I mean? I knew Garvey in high school. He never let anyone help him with anything." Without looking, Wade could tell that Neiswinder was staring at him.

"You mean 'hands off,' Joe?" Neiswinder asked.

Wade nodded, once. "Hard working guy, Tom Garvey. Stubborn sonofabitch."

· 10 ·

It was hot hard work, and the sun off the water was blinding. Tom Garvey's back ached from days of trying to put the plug back in the levee, fixing the hole in the dike. As the water began to recede, he'd dragged rocks and tree limbs, flotsam and jetsam the river had brought his way from his fields, and managed to pile it into the breech. Now he was trying to secure it. He'd gotten a diesel pump, and it billowed black smoke into the morning air as it labored, returning the water to the river. The bulldozer sat cocked in the mud, wreathed in a tangle of webbing, blocks and tackle.

He heard the thudding, sensed the approach of the copter before he saw it. Coming at him low over the water, it looked like a gigantic locust, its glass eyes bulging and wings whirring, coming to ravage the crop. As he watched, it began to climb, casting a swift black shadow upon the water. He could barely see the human figures inside the cockpit, hiding behind sunglasses and triple-ply glass and metal. He stood, stretching his back, shading his eyes with his hand. Mae stood as well, her hands on her hips. There it was: the Leuztcorp insignia on the side of the copter. He should have known.

He looked over at his wife; she was white in the blinding sun. She took her hand and placed it over her eyes; a shadow covered her face, rendering it invisible. "Joe Wade," she said. She dropped her hand, and her face reappeared.

"Yeah," Tom said. "The flying farmer."

Mae looked at him; for a moment, her face registered nothing. And then she grinned, her mouth opened, and she burst into laughter. Their joke was drowned out by the thud of the copter's blades reverberating off the water.

· 11 ·

They were on their way back. Wade had flown south and west, crossing the river, circling now toward Millrock and the Leutzcorp landing pad. Soon it would be time for lunch. The atmosphere in the copter had loosened up; Harve Stanley had suddenly snorted into motion, telling the joke about the olive oil, the asparagus, and the plastic duck. At first the Senator had looked shocked, but he allowed himself a grin when even Simpson had laughed out loud. Besides, the damage had been seen, had registered, there was nothing the Senator could do about it while they were up in the air. Now, any moment now, it would be Wade's move. He felt himself hovering in time, as the copter hovered in the air, waiting. His chance came sooner than he'd expected.

"Why'd you show me all this, Joe?" Neiswinder asked. Wade could tell from the expression on Neiswinder's face that he might as well be straight.

"Ed, what we need here is a dam. Every couple of years the river floods and everyone shakes their heads and nothing ever changes. It's time we did something. You're an expert on water rights—that's why your friends put you into the State House." He paused. "Look into it," he added, lamely.

"If all this goes underwater, what happens to the farmers?"

Wade wanted to point out that it *was* under water, but held off. "They'll get a fair price for their land, won't they, Howard?" he said.

In the back seat, Howard Simpson puffed up like a rooster balloon. "They're in no position to bargain," he said, "but we'll certainly try to be fair."

Neiswinder's head turned as if on a swivel, taking a look at Simpson, finally resting on Wade's chin. "You and old man Leutz got a personal interest here, Joe?" he asked. Wade turned around toward Simpson with a big smile. "You hear how he talks to a fraternity brother?" he said. "We were *close* in Knoxville, weren't we, Ed?" Without waiting for a reply, Wade moved the controls and banked the copter radically to the east, swooping toward the sun.

· 12 ·

Mae Garvey stood on the old cement sidewalk in front of the Millrock branch of Farmer's Federal Loan and Trust, her arms crossed, tapping her foot, trying with all her might to appear interested in what she saw, when all the while her mind was behind her, inside the squat brick building with her husband. Lewis hunkered on the sidewalk, drawing a picture in the silt with a stick, and Beth stood next to her mother. Mae thought of picking her up for comfort—hers, not the child's—but decided against it. She shook her head slowly, and swept her eyes up and down the main street of Millrock. She had to admit it was a depressing place, even though it was mostly what she'd known her whole life. Founded in 1882 as a center for grinding the corn and wheat the rich bottom lands along the river were producing, Millrock had long since lost its mill, and now a thin odor of mildew and rot seemed to hang in the air, as though the town were merely an afterimage, as though its future, clear as the morning sky, had already come to pass.

The few remaining storefronts needed painting; the abandoned building on the corner where the shoe place used to be had a large crack in its plate glass window, and the masking tape which covered it had been yellowed by sunlight. "For Sale" signs littered the street like dried blown leaves in November. The window of the abandoned Woolworth's now served as a community bulletin board. It was plastered with notices and signs, most of them hand-lettered and misspelled. A group of unshaven men in dirty clothes stood there, as if waiting for someone to give a speech; to Mae they looked utterly without hope. If she closed her eyes, she saw them as an afterimage too. Beth was getting more and more restless at her side, ready to start a small squabble to regain an interest in life. She felt a small hand grab her jeans and tug. "Mom, can I get some ice cream?" Beth said.

"As soon as Daddy's finished," Mae said.

"When will he be finished?" Beth's voice threatened to turn whiny. Lewis looked up from his impromptu artwork and glared at his sister. Mae felt a wild rush of sympathy for the boy; he knew, more or less, what was happening inside the bank; Beth was still too young. "When he's done,"

Lewis said, "that's when he'll be finished." For Beth, the last weeks had been an adventure—the rain, the flood, the clean-up, the reckoning of the disaster. Lewis was old enough to remember the last time, and the time before that.

"Soon, Beth, soon," Mae said, brushing her hand across her daughter's hair, so much like her own. "Hush, sweetie. We have to wait. Look. Here comes the sheriff." Beth's gaze moved from her mother's face to the street where Sheriff Jim Roy Watson was taking his time getting out of the cruiser. He was a jolly man, but he liked the shiny silver badge he wore, and he used its authority with a cruel edge that Mae found distasteful. Mae put her arm around her daughter and pulled her close as the sheriff sauntered up the opposite sidewalk; with the toe of his boot Watson nudged a man huddled in an overcoat, asleep, his head on a tattered briefcase, stretched out on what had once been a fine oak bench.

"Who's he?" Beth asked.

"A poor man without any work," Mae said. "He probably doesn't have anywhere to go."

"He's a bum," Lewis said.

"Lewis Garvey," Mae said. "You know I don't like that word. I don't want to hear it out of your mouth again, understand?"

"That's what Freddie Cheevers says at school," Lewis said, defending himself. "And Peter Hinkle."

"I don't care what they say," Mae said. "That's an ugly unkind word. You hear me?"

Lewis looked at her, narrowing his eyes. "Yes, ma'am," he said. Was he being smart? Lord, was he growing up. The days were coming when he'd sass his own parents, no doubt about it.

The man sat on the bench now, bewildered, rubbing his eyes in the morning glare. Watson reached out and nudged again with his boot, and the man stood, grabbed his suitcase, and tottered off, headed for the group of men who stood in front of Woolworth's. He walked past Leutz's Pharmacy and Zolt Realty, and the sheriff trailed him at a respectful distance. As she watched him go, Mae found herself suddenly staring at the smiling face of Joe Wade. He'd pulled over to the curb in his elaborate customized Bronco. He was wearing expensive designer sunglasses, a polo shirt, and his bare elbow hung over the chrome and silver rectangle of open window. "Morning, Mae," he said.

Whenever she saw him, Mae knew she hadn't *really* sorted out all her feelings about him and stored them away as simple memories. She liked him and resented him. She knew she didn't respect him, but still something attracted her, how good he'd been to her, his charm, his money.

"Joe," she said, careful as could be.

"I saw you took some water."

She remembered him cruising overhead in his company helicopter, looking down on the brown lake from the clean cool air where no one's cuffs got dirty. "Coulda been worse," she said. Almost instinctively, she felt her body shift, one hip jutting out in a taunt.

"Anything I can do?" Wade asked. He'd taken off the sunglasses, and she could see his green-grey eyes, the tiny crinkles around them.

Yes, she thought. There was plenty he could do. "We'll manage," she said. "Thanks all the same."

"Thought I'd ask," Wade said, putting his glasses back on. "Well, see you," he said. Mae nodded, strained her mouth into a smile. Beside her, Lewis stood, as at attention, and even Beth had grown unnaturally still.

· 13 ·

Tom Garvey put a finger inside the collar of his shirt and pulled, giving his neck a little air. He sat miserably on a grey aluminum folding chair in front of Howard Simpson, who was half hidden by his large desk. Right now all Tom could see was the part in Simpson's hair as the loan officer shuffled through the pile of papers in Garvey's folder. Tom shifted his legs. His thick-soled Montgomery Wards were too large for his feet, and he was uncomfortably aware that his brown suit was getting a bit threadbare in the knees. He'd worn a tie, but it didn't make him feel the least bit more businesslike. It lay pressed on top of his freshly ironed workshirt like something newly dead.

Simpson cleared his throat and jerked his neck, making his eyes focus somewhere in the vicinity of Tom's chin. "You need ninety-seven hundred dollars?" he asked.

Tom smiled as brightly as he could, as though he'd just asked for a cup of coffee. "That's right," he said. "I need to plant a new crop, I need to fix my dozer. It's all there on that list, near as I can figure." He remembered Mae's face that morning as she stood ironing his tie and shirt, and he sat at the kitchen table with the list of numbers, afraid to add them up. "Are you sure?" she'd said. "Couldn't you have made a mistake?"

Simpson's eyes fell to the loan portfolio again, and he shuffled more papers. "Let's see," he said, pulling out several stained and folded sheets and arranging them before him. "You got three hundred and twenty acres of land. You borrowed sixty thousand in 1970, took a second mortgage for eighteen-five in '76. Two hundred fourteen thousand worth of farm equipment on which you paid only sixteen-three." He shook his head, bunched his lips together, and looked up. "You owe us a lot of money, Tom. I'd like to help you, but if we give you another loan, how are you gonna make the payments?"

"I'm a good customer, Howard."

"I know that," Simpson said.

"I made my payments the first of every month for twelve years now."

"That's not the point, Tom . . ."

"That's exactly the point," Garvey said. "Ten years ago you people were tripping over yourselves to get me to borrow money."

"But it's different now," Simpson said. "Times have changed. Land values are down. You owe us more than your place is worth. If you went under, we'd lose money on you."

On Simpson's desk a chrome-framed color photograph was propped. In it Simpson stood with his arm around his wife's waist as if trying to hide the bulge at her belt. Next to them stood the Wades. That must have been taken several years ago, since Emily Leutz Wade had died in the fall of '81. They were wearing brightly colored clothes, as if on a tropical vacation.

Garvey's hands clenched on his knees and he straightened his spine. He could feel his face go hard, his voice get shaky. "Are you turning me down?" he said.

Simpson pushed himself back from the desk. "Now take it easy, Tom."

"Take it easy?" Garvey leaned forward, seizing the advantage. "You're trying to put me out of business."

"Don't be silly," Simpson said. "Nobody said that."

"You don't have to say it. You're doing it."

"Lower your voice," Simpson said, his face turning pink above the starched white manacle of his collar.

Garvey wasn't shouting, but he certainly wasn't about to lower his voice. "I need that loan, Howard. I've earned it."

Simpson cleared his throat again and peered around. A man and a woman standing before the one teller turned to look at them. Garvey stared as hard as he could at the side of Simpson's face, willing him to look back. Slowly the red neck pivoted, and their eyes locked.

"Leutzcorp might give you a damned good price for your land, Tom. Why don't you go talk to Joe Wade about it?"

Well, there it was. The other shoe had dropped. The real enemy had been named. "I'm not looking to sell," he said. "I'm looking to stay."

Simpson sighed, picked up several papers and made a show of straightening them. When he looked up again, his gaze went past Garvey toward the front door. Tom felt a breeze on the back of his neck; someone had just come in.

In single file his family entered, Beth followed by Lewis and Mae. They all looked at him and then moved sideways to sit on the bench to the right of the door. If he hadn't known better, Tom would have sworn they looked as though they'd lost their will to live.

He turned back to Simpson; the other man was still looking past him.

"That's your family, isn't it?" he asked.

"Yes," Tom said. "That's my family."

Simpson smiled, almost enviously. "Fine looking," he said. Finally, he sighed and closed the file. "I don't know what we can do for you, Tom. We can roll your notes over again. Don't know what else."

Before anything happened he'd later regret, Tom grabbed the list he'd brought with him from Simpson's desk, and without saying good-bye, he turned and walked toward the door. Mae, Lewis, and Beth all stood as soon as they saw him coming, and when he reached them, he took Mae's arm, shooed the children before them, and then followed them into the glare.

· 14 ·

The minute he was out the door, Tom began pulling at his tie, as though it had designs on his neck. He kept his voice low, but couldn't rid it of agitation. "Why'd you come in?" he asked. "I thought you said you'd wait out front."

"Joe Wade drove up," she said.

"God," Garvey said. "The horns of a dilemma."

"Besides. I came in so he could look at me and the kids close up." Tom rolled his eyes and turned toward her. "I don't think it made any difference," she added quickly, placating him.

"It sure didn't," Tom said, scowling. He'd finished working out the tie's knot, and he ripped it out from under his collar. "Neither did this."

"Mom," Beth said, at her side, "can I get my ice cream now?"

Lewis sidled-up and tried to pull Beth away. "Beth," he said. "Shhhhh."

"She said when Dad's finished. Aren't you finished now, Dad?"

Although he tried to squelch it, Tom felt the anger rising in him. Damn. The world didn't let you alone for a minute, did it? First the river rose and flooded your land, destroying the crop you'd planted. Then some ass in a helicopter flew overhead, looking down on you and your misfortune as a way of increasing his fortune. Then his brown-nosing *yes* man refused to give you the money you couldn't do without. And your own family continued to need, need, *need*. "No, Beth," he said. "I'm not finished."

Beth stopped dead and stared at him. Had his words been water, he would have scalded her. To make amends, he reached into his pants pocket and pulled out a crumpled faded dollar, and thrust it toward her. "Go get some ice cream," he said. It was Lewis who took it. He grabbed his sister and pulled her down the street, toward the soda fountain at Leutz's Pharmacy.

Tom looked at Mae. He knew she hated it when he scolded or yelled at the kids. "That Lewis," he said. "He's getting to be something."

"You look real handsome," she finally said, reaching out and running her fingers through his thick black hair. "I cut it real good this time."

God, she embarrassed him sometimes. He tugged at his collar, running his finger against his neck. "Must be some soap still in this thing," he said. "It itches. Come on. Let's get us home." He grabbed her hand and they followed the kids toward Leutz's Pharmacy.

· 15 ·

Two days later the letter arrived, and when Mae pulled it from the mailbox it felt heavy in her hands. There in the upper left corner was the embossed gothic *Leutzcorp*, and above it the typed name of *Joseph Wade*. It was addressed to Tom; she wanted either to read it or to rip it to shreds and scatter the pieces around the yard. Instead she folded it carefully and placed it in her apron pocket. At dinner that night, Tom asked off-handedly if there'd been any mail, and when Mae made a bright show of advertising circulars and a flyer from the Jehovah's Witnesses, he paid her no mind. "How's the land shaping up?" she asked after the kids had taken their chocolate pudding and gone to the living room, leaving them in the kitchen with their coffee.

"Wet as a sponge," Tom said. "It'll be two more weeks at least before it's dry enough for disking and planting again. Put a seed near that land now and it'll rot before morning." He paused and stared down into the black circle of his mug as though it contained the future. "Besides, we don't have the money to buy seed for another crop."

"We've got through before," Mae said.

"True enough," Tom said. "But there's always a first time."

She reached into her pocket and pulled out the letter. "This might cheer you up," she said. Tom looked at her. Mae did everything she could to keep her face impassive, free of the conflicting feelings tearing through her; she hoped Wade had offered so much money that Tom couldn't possibly turn it down; she hoped Tom would be so angry that he'd figure out a way to keep going.

Tom took his time. He licked his lips, held the white rectangle up to the bare bulb. "Typed," he said. And then he slowly separated the gummed flap with the help of his gravy-stained knife, took out the letter and read it.

"Well, well," he said. "Cash on the barrel head."

After the kids were in bed, after Tom had read something called *The Three Little Peppers* to Beth and had explained to Lewis about the way Hank Aaron had held the bat, Mae sat before an old dressing table in their bedroom. She brushed her long blond hair one hundred times every morning and every night, her one vanity, she thought, and it felt good, the even strokes pulling gently at her scalp, the way the strands seemed smoother, softer when she was done. In the mirror she watched her husband, lounging on their bed, re-

reading the letter from Wade. Or re-re-reading it. Seemed as though he'd done *nothing* but read it since she'd given it to him, except for the time he'd wadded it up and flung it against the wall, and then retrieved it and flattened it out, ironing it with his palms.

"Wade didn't waste any time, did he?" he said. "Howard must have called him the minute I left the bank. Did I tell you about the photo on his desk of him and Wade and Emily Leutz and what's her name?"

"Jane Cotting," Mae said absently. *Seventy-nine, eighty.*

"I figured," Tom said. "We'd come away clean with about twenty-five thousand dollars."

Mae stared at him in the mirror. It had been her mother's, with those beautiful wavy patterns that old glass often had, and as he moved, his face distorted slightly, as in a fun house mirror. "More like twenty-eight," she said.

"I'm not interested," Tom said.

"Because it's him?"

"Because my people are buried here, Mae. I grew up here. I've lived here all my life, and I don't need some bill-toting helicopter-flying sonofabitch to come oiling his way around.... This is our home place, Mae. I got feelings." He dropped the letter on the bed and walked out, down the hall to the kitchen. He'd been doing that a lot lately, staring out at the levee and the invisible river beyond. She paused to watch him go. Alone again, she picked up the brush and—*ninety-eight, ninety-nine*—finished that task. Then she followed him to the kitchen to begin the next one.

· 16 ·

When she awoke the next morning, Mae turned over and separated the curtains, peering out into the beginning of daylight to see what the weather had brought. A fine mist clung to the ground; it was too early to tell if it would be cloudy or clear. Tom was already gone. That meant there'd be coffee in the kitchen; he was out somewhere, up to his ankles in mud, or milking, if Lewis hadn't gotten there first. Lord, she'd slept longer than she'd intended. She'd planned on being up to make a big breakfast of pancakes before they left for the auction.

She sat up, rubbing her eyes and yawning; her feet puzzled around the floor for her slippers. Then she was up, and into her bathrobe; on her tiptoes she reached high into the closet shelf, pulled down the quilt she'd rescued, and walked down the hall to the kitchen. Beth sat at the table, spooning Raisin Bran and milk into her mouth. "Morning, honey," Mae said. "I was going to make pancakes."

"Morning, Mom." A dribble of milk ran down Beth's chin.

"Now you finish that up and come help me, okay?" Beth nodded, picked up the bowl and drank from its rim. Mae set the quilt down on the table and moved to the counter, where she'd stacked the jars last night, the cucumber rind pickles, pears, applesauce, the quarts of sauerkraut, jams and jellies, and tomatoes. Beth pushed her bowl away and reached for the quilt.

"Beth, you wipe your hands before you touch that quilt. You know how valuable that is." Beth went to the sink, dutifully picked up a sponge, massaged her palms, and wiped them on her pants. She hurried back to the quilt and stroked it, as if it were a sleeping cat.

"It's so pretty," she said. "How old is it?"

"It's more than ten times as old as you," Mae said. "Your great-grandma sewed every stitch with her own hands."

Beth looked up. "Do I get it when you die?"

Mae smiled, remembering the uncomplicated greed of small children. "I'll make you one of your own. And you can choose the pattern. Maybe log cabin." She put a piece of thick plastic down, placed the quilt on it, and wrapped. "Here. You carry it. Careful now." Beth picked it up; Mae finished putting the last of the preserves in a wooden crate and followed her out the kitchen door.

Tom and Lewis were fastening a freshly cleaned six-row planter to the back of the pickup. "The menfolk hard at work," she said. "Morning."

"Morning," Tom said. "Will you look at the job Lewis did? Almost good as new. Simpson would buy it back for more than we paid for it."

"How much do you think we'll get?" Mae asked.

"Should get fifteen hundred a row," he said. "Cost thirteen grand new." Tom wiped his hands on the thighs of his filthy overalls, came over to give her a kiss. He stopped short, then bent and put his hand on Beth's shoulder. "Honey, you take that back inside now, okay? Will you do that for me?" The girl turned, hesitating, looking up at her mother.

"Tom, please," Mae said.

"It's not for sale," Garvey said. "Take it inside, Beth. Put it somewhere safe, okay? Now come here. Let me say good morning." He grabbed her arms, leaned across the wooden crate between them and kissed her forehead. "Come on now," Tom said. "We're wasting time."

"I was going to make breakfast," Mae said.

"We'll get something there."

"But the money . . ."

"Or we won't," Tom said. "Come on." Mae walked toward the cab with her preserves; she stared forlornly at the pickup's bed; it contained six pressed-back chairs. She'd been going to recane them one of these days; they were antiques. She'd bought them just after she and Tom were married, the dowry she hadn't brought with her.

Tom climbed into the driver's seat, and Lewis hoisted himself into the back where he could keep an eye on the planter and chairs.

"Lewis," Mae said. "Will you be warm enough back there? You stay out of the wind."

"Yes ma'am," Lewis said. "I'll be fine, won't I, Dad?" No response from Tom. He was fiddling under the dashboard.

"Damn electrical system," he said. As Beth came tearing across the yard, Mae settled on the passenger side, the box of preserves at her feet. Beth hopped in next to her mother, Tom turned the ignition, and the truck coughed to life; by the time they hit the blacktop, it was in second. Its headlights cut a golden swath before them as they took off toward Millrock.

Garvey hit the wipers once to remove the thin coat of moisture on the glass. "What'd you pack?" he asked, gesturing to the box at Mae's feet.

"Oh, stuff," she said. "You know. Some kraut, pickles, pears, blueberry jam."

"Leave the jam," Tom said.

"Okay," Mae said. She didn't question him, just reached over, pulled out the five pint jars of blackish-blue preserves and stashed them under the seat. "You like my jam?"

Tom looked at her and grinned. "What if I do?"

Mae shrugged and looked away, out the window. The sun cracked the horizon, and a touch of light fringed the upper branches of a stand of trees at the eastern border of their land. Now that all the water was gone and the trash removed, the land was flat and dark again. God, it was pretty here. The sun's dome began to appear, and long shadows swept the fields.

· 17 ·

They drove down the road in silence. Beth, who'd been so lively, was going back to sleep. She slouched against her mother, her head lolling like a broken flower on its stalk. Tom seemed to be whistling under his breath, keeping time with his inaudible tune by tapping his fingers on the driving wheel. Mae contented herself with breathing the cool freshness of a river dawn and watching the landscape coalesce as they drove north. Already the birds were beginning to play tag among the hickory and redbud. In this light, they all looked alike, the river swallows and grackles, mourning doves and blackbirds. Their silhouettes were identically black, their tapered wings like the flat pods of milkweed. The green leaves dotting the branches began to assume a clear shape, rather than the smudges a child with a blunt crayon would have made. The road rose and fell, and occasionally Mae caught a glimpse of the river, now well-contained within its banks, as it rolled south, its surface a glistening clarified sheet like crumpled foil.

They reached the far edge of their property and started along the barbed wire fence belonging to Rod Tessley and his wife Sally. The Tessleys's white farmhouse, like the Garveys's, needed paint and a new roof, and their barn was in considerably worse shape. To Mae it looked as though two of the central supports had rotted or settled, and the roof threatened to collapse. They passed the driveway, as the Tessleys's truck, with Rod, Sally, and the girls crammed in the cab, came lumbering toward the road. Mae looked out the rear window, and lifted a hand, but none of the Tessleys saw her. Her sudden movement roused Beth, who sighed and hustled her shoulders as if she were caught in a crowd. "Where are we?" she said.

"Hush, sweetie," Mae said. And to Tom, "They're selling their old combine." She could see it lashed to the back of their truck, laughably small compared to the recent models. Tom glanced into the rear view mirror, and shook his head. "Yep," he said. "They are."

"*Who* is, Mom?"

"The Tessleys, honey."

Beth swung around and strained to look out the window. In a voice as light as she could make it, Mae said to Tom, "I think Lewis has a crush on Lisa Tessley."

"I think so, Mama," Beth said. "On Betty Gaumer too."

Tom turned to her and smiled. She shook her head, gently, firmly, to keep him from making fun. She reached up and stroked Beth's hair. "Shh, honey, you turn around now and settle down."

Another few miles brought more light, a firmer clarity to everything. Mae could now see the stalks of weeds, the jutting clumps of sawgrass which topped the levee, each blade sharp against the morning sky. And then they passed the entrance to the Birkins's farm, its grey farmhouse needing paint and shingles. Mae could see Dave Birkin coaxing his Jersey milk cow into the trailer. The milker was already loaded in his truck. On the other side of the cab, Judy Birkin lifted her two small children, their legs loose as limp celery, onto the seat.

This was getting to be too much for Mae. With each neighboring farm she passed—each beautiful piece of rich bottomland the river had flooded, destroying crops, killing stock, ruining rugs and floors and wallpaper—she felt more and more desolate. "The Birkins, too," she murmured. Turning toward Beth, she grabbed her under the armpits and pulled her into her lap, hugging her. "Are you warm enough? Want to sit here?"

She wondered how Lewis was, had a sudden vision of him scrunched up against the cab, shivering, his lips blue. Beth had turned her head, and now she pointed. "Mom," she said. Mae turned in time to see Lewis, jazzy as a jay, waving to the truck behind them, to Lisa Tessley, who waved back.

· 18 ·

By the time they reached the outskirts of town, the full enormity of what was going on had settled on Mae Garvey. Here they were—and for all she knew there were more streaming in on other roads—three families simply living, or trying to, according to what they'd been brought up to believe. If you worked hard, you'd be rewarded. If you had a square of earth, a share of sun, a strong heart, and willing hands you could make something of yourself. Now they were off to sell what was theirs as a way to keep from losing everything.

If anything could have depressed her more, it was Millrock. The road wound past the Harkness Iron Works. It wasn't so long ago when the place was in full operation; she'd been in high school then, and her uncle and all his buddies worked there, and the money poured out of their pockets into the local shops and stores and bars, and the town had a fresh coat of paint and the sidewalk benches were bright green. Now her uncle was in Little Rock or St. Louis, or somewhere. He'd left his second wife in the Memphis bus station, claiming the only woman he'd ever really loved had been his first wife, Mae's aunt, dead in a car crash at twenty-four.

Someone had painted on a long piece of planking NO HIRING—DO NOT INQUIRE. The sign was poorly executed; black dribbles fell from the *g* and the *q*. Only one of the factory's six smokestacks seemed occupied with polluting, and only a few wisps of white smoke drifted upwards from its brick lip: the others stood empty of anything but air. A single short row of cars huddled close to the factory in the acre of parking lot.

Steel mesh gates hulked around the factory and the lot, barbed wire topping the fence and slanting inward as in a prison yard. Beyond the gates, cars and campers clustered. Mae could see that whole families, with nowhere else to go, were living there, right out of their vehicles, hoping the plant would return to normal operations. "Tom," she said. "How long since it's been all closed down?"

"Two months," Tom said. "Maybe three. Hell, I don't know. I don't even know why. It's been years since it was really going."

Mae didn't reply; she was staring at the side of a small cream-colored camper, where a sheet hung with the words "A Job Please—Family of 5—I Need Work." She remembered the men she'd seen in Millrock, clustered around those notices. "There's more of them every day. Where are they coming from? I always thought you went to the city, not out here to the sticks."

"There aren't any jobs in the cities either," Tom said. He gestured with his head. "A lot of them look like farmers."

Mae glanced at him. "Everyone looks like a farmer to you," she said. "If you had your way, everyone would *be* a farmer."

"Sounds good to me," Tom said. "Think of all the problems that would solve."

"Who'd run New York?" she asked.

"Someone was doing okay," Tom said, "before those Dutch-types sailed into the harbor."

· 19 ·

By the time the auction began, the day was nearing mid-morning, and the May sun was hot. Mae felt sweat trickle down her sides, and self-consciously dabbed at her face with a wadded Kleenex. Hal Armstrong, not a bad man himself, but the most feared and hated one around these days, stood before a microphone on a plywood platform. He was enormously fat; his jowls had jowls, and his little blue eyes were no bigger than dimes. He wore a red-checked shirt which bulged in front, and he hadn't tucked it in, as though its hiding his belt would disguise his size. He had a blue bandanna in one hand and he mopped his brow fervently. Behind him, another of those hand-painted signs she'd been seeing all morning read HAL ARMSTRONG—FARM LIQUIDATOR—SALES—AUCTION TODAY. Mae could never get used to the word "liquidate." Someone, it could have been Tom, had explained about "liquid assets," but all she could think about when she saw the word was *the river,* and its surefire means of liquidation.

She stopped counting at thirty-two; the crowd of men and women stared up at the moonfaced Armstrong, whose jowls shook as he jabbered on in that peculiar language men with nothing but money on their minds spoke at auctions. Most of the men wore jeans or overalls, the seats and knees threadbare or patched with denim scraps; their boots were black and crusty around the soles, splattered with mud, and laced up with good thick black laces, the no-nonsense laces that lasted. The women wore jeans or wraparound skirts and cotton blouses. Some had kerchiefs over their hair. Mae could see from the slant of their backs they were doing their best to look jaunty. Their machines, their livestock, their lives were on the block. She turned to Tom and told him she thought it was time to unhitch the planter.

Mae took her sauerkraut and pickles, her pears and applesauce, and set them up on one of the rickety tables where the other farm wives had laid out, as at a wake, their belongings and their wares. There were tottering old bridge tables belonging to the Grange, and long particle-board slabs supported by homemade sawhorses. In the heat, everything seemed to sway, as though at any minute the earth would tilt, and everything would land up on the ground.

She'd picked a corner of one of the long tables; most of it held food. There were other canned goods, jars of cherry preserves and grape marmalade, and Billie Jean Winegardner's prize-winning tomato chutney. There were loaves of bread, apple and pecan pies, handmade quilts, family photographs, empty wooden frames, old Ball jars, small handblown bottles, arrowheads—whatever the women had thought might be of interest to the scavengers who would be prowling, looking for something cheap from someone already down on his luck. There was a couple now, probably down from Cumminsville. They were younger than she and Tom, and they wore clothes they hadn't bought at K-Mart. The woman spoke, in a voice with a crystal edge, and Mae wanted to break her fingers as she touched the edge of a pie and brought the manicured nail to her mouth.

Mae looked over at the truck where Lewis and Tom were working; she hurried over to do what she could. Behind her, Armstrong's voice was almost unintelligible as it jabbered and babbled, repeating, making gibberish of English as he filled the air with sound, keeping people from thinking straight and making clear decisions.

"Careful now," Tom was saying to Lewis as she drew up.

"Hey," she said. "What can I do?"

"Just get out of the way," Tom said.

Mae looked at her son; his face was almost apoplectic; they were straining to turn the planter so it could be pulled to its place in the line of machinery to be auctioned.

David Birkin, their neighbor, stepped up. "Morning, Mae," he said, and nodded. "Morning, Tom. Need a hand?"

The planter rotated slowly, its runners and tamping wheels ripping the ground as Tom pulled on the yoke. "No thanks, we can handle it," he grunted. Birkin turned back toward Armstrong and his babble. Mae moved with him, touching his elbow. He looked at her and smiled.

"Don't mind Tom," she said. "You know how he is, Dave."

"Yes, I do," he said. "Just like his father. You're looking well, Mae."

"You're looking good yourself. Where's Judy?"

"Why, she's right over here. Come say hi."

Judy Birkin stood before the table Mae had just left. She bent over, taking things from a cardboard box. As Mae and Birkin drew closer, she set out a crystal perfume bottle, some lace antimacassars, a soup tureen, a dainty cup and saucer of bone china. "She's crazy for that stuff," Dave Birkin said. "Excuse me."

As Mae stood there, Sally Tessley came up. They'd greeted each other earlier, and now they watched Judy Birkin, seeing themselves. This time Mae had brought mostly canned goods, but still she knew how Judy felt. The woman bent over one more time and took from the cardboard box a crystal vase. Even from that distance, Mae could tell how beautifully crafted it was, how much Judy loved it. The facets in the cut crystal threw rainbows on Judy Birkin's face and on the table. "Look," Mae said, grabbing Sally's hand. Judy brought the vase close, as if to smell it, and set it down carefully on a piece of lace.

"I hate being a farmer's wife," Sally said. "I really do." She moved away, toward her husband Rod. Mae wondered if their combine had hit the block yet. Mae walked up to Judy Birkin. As her shadow crossed the woman's face, Judy looked up and a startled, almost guilty, smile swept onto her pale features.

"Were you spyin' on me?" she said shyly. "This vase was . . . well, it doesn't much matter, does it?"

"How you doing, Judy?"

Judy Birkin stretched her face and nodded, as if trying to say that everything wasn't quite perfect, but very fine nonetheless. And then she sighed. "We sold our stock," she said.

"I heard."

"It's easier without the animals. You know."

"Yes," Mae said, thinking of the eggs, the slop, the feed.

"Miss the milk," Judy said, and looked away, as at some sign that would tell her what to say next. "But I don't miss the milking," she said, and smiled again.

"You got some pretty pieces," Mae said.

"Thank you."

"You should get a lot for that vase. It's a good one."

Mae walked over toward her preserves and saw that Tom or Lewis had brought the pressed-back chairs over. Now what would she ask for these? She rested her hands on the backs of two of them, and hoped no one would be interested.

"Don't matter none," Judy Birkin said. "Just a bunch of old things. Sooner they're gone, sooner we can get on to living in the twentieth century."

Sally Tessley hurried up. "Mae," she said, "I hate to be the one tells you, but I think your planter's up soon."

Armstrong was down off the platform and moving along the equipment lined up for auction. He wore a straw hat now, and its shadow over his face accentuated the weight of his neck. He'd left the microphone behind; with his bullhorn he looked like those pictures of that Mississippi sheriff with the German Shepherd dogs Mae remembered seeing in *Life* magazine. She hurried up to Tom, and took his hand. Tom didn't even look at her; he was staring at the men who crowded around his machine. They wore shirts from a Sears catalogue, shirts with fake mother-of-pearl buttons, and straw boaters like the ones at the Haywood

County Fair. Their shoes were brown and polished, and the few with suits wore them open-throated, no ties. Mae looked down and saw Lewis elbowing his way through the crowd. She had to hand it to the boy; he had his father's staunch spirit, but something else besides. He could *sense* trouble, and pull it toward him to soothe and comfort, like a lightning rod.

Armstrong's voice came over the bullhorn so fast that Mae could hardly make out the words. "Here we have a brand-new, almost brand-new 1981 six-row planter belonging to your friend and my friend, our neighbor Tom Garvey. He's in a fix, who wants to help, let's start the bidding at five thousand, do I hear five, thank you five, do I hear five-five, five-six, do I hear six . . ." The hands went up, came down, the price inched up. It was over in less than two minutes. The planter sold for seven thousand, two hundred and fifty dollars—twelve hundred a row. Tom stared at the ground. Mae watched Lewis reach up and touch his father's arm. "Lewis," she said. "Go see if you can find your sister, okay?"

Armstrong had sold a John Deere tractor and a Kelley disk, and then he walked back toward his microphone and plywood platform, mopping the back of his neck. As Mae stared up at the platform, a young man came with an easel and placed on it a large photograph of a farm. It looked real familiar to Mae, but she couldn't quite place it. And then she knew. Dan Gaumer, his wife Ethel, and their children, Billy and Betty, climbed the few steps and stood beside the picture of their farm. In front of them, Armstrong cavorted like a fat man from the circus, a freak. The Gaumers looked embarrassed and scared. Armstrong waved his arm at his stockmen and they began driving up pieces of heavy equipment.

"Okay now," Armstrong said, his voice slower, more intelligible. He spoke into the microphone and stared out over the heads of the assembled farmers and their families as at a dancing girl gyrating on a knoll miles away. "Next we have lot number fourteen, the Gaumer farm." Tom's brow furrowed, and he pulled away from Mae and whispered something to the man beside him. "Everything to be sold. You want to know anything 'bout this equipment or livestock, just step up and ask Dan Gaumer here. He's our friend and neighbor and he's worked this farm and he knows every inch of it, and you just ask him."

"Wait a minute," someone yelled from the crowd behind Mae. The farmers had started elbowing one another, talking, their voices rising like a swarm of bees made suddenly angry.

Tom turned to Mae. "Dan Gaumer," he said. "He's just three miles down river." Everyone was talking, and no one was trying to keep his voice down. Mae could see Tom getting angrier and angrier; when that happened his forehead grew red as a persimmon in December. Armstrong looked around uneasily, tapping the microphone for order. "You all know his place down near Osborne."

Earl Smoot, a farmer from the other side of the river, who Mae knew mostly by reputation—he was a fierce fundamentalist and had a fiery temper—was making his way toward the platform. Mae strained to hear him over the general commotion.

"You ain't gonna sell him out here," Smoot yelled. "We understand what's going on. You can't do that here. No sale. I swear to God. No sale."

"Now hold on, boys," Armstrong said, over the microphone. His voice boomed out and echoed off the small stand of trees behind the crowd.

Mae cupped her hands around her mouth. "No sale," she yelled. Tom cupped his mouth and yelled too. Around them other farmers were picking up the words and turning them into a chant. David Birkin and Rod Tessley were yelling. Don Bogen was yelling. Smoot stood up in front, waving his arms like a lunatic band conductor. *No sale, no sale.*

Armstrong's voice broke through. "Now, we're runnin' a professional auction here, boys, so let's just settle down a little. There's no need for this carrying on, no one's trying to hurt anyone, you know me. . . ."

No sale, no sale. The refrain had grown thunderous. Farmers were stamping their feet, raising clouds of dust, clapping their hands. Armstrong looked pointedly over at Jim Roy Watson, who stood lounging against his patrol car with a couple of armed deputies. He raised his chin, shaking his jowls, and the sheriff moved closer. Armstrong grabbed the microphone and shoved it against his cheek as if it were a rifle stock and he were aiming to shoot. "You boys just ain't listenin' to what I'm sayin' now so if you'll just shut up your godalmighty traps for a minute so's you can hear the whole story. . . ."

No sale, no sale, no sale, no sale!

Mae was caught up in the carnival aspect of it; she'd felt the need for this kind of public release for weeks, ever since the rains had come. While she chanted, clapping her hands, she saw Ethel Gaumer lower her face into her palms as if she were crying; saw her husband step forward, then back to comfort her, then forward again toward the microphone. His face was caught between worry and anger; he didn't know what to do. He started yelling something but Mae couldn't make out the words. Then he sidestepped and pushed Armstrong out of the way and seized the microphone. "It's too late," he yelled. "They done already took it."

"No sale!" Mae yelled, and then felt her voice fade away. All around her others quieted. Gaumer was still yelling into the microphone. "You don't understand. My farm's gone. They're not selling my farm. The bank already took it, they already foreclosed on me."

The crowd was suddenly still. Armstrong savagely grabbed the microphone back, and Dan Gaumer, like a man who'd just been beaten, slunk back to the thin wavering line of his family. "You hear? I ain't selling his farm. Now go on, move back. Earl Smoot, you ought to be ashamed of yourself."

Gaumer took a step forward and started to speak again. "I appreciate what you tried to do, but my place is already gone. This stuff is just what's left and I'll need the cash to clear out. I could use your help. So you go on now, Mr. Armstrong."

Hal Armstrong picked up the list of equipment which went with the Gaumer farm and shaded his eyes with his open palm. "All right now," he said. "We got an IHC four-oh-three combine with a thirteen-foot grain head and four-row corn picker. What am I bid?"

· 20 ·

At school that week, Lewis barely talked to Betty Gaumer. Her brother Billy was in the next grade, a different classroom, so Lewis got to see him only on the playground and during lunch, but he seemed to be keeping to himself as well. Betty had always been a bit of a tomboy; she still wanted to play kickball after the other girls wandered off to stand in pastel clumps and giggle. But now she walked alone, playing with a yo-yo, or talking to her brother.

He could remember clearly the way she'd stood on the wooden platform behind that huge disgusting man, her hands clamped together and twisted behind her back, or so it seemed from the tilt of her shoulder blades. A little knock-kneed, wearing pale yellow socks which came to mid-calf and a green and red Scotch plaid skirt, she had looked straight overhead, never looking down at where the men and women stood repeatedly thrusting their fists into the air. He had opened his mouth and yelled along with them. They all seemed as convinced as they could be. Better than church, where occasionally someone yelled out in agreement at something Reverend Burchill said. He'd seen the veins and tendons in his father's neck, the sweat forming at his mother's temples, and he had stepped away from them until he was behind Beth and had his hands on both her shoulders. When Beth said *No sale,* it sounded like "No school," perfectly reasonable for a Saturday morning.

The next Saturday he was up while it was still dark, moving stealthily into his jeans and shirt, his sneakers, his denim jacket with the brass buttons, just like his father's. In the kitchen he stuffed a piece of bread in his mouth, gulped down some orange juice, and, ignoring the chickens and cows for the minute, jumped on his bike and headed south on the thin ribbon of macadam.

As he reached the rise of road overlooking the Gaumer place, outside Osborne, the world had begun to be visible. The rustle in the culvert to his left could be a squirrel, a woodchuck, a trickle of water rushing over reeds. He was panting—he'd really pushed himself—by the time he braced his legs against the road and sat, looking at the family, so small in the little valley. Slowly, Lewis began to roll toward them, squeezing the handlebar brakes. When he got as close as he dared, he stopped, braced his legs again, and sat there.

He'd known the Gaumers were leaving this morning, but he hadn't known they'd be almost packed before daybreak. Last week he'd stood while cow after cow, hog after hog, tractor, disk, planter, combine, a flock of chickens were put on the block and gavelled away. There was nothing left but the buildings themselves and the land they stood on, and those belonged to the bank.

Mr. Gaumer was tying a wooden box to the top of the old battered station wagon, already piled high. Under the box was a mattress, and upside down, their legs sticking out at wild angles, a few straightback wooden chairs. Lewis thought he saw a stool, and a bicycle. The rest seemed to be boxes. All of it was crisscrossed with clothesline, the web of a mad spider.

Lewis watched as Betty and Billy Gaumer carried out

more boxes and set them down on the tailgate of the wagon. In the farmhouse, lights burned, casting a soft apricot-colored glaze on the window glass and out the rectangle of open doorway. The house itself looked safe and pleasant, somewhere you'd like to stop for breakfast. But the three figures at the station wagon, bathed in the afterglow of that light and the thinnest of dawns, were ghost-like.

Billy stretched and turned around to scan the horizon. Suddenly he saw Lewis on his bike, and he grabbed his father's arm and pointed. Mr. Gaumer nodded, then turned and waved to Lewis in one long sweep. Lewis waved back and watched as Billy ran up the hill to where he sat. By the time he reached the bike, Billy Gaumer was winded, and he stood there in awkward silence, catching his breath. Finally he smiled, let it fade, put his hands on his hips, and looked back down at his father. "Hey," Billy said. "Dad says they got Little League in the city. Uniforms and everything. And a place called the YMCA where you can go swimming and play basketball."

"What city?" Lewis asked.

"Cincinnati. I'll get to go to Riverfront Stadium and see the Reds and Bengals."

Lewis suddenly wished he hadn't come. "That's great," he said, and then, "that's really great," trying to push some enthusiasm into his voice.

The boys were silent again, watching as Betty walked up the hill toward them. "Billy," she said. She stopped and stared at the road. "Hi, Lewis. Billy, Dad says we gotta hurry. Come on."

Lewis reached in his pocket and fingered the rock he'd found, perfectly round and polished by the river until it shone dully under a lampshade like a stone from the moon. All week he'd carried it.

"Bye, Lewis," Betty said. She looked at him fully for a second, then turned and ran down the hill. The slap of her sneakers on the asphalt sounded unnaturally loud.

"Well," Billy said. He shrugged and kicked his toe against the road. "Gotta go. See you." Awkwardly he stuck out his hand, and Lewis fumbled his hand out of his pocket and grabbed Billy Gaumer's hand and shook it once like he'd seen his father do. The pebble felt hot in his pocket. Then Billy turned and was gone as well, running as fast as he could.

Lewis sat on his bike. Mrs. Gaumer came out of the house and climbed into the passenger seat, and Billy and Betty jumped in either side of the back. The car's brake lights faded and then came back on, and a door opened. Billy ran back into the house and turned off the kitchen light his mother had forgotten to extinguish. Without looking up at where Lewis sat, the boy got back into the station wagon, and Lewis watched as it moved clumsily up the dirt driveway toward the main road. At the point where the dirt and the asphalt intersected, it seemed to Lewis the station wagon hesitated, but then turned north toward where he sat, toward Hazlett, Rosner, Lexington, Cincinnati. Lewis raised his hand to wave. There was a brief flurry of faces as they passed him, and he kept waving, but it was clear that no one was looking back. The station wagon, its topheavy load swaying slightly, accelerated, and then was gone.

Lewis pushed off with his feet, and hunched over the handlebars as the bike coasted down the hill toward the Gaumers's. He tilted at the mailbox, turned left, and came to an abrupt stop, mired in the mud of the driveway. He let the bike drop, and with his heart beating hard, he walked toward the house. Before him, the sun was coming up; rays of light shot skyward, individual as the opening triangles of a fan. They radiated behind the farmhouse, pointing everywhere but there. He pulled open the screen door, saw how precariously its hinges still held it to the molding, and then tried the warped wooden kitchen door itself. It pushed inward, creaking, and he stood and looked at the desolation of the Gaumer house.

One window had no glass in it; a thin piece of plastic kept out the wind. The floor was chipped and cracked, a bumpy linoleum ocean that had once been yellow. Lewis could see the indentations where the kitchen table had stood.

He realized he hadn't been to the house since the previous fall, but it seemed like years now. Pieces of newspaper were taped to the refrigerator. The ceiling paint was peeled and flaked.

Lewis backed out as though the house were contaminated, and he kept walking backwards toward his bike. The cattle pens were empty, the barn door swung in the slight morning breeze. He thought he heard the lonely sound of a cow lowing, but it was only the wind. Over the horizon the sun rose, a huge unblinking cyclops eye. He turned and bolted for his bike, pumped it up the hill as hard as he could, and didn't stop until his own farm was in view, with the chickens, the cows, his sister, his father and mother—his home.

PART TWO

· 1 ·

Before leaving to contract with Wade for the corn, Tom had had a long talk with Mae. "Now don't you go getting him riled," Mae had said, and Tom had replied, "I thought you didn't care about his feelings anymore." She'd colored at that and looked away. He hadn't been able to tell if she were embarrassed or angry until the wooden spoon she was holding had snapped in half in her hands. "I'm sorry," he'd said, and she had turned to him, her eyes blazing. "It's just that he's got the power," she'd said, "and making him angry isn't going to help us. And we need all the help we can get. You want to come with me and look at that pile of bills?"

"No. I'd get another ulcer."

"You got an ulcer?"

"No," he'd said, "but I'd get me a pair." He had grinned. She hadn't. Time was he could always make her laugh.

He parked the pickup next to the other cars and trucks, Rod Tessley's old Dodge, Dave Birkin's Toyota, Winegardner's Chevrolet. Earl Smoot was there, and Bill Youngdall, and Carl Zemke. He saw them all standing in a tight little group as he walked up. Behind them the twin silos of the Leutz Grain Corporation commanded the landscape. On each was painted the corporation's name in the corporation's colors, black and gold, like a yellowjacket. Tom wondered if they drew their share of lightning in a thunderstorm.

The men were looking at a chalk-streaked blackboard scattered with numbers. Joe Wade and his foreman Harve

Stanley stood before it. Stanley, one of the dumbest men Tom had ever met, was holding a clipboard, and he shifted his weight from foot to foot as if in time to some company regulation. Wade was smartly dressed, with a red bandanna tied around his neck. Tom had to give it to him. Put him in a city, in a fancy restaurant, and he'd be all silk and diamond stickpins; out here, he was a country gentleman, flannel and denim.

Wade was talking to Tessley as Tom arrived. The numbers on the blackboard

AUG 3.50 SEPT 3.50 OCT 3.50

weren't that bad, what the corporation was promising farmers who signed contracts now, the price per bushel of corn delivered. How many did he want to contract for? How many did he *have* to contract for? was more like it. The night before he'd sat down with Mae at the kitchen table after the kids were asleep, and they'd lit the kerosene lamp and whispered over the papers on the table, as though everything would be easier if the light were soft and their voices low. He licked his pencil and drew numbers on the yellow sheet, too many zeros.

Tom looked up. Tessley had signed something and had backed his pickup over by the silos, and a thunder of gold was falling into his truck, beautiful yellow dust swirling in the air. Stanley was staring at him, mouthing something. Tom cupped his hands around his ears. "Garvey," Stanley was yelling, straining above the noise of the falling grain. Tom came forward and stood before Wade and Stanley. Joe Wade leaned over and stuck out his hand. Tom reluctantly shook it, once.

"What do you say, Tom? You get the water off your land?"

"It's goin'," Tom said. "I sent away to Knoxville for this special drain and plug I installed in my field. Whenever it floods you pull the plug and all the water runs back into the river. Pretty handy."

Wade smiled. "You could patent that and make yourself a lot of money."

"I reckon that's more up your alley than mine," Tom said.

Wade's face was a trifle less friendly. "You want to contract?"

"Yep," Tom said. Did the man think he'd come out here to talk?

"Three hundred acres," Wade said. "That right?" Tom nodded. "How many bushels you figure on wagering?"

"A hundred-and-thirty an acre."

Wade whistled. "That much?"

"That's right," Tom said.

Stanley wrote on the clipboard. "That'll be three-forty-five."

"What?" Tom said. He turned and pointed to the board. "It says three-fifty."

"Morning's price," Stanley said. "Gone down since."

"Then why's it say three-fifty?" Earl Smoot asked. He was standing next to Tom now.

"Haven't had a chance to change it," Stanley said. "Excuse me." He wiped the numbers with the butt of his palm, wrote 3.45 three times.

"Who sets the damn price?" Smoot wanted to know. All the farmers stood next to Tom now, hands on their hips.

Joe Wade stepped forward. "The free market sets it, you know that."

"I heard it was little trolls in the Chicago pits," Carl Zemke said.

Tom turned and pointed a finger at Wade. "I say it's your father-in-law. He sets everything else in this county, even the cost of ice cream."

Wade turned his palms flat up, as though he had just turned his pockets inside out looking for change. "If you don't like the price, you can haul your crop to Memphis or Nashville. You're a free man, Tom, you got options. No one's forcing you to do anything you don't want to do."

"If you haven't got cash," Tom said, "you haven't got

options. Jesus Christ. Three-forty-five. I better take it fast before it falls to three-forty and my ass is in a sling."

"It already is, Tom," Carl Zemke said. "All of ours is."

"We'll see," Tom Garvey said. "We'll see."

· 2 ·

Joe Wade walked out of the Leutzcorp main office twenty minutes later. He was tired of the three men he was with, with their starched handkerchiefs and expensive black shoes. At this point, he was even tired of the rolls of blueprints they carried under their arms. Their herringbone suits looked too hot for mid-May, and the pencil-thin mustache on the one named Benbow twitched whenever he moved his eyes from side to side. He walked them to their Audi, and leaned on the maroon door as they buckled themselves into their seats. "Now remember," he said, "if you have any trouble filing these, get to Ed Neiswinder. He knows all about it." He stood back, and as if the release of his hands began some complex electrical current, the car rolled evenly forward, turned, and was gone. Wade waved at the backs of the men's clean-shaven necks, and as he followed them he saw Tom Garvey standing near his pickup, watching as a torrent of hybrid corn seed poured into the bed of the truck. Wade loved the sound of falling grain, a dry crackling sound, like corn popping underwater; mostly he loved the hard watery feel of it in his fingers, each kernel pushing against the others, the way holding a fistful of river felt.

Garvey was staring intently at the Leutzcorp men in their

green coveralls with the collars turned up, their plasticine goggles; they looked like they worked at some breeder reactor rather than for an agricultural concern. Tom stood close enough that it seemed to Wade he was ready to catch any errant kernel which flew into the air. His face was coated with fine yellow dust from the bottom of the bin, the husks rubbed off and pulverized into something softer and finer than doubleground flour.

Joe Wade would have liked to feel nothing for Garvey, but every time he saw the man he was buffeted by contradictory emotions. He thought of Garvey in bed with Mae Stillwell, and his throat got slightly dry; he thought of Garvey out at work in his fields from sunrise until dark, and although he didn't envy the backache or wet feet, he envied the *desire*, the burning need to make things grow. That Garvey had those children he envied maybe most of all; they were fine-looking kids, and they walked with the ease and strength of their mother, the determination of their father. Since his wife had died, Wade had become more and more aware that his largest grief was that he had no children, not the absence of Emily Leutz, although there had been sweetness there, possibly enough to build a life around. Now, instead of stepping back into the air-conditioned office with its tinted glass, he forced himself to walk over to Garvey. There was—aside from personal feeling—business between them.

Garvey looked at him briefly, and then back at the men who were finishing up, sweeping the spilled grain into a sack, removing the small piles of dust, though some of it filtered through the air like pollen.

"Get your money's worth?" Wade asked.

"I reckon so," Tom said. "As far as I could see."

"How come you didn't answer my letter?"

Tom looked away, and then stepped forward and took a handful of corn from the back of his truck, and sifted it back and forth, from one hand to the other. "Didn't know I had to," he said.

Wade shrugged. This was always the way it was with Garvey, always had been even in high school. Garvey was always in trouble with one teacher or another, for surliness or close-mouthedness. *Who won the Presidency in 1952?* Miss Kelly had asked. *Eisenhower,* Garvey had said, not Dwight D. Eisenhower as anyone else would have said. Garvey didn't know the meaning of *elaboration,* and Wade was more than a little convinced that this was a habit, a calculated defense, a sly maneuver never to say anything which could be remembered or repeated, as though words were slippery as snakes, and apt to be poisonous.

"Gonna plant one more crop, huh?" Wade asked, proud of himself for the implicit trap he'd laid. There was only one answer, and it was close-ended; it held in its monosyllable the seed of Wade's final victory.

"Gets to be a habit," Garvey said, and grinned. He tossed a few kernels to Wade, and they sounded like a baby's rattle as they bounced off his shirt and fell to the asphalt. "Be seeing you." He climbed into the cab of the truck and sped off, stopping, just barely, at the Leutzcorp gate before he turned left down the county highway toward home. As he went, Wade watched the corn dust rise from the back of the truck and swirl behind him, a thin double helix of gold.

· 3 ·

After Lewis got home from school, he and his father carefully measured and poured the corn through a complicated funnel and into gunny sacks they'd washed out and dried in the sun. To Garvey, the rows of bags of seed corn looked like money in the bank; he couldn't have been happier had he opened the barn and seen gold bullion there—well, maybe that wasn't strictly true, but still. . . .

They had fried chicken and mashed potatoes and red-eye gravy for dinner; Mae had killed and plucked a pullet that afternoon, and everything seemed about as good as it could be—seed corn in the barn, the ground drying up nice for planting again. The flood had brought with it, as it always did, fresh silt, the richest land there was. If everything went their way from now on, Tom knew he could expect a bumper crop—the *Almanac* promised a good humid summer, and though he knew he shouldn't depend too heavily on mumbo-jumbo, as Mae called it, he did. His father and grandfather had. He pushed himself back from the table and patted his stomach. "You got anything special for dessert, honey?" he asked.

"Maybe," Mae said, "but first there's chores to do."

"Nothing that can't wait," Tom said.

"Jessica's sick again," Mae said. "I went to see Springer this afternoon, and he gave me more medicine for her."

"What's the matter this time?" Tom asked.

"Same as always," Mae said. "Won't eat. Moans when I try to milk her."

"You milk her this morning, Lewis?"

"Tried to," Lewis said. "She wouldn't have a part in it."

"You didn't tell me," Tom said.

"You were going in to Leutzcorp," Mae said. "Lewis told me."

"Should I look at her?" Tom asked.

"No, you go with Lewis and work on the dozer. Beth and me'll take care of the cow."

· 4 ·

She'd left the barn door open to catch the last streaks of sun. The orange rays just touched the black and white Guernsey standing restlessly in her stall as Mae stroked her muzzle and looked into her brown eyes, trying to gauge the extent of the illness. She knew it wasn't just a simple thing, but they hadn't the money to get Dr. Springer to drive out to look at Jessica; *dear* God, she thought. Jessica had been a reliable cow, a good milker. And she was Beth's favorite. Mae took the box of pills Springer had given her out of the bag; they were big as coffee cups. Getting one of these down the cow's throat would be like threading a needle with a piece of clothesline.

Beside her, Beth wrinkled her mouth in consternation. "She don't look good, Mama," Beth said.

"Doesn't, Beth," Mae said. "Not don't. But this medicine will make her better. It's strong. Don't you worry about Jessica."

Beth reached up and stroked the cow's flank; it seemed to Mae the animal shuddered, but then she'd been shivering all day, since she'd checked in the morning. "Hear that, Jessica? You just rest and I'll come and see you before bedtime." Mae knew that wasn't too far away, and maybe Beth would have to wait until morning. If all went well, Jessica would be better then.

· 5 ·

Lewis held the acetylene torch, and sparks sprayed from it in miniature celebration. Tom could see his son's eyes behind the welding mask as the boy bent over intently, cautiously applying the blue-tipped flame to the damaged dozer. Even with his goggles on, he could see his son's energy was entirely concentrated on the job he was doing. Tom had worked for a while with Lewis watching, but what the boy was doing now required no special skill, no intricate knowledge of machinery, just perseverance and dedication, and strong back muscles. Lewis could do it.

He took off his goggles and stepped backwards. The blue tip came away from the joint Lewis was welding as the boy turned to his father. "No," Tom said. "You go ahead. You know what you're doing. Don't be afraid. I'm gonna take a little nap. These last couple days have tuckered me out."

Lewis stood up, uncertain. With all the confidence he could muster, Tom turned his back and walked over to a nearby bale of hay, and leaned against it.

"Dad, don't go to sleep. Maybe you better do it."

"You're doing fine," Tom said. "You do just what you been doing, and remember I'm right here."

His father had done this with him lots of times when he was a boy. He remembered the first time he'd milked a cow by himself, pulling too long and hard on one teat so that old Billie had turned around with murder in her eyes, and his father had jumped from the pose of sleep to startled life, intervening in time to ease the boy's fingers into a more comfortable rhythm. Lewis couldn't do any harm to the dozer, could he? And he could hardly hurt himself worse than a little burn. Tom settled back against the bale of hay and closed his eyes, then opened the left one just a crack. Through the fuzz of lashes he saw Lewis look at him uncertainly, then shrug and turn back to the dozer. Sparks flew. The boy was doing good, real good. After a while Lewis didn't even bother to turn around and check. It was harder than he'd thought, pretending not to watch.

· 6 ·

"Mr. Leutz called and asked for me to tell you to call him if I seen you," Elma Schloss said. She was chewing a wad of pale green gum so big her words almost couldn't find their way around it, and she looked up from the tabloid she was leafing through, straining the already taut skin of her neck. Joe Wade figured she must now be in her late fifties; she'd worked behind the counter in Leutz's Pharmacy since he'd been in high school and had tried to get her to sell him and his friends packs of Lucky Strikes before she thought they were old enough.

"Thank you, Elma," Wade said, laying down the tube of Ben-Gay and the bottle of Anacin on the thin strip of linoleum counter; the rest was covered by a lurid color picture of some creature with reddish-green eyes and wings where its ears should have been. "What's that?"

"Just something they found in a closet over to Crockett

County," Elma said. "Never woulda found it had it just kept its big mouth shut at night. It kept waking up the family. Killed a couple sheep. Your back hurting, Joe?"

"A little," Wade said.

"Don't you forget I told you Mr. Leutz called."

"I won't, Elma," Joe said. "Thanks."

She rang up the purchase and gave him change for a five, then placed the items in a small paper sack with Leutz Pharmacy printed in faded script. She was lost in the tabloid again before he left the store.

On the sidewalk he stood and rubbed the small of his back with the fingers of his right hand, as inconspicuously as possible. Too much driving, not enough walking. Hard to believe your body could start giving out on you as early as your mid-thirties. He'd have to start jogging again, and playing fast-pitch softball as he had in Knoxville, or get over to the gym in Trenton and work out a bit. He wondered what Leutz wanted, but wasn't in the mood to call.

For the past year and a half, since Emily's death, the old man had called more often than not about nothing—complaining to Joe about headaches, asking questions about the business he knew the answers to, just trying to talk to someone, anyone, who was a link to his daughter. Joe sympathized, but he hated the constant reminder of his wife's death; it made *him* feel no better, even if it helped the old man. He knew he should go over and visit more often—and he had a standing invitation for dinner, which he might have accepted could he stomach the German maid's cooking. But the house had become a mausoleum, first to the memory of Gertrude Leutz, who'd died fifteen years before, and now to Emily, their only daughter. Wade remembered the old man's face at the wedding, how he'd danced with Emily, his leathery lizard's face gleaming with sweat, as though he'd live to be a hundred. Since her death, he rarely left the house, entrusting more and more of the business to Joe. And while it was surely one of the reasons he'd married Emily Leutz, Joe wasn't exactly ready for the sudden responsibilities that had been thrust upon him.

A few cars and trucks moved through on the main street. Even at the height of its prosperity, Millrock hadn't been big enough to warrant a streetlight, and now there wasn't enough traffic to keep a cop occupied for twenty minutes a week. He passed the employment office, a brick shoebox, exactly like all government buildings of its type, designed by an anonymous architect from a second-rate firm. Its gilt-edged decal spelled out *Department of Human Services,* and from the flagpole rooted in cement a tattered nylon flag drooped. A bulletin board hung in the hushed glass-enclosed space between the two sets of doors, and a man, a woman, and three children stood, checking the three-by-five index cards, looking for work. As he watched them, the reflection of an old truck, beds, chairs, a chiffonier roped to the top, washed past on the plate glass like the sun passing over water. Joe Wade roughly pulled himself away and walked up the sidewalk toward his Bronco. He'd better get to the office and call Leutz. Then he saw her.

Beth Garvey sat alone, staring up at the sky where there might have been a pigeon, a passing cloud, a somersaulting angel, her hand stuck through the rip in the cellophane wrapping of a package of Oreos. She was surrounded by three brown paper bags bulging with groceries, all of them precariously balanced on the bench before the Millrock General Store. Mae was nowhere to be seen.

Wade found himself inexplicably cheered. The day he'd caught the children and their mother standing before the bank he'd been in too much of a hurry, and as he'd driven away, he couldn't help feel he'd been insensitive, had wounded Mae Garvey's considerable pride, as he'd often done when they'd dated in high school. He'd never given her enough credit, that was it: he'd always assumed she was like other girls in Millrock, girls who wanted Wade, or his friends, to take the first step, say the first thing, offer the first bite. Not Mae Stillwell. Today he'd do better. If he could find her. Before the General Store, several sagging particle-board tables were covered with junk—old spoons, jars, kerosene lanterns, bits of fabric, piles of magazines, blouses and slacks and jeans. Five women who looked as if they'd come from some citified place were picking through the piles, wasting time on a Saturday afternoon.

As casually as he could, not wanting to disturb the somersaulting angel on which her eyes were fixed, Joe Wade sauntered over to Beth Garvey. Her hand had come loose of the cellophane handcuff and was moving toward her mouth when he spoke. "Are those Oreos?" he asked. She stopped, her hand arrested in midair, and she turned from the angel to him. He could see that his question had neither embarrassed her nor caught her off guard; he also saw that he was of infinitely less interest than angels, clouds, even the blank blue sky. "My favorite," he said. "Yours too?" No response. For an idiotic moment he thought about trying out some of the phrases he'd learned during Peace Corps training, before his father had gotten so ill and he'd been called back from San Diego, before he'd even gotten a chance to go overseas. He knew how to say *This is definitely not my bag* in Korean, and had never had a chance to say it, except in training. He sat down instead, moving one of the bundles so that its contents stood steadier.

"Mama said I'm not supposed to talk to strangers." Her voice was that imitation-adult simper that always made him smile.

"Beth," he said. "I'm no stranger. You've seen me lots of times. You've seen me talk to your mother and father. Besides, I was born here, right here in Millrock. How long have *you* lived here?"

"Six years," Beth said. "I'm only six."

"Well, I win," Wade said, insanely. "I beat you by thirty years." He pointed at the package she held. "Do you think I could have just one?"

Beth looked at him carefully, as though her decision could have a long-term impact on her future. She turned back to her angel. "No," she said.

Wade laughed. "You're your father's daughter, all right," he said. The door opened behind him, and he watched Mae Garvey carefully close it. She was dressed in a simple sleeveless cotton shirt and wraparound denim skirt, and she had an old leather handbag with a very long strap over her left shoulder. Her expression didn't change when she saw him, but something flickered in her eyes. Her hair was loose, and although a bit tangled, it was freshly washed, and in the mixture of shadow and sunlight outside the store, its highlights shone orange-gold. She'd never looked more beautiful. Without acknowledging Wade, she moved to stand before her daughter.

"There's no answer, Beth. We'll just have to wait for him."

Wade stood, as though he'd been waiting in her parents' parlor to take her to a dance at the school gym. "Hello, Mae," he said. "I was trying to talk your daughter out of a cookie."

"I bet you didn't have any luck," she said. One hand held the strap of the handbag in place and the other was wrapped around what looked like a bottle of dish soap sequestered in a small brown bag.

"Not yet," he said. She smiled at that; she'd always smiled at his persistence. "You stranded here in town? I don't mean to butt in, but I'd be happy to give you a lift. I'm on my way to Osborne anyway. I have to go right past your place." Did she believe him? It was hard to say. She would want to be home with these groceries instead of sitting on Main Street waiting, but her pride might keep her from accepting a blatant favor. And if not her pride, her obeisance to her husband's pride. "You tried to call Tom and there was no answer? Well, if he's on his way, he'll have to pass us and otherwise . . ."

"I guess it'll be all right," Mae said. He almost expected her to extend her hand now, but she was Mae Stillwell Garvey, not Mary Beth Jenkins or Betty Sewell, or anyone else.

"Let me help with these," he said, picking up two bags. "Beth, can you manage those cookies alone?" Beth was not amused.

They moved to load the packages into the Bronco just

several parking spaces away. As they passed the tables of junk, Mae stopped for a minute, then kept on walking; her eyes were narrower, her mouth more tense.

"You changing your mind?" Wade asked.

"No," Mae said. "We'd appreciate the ride."

"What is it, then?"

With a backward jerk of her shoulder, Mae indicated the table they'd just passed. Wade turned his head to see a woman in a taffeta dress holding up a cut glass vase, turning it in the light.

"It's just that vase was Judy Birkin's," Mae said. "She had to sell it at auction."

"That's too bad," Wade said. "Did she get a good price?"

"Some things don't have a price," Mae said.

Wade looked at the city woman. She'd moved to talk to one of her friends, the two of them touching the vase now. He put the two bags in the back of the Bronco, and without looking at Mae again, he walked over to the table and fumbled through the pile of corduroy. The women's voices dropped, a bad sign. He hunched closer and peered over the woman's crimson shoulder. He could see her face now. It had rarely known the sun, but was no stranger to pancake makeup. "That looks almost like an antique now, don't it," he said.

"Pardon me?" the woman said.

"I seen lots of those around," Wade said. "Everyone around these parts got a drawer full of 'em. Mind if I look?" He took the vase out of the woman's hands. "Yep," he said, turning the vase's bottom toward the woman and thrusting it at her like a fist. "See that green marking on the bottom there? They all got that. There's some real old stuff around here, but you need to be careful. Don't mean to be nosy or nothing, but don't buy that. It's a cheap copy."

The woman turned away from him, toward her friend, and the two of them moved to the other table, where they busied themselves with a silver creamer and sugar bowl. Wade turned and winked at Mae; he took the steps in one jump and pushed through the door into the General Store.

In a moment he came out with a brown paper sack.

He opened the back door of the Bronco and ushered Beth in; then he opened the front door with exaggerated politeness, tipping an imaginary hat and bowing so low its brim dragged in the pebbles and dirt at curbside. Mae got in and settled herself, and Wade handed her the vase.

"I don't need more soap," Mae said.

"You give it to her," he said, and decided not to push his luck any further. He'd thought he might keep up the accent he'd been having such fun with, but one look at Mae's face told him otherwise. He put the Bronco in gear and drove off. In the rear view mirror Beth looked happy as could be. He was a trifle hungry. He really could have used an Oreo.

· 7 ·

Just outside of Millrock, they passed the Harkness Iron Works. Wade hoped Mae wouldn't say anything about it, and she didn't, but her hard look at the smokeless stacks, the small number of cars inside the gates, the makeshift trailer camp adjacent to the factory was eloquent enough. "Lot of people out of work these days," he said. "Things'll get better. They have to."

"Can't get much worse," Mae said.

They moved smoothly now; outside of Millrock the road surface improved, and the Bronco hummed along, its wide thick tires swishing against the asphalt, adding another soothing layer of sound to the steady hiss of air. The trees were in full leaf now, their small green palms unfolded, open to sunlight and the imminent arrival of summer. A squadron of river swallows swooped across the water and hovered over a large oak, now dead, a livid black lightning scar etched in its bark. Mae turned as they passed the tree and as she swiveled, Wade could see she took in Beth and the groceries in the back seat, and the few things he kept in the storage area behind. His golf clubs were there. Just the sort of thing she'd take offense to. Like the Bronco itself.

"You play a lot of golf?" she asked.

"When I have to."

"Must be awful hard on you," she said, turning and staring out her window at the levee. "All that walking."

Wade glanced at her, then back at the road. He smiled. For all the times she'd tried to be smart or sharp-tongued, he never really felt she had an evil bone in her body. He reached across, pushed the button on the glove compartment, and the door fell open. He pulled out a cassette tape and slipped it into the tape deck in the dashboard. Mae didn't say anything.

A guitar began twanging, and then the familiar voice. "You still like Willie Nelson?" he asked.

"Sure," she said, her voice carefully noncommital.

I grew up a-dreamin' of bein' a cowboy,
Lovin' the cowboy ways.
Pursuin' the life of my high-ridin' heroes
I burned up my childhood days.
I learned all the words of the modern-day drifters
Don't you hold on to nothin' too long . . .

He remembered the summer after he graduated from the University; he'd been called back from Peace Corps training, called back to Millrock and the life he'd always known, after feeling—deep in his chest—that he'd finally gotten out of Tennessee. His father was taking a long time dying, and his mother's eyes let him know that after they put the old man in the ground, he was staying here, putting down roots as real and stubborn as the coffin they'd bury his father in. And Mae Stillwell, two years out of high school and looking to settle, had decided—he could tell from the way she looked at the man at the softball games during the summer league—on Tom Garvey. It had been a toss-up when he and Garvey were in high school together, but when he went away, well, what could he expect? He hadn't exactly pined for her over there in Knoxville; he'd been, well, *someone,* and there were lots of Pi-Phis and Tri-Delts who would have sold their fathers' spreads for a date with him. But back home, Mae Stillwell was the Elgin Marbles, Beethoven's Seventh, all the things he'd never learned about in Millrock, all the things he'd come to value.

Cowboys are special
With their own brand of misery
From being alone too long
You could die from the cold
In the arms of a nightmare
Knowing well that your best days are gone

So when he got those two tickets to the Willie Nelson concert at the Grand Old Opry, there wasn't anybody else he would have thought to ask. The song was almost over, Willie mournfully wailing one more time about how his heroes had always been cowboys, and then the last guitar chords faded, and "The Orange Blossom Special" began hooting and chugging its way over the speakers. Mae reached up and pulled an imaginary cord, letting steam escape, and smiled.

"What are you smiling at?" Wade asked.

"Oh, nothing," Mae said.

"Come on. I've known you too long to believe that."

"I was just thinking about Nashville. I can still see the look on your face when they wouldn't let us backstage."

Wade blushed, and laughed. "I did too know him. I swear

I did. He came to a party at my fraternity after a concert he gave at Tennessee. I swear. We drank juleps. I spent a whole month with him that night."

Mae laughed. "I know, I know. You even know how many red bandannas he has."

Beth sat forward in the seat and put her elbow between Mae and Wade. "What's so funny, Mom?"

Mae turned around and stroked the child's face. "Nothing, honey. I just got the giggles."

"How you doin' back there, sport?" Wade asked.

"Fine," Beth said. She seemed friendlier now, everyone was laughing, good spirits flowing everywhere, the landscape speeding by, "The Orange Blossom Special" careening madly down the tracks.

Wade leaned over toward Mae. "You think you could convince her to give me a cookie?"

Mae looked at him, a bit more sober. "Do your own dirty work," she said. But Beth had overheard, and her good spirits remained undampened. In the rearview, Wade watched her punch her hand into the cellophane and pull up an Oreo. She stuck in over the top of the vinyl upholstery, and he took it. "If you want a pop, you just reach in that fridge and help yourself."

"What fridge?" Mae asked.

"The one in the back seat," Wade said.

"This one, Mom," Beth said.

Mae turned around and stuck her head over the seat. "My Lord," she said. "Next thing you'll get yourself a telephone."

"Can I have a pop?" Beth asked.

"Now, you're corruptin' my daughter," Mae said.

"If she's your daughter, I'm sure she can handle it," Wade said. He turned to her, all smiles, and saw that she sat poker-faced again, staring straight out the windshield at the broken white line. He shook his head. He couldn't say anything to please her. It was as though she were *looking* for things to fight about. He wished he'd half the skill of the engineer of the Orange Blossom Special; he couldn't seem to keep his locomotive on the tracks.

Beth noisily opened a Dr. Pepper and drank from it. The music had run out; now the hiss of the tape accompanied the tires and the passing air.

"We got your letter," Mae said. Wade gripped the wheel a little more tightly and tried to take a deep breath without getting caught. "Tom's not interested in selling."

Tom, Wade thought. "How do *you* feel about it?" he asked. This time he didn't breathe at all. She didn't say anything. He remembered those contests he supposed high school kids still staged with one another—staring until one looked away, arm wrestling, and the big one: a lit cigarette was placed in the declivity formed by two forearms pushed together. Who'd flinch first?

"It must be hard to hang on," he said.

Mae continued to stare out the windshield. "Not for Tom Garvey," she said. Was there anything in her voice to tell him what she really meant? It was exasperating. He remembered the last conversation with Garvey himself, how he thought he'd end-gamed Garvey, and how the man had wriggled out. He'd taught his wife and children well, the sonofabitch.

He pushed the eject button, and Willie Nelson popped out. Wade put the tape back in the glove compartment and took out another. Mae still hadn't looked at him. Georg Solti. The Chicago Symphony. A nice Midwestern group. He pushed the forward button and the first chord of Beethoven's Seventh sounded; the oboe passed the descending fourth to the clarinet and the slow crescendo began.

8

When the telephone started to ring, Tom Garvey was astride the barn's ridgepole, gripping a lightning rod with one hand and holding his son's ankle with the other. Lewis was stretched downward at a dangerous angle, nailing oak shingles in place to cover the gaps in the roof the storm had revealed. There was nothing he could do but hold on. It might be Mae, calling from Millrock to say she was ready, but he'd expected she'd be another hour, and it would take that long to finish the roof.

He and Lewis had made the shingles themselves, Tom teaching the boy how to hone the adze, then how to measure and saw the oak heartwood into the proper thickness, and finally how to use the adze to shape the individual shingles. The rich slightly burnt smell of the oak, the spiraling curls of wood the adze made as its razor edge stroked the grain, seduced him into forgetting his watch; he worked slowly, carefully, with a craftsman's precision, the way he *liked* to work, when the bank and the weather weren't breathing down his neck. Ever since he could remember, Tom Garvey had been good at things like this, working close with his hands, tinkering with car engines or some complicated doodad his mother had in the kitchen, a mechanical apple peeler or a busted iron.

It had been Mae's idea: she and Beth would go to town and do the shopping, if Tom would give her a lift in. Since he hated Millrock, he could get back home and work on the barn roof; as he'd estimated it, he could finish the job and hightail it back to pick her and Beth and the groceries up.

So when the phone rang, each shrill jangle a reproach, but lovely too, the sound trilling across the fields and the river, now a glittering mass of fishscales in the late May sun, he counted to himself. There was no way he'd get down to answer it before dark at this rate. Nothing like a little height to bring perspective: he *loved* it up here. Besides, if he let go of Lewis, the boy would slide down the roof, off the barn, fall on his head and die. Mae surely wouldn't want him to do that.

He told himself as the rings reached twelve it was probably some guy from Memphis Casualty and Life wanting to know if he, Tom Garvey, for only pennies a week. . . . The phone stopped. It had gotten to sixteen. Lewis said, "Probably Mom," though his voice was faint, all his air pushed by gravity to the top of his lungs. He took one last swing with the hammer and began to shimmy backwards, so that soon it was his knee instead of his ankle that Tom held.

The two of them crawdadded to either end of the roof-beam, and began working toward one another, taking the handmade shingles from one side of the matching carpenter's aprons they wore, the galvanized roofing nails from the other. Tom fastened them down with three short *bams* of the hammer; a tentative one to fasten it, and two staccato hits to nail it home. Then to his apron, and the next shingle went into place, one on top of the other, like fallen dominos.

He and Lewis met almost in the middle; the boy was getting good. He loved this silent working, this synchronous understanding of what needed doing, and doing it. And when they sat facing each other, close enough to bash one another's heads in with the hammers, he grinned at his son, and his son grinned back.

There was just one more thing to do before they hoisted themselves down from the roof, got in the pickup, and sped into town to get Mae and Beth. There was a big rotten spot on the eastern-facing slant and no number of shingles would do it—it would be like pouring sand down a sinkhole. They'd brought up a section of galvanized tin. Tom hated to do it that way; from the ground it would look slipshod and ugly, a barn roof part wood and part metal, but he consoled himself by thinking that after the second planting he'd take off the metal and fix it right. He'd buy plywood and then he'd make himself a bunch of the sweetest oak shingles. For now, the tin would have to do; it was a scrap left over from patching the silo, and, well, money being what it was, it would keep out the rain a hell of a lot better than an old cotton shirt.

They let themselves down the slope slowly until they had a footing, could brace themselves and nail it in. Tom searched for nailers, showing his son how to do it, how you could tell the difference between air and wood with the deftest and smallest of hits if you knew what it sounded like. And then rhythmically, around the perimeter, they began to put it in place. They were done in no time, and they pulled themselves up to the crown again, and Tom wiped his forehead with the sleeve of his undershirt. He looked out over his three hundred acres of corn that had rotted or never germinated, at the river which had done the damage simply because there'd been too much of it to flow between its own banks: *gotten too big for its britches* was what his father had always said, both when the river flooded and Tom disobeyed. Another two days, he figured, and the land would be ready for disking. He looked down at the tin they'd just nailed in place and saw it was crooked. That vexed him, a job done shoddily, and this afternoon there seemed to be all the time in the world.

"I'll get it, Dad," Lewis said. Before Tom could stop him, Lewis had slid down, pried out a couple of nails, tapped the tin with the hammer to correct its slant—he looked back up at his father, and Tom held his thumb and forefinger together in a perfect circle—and hammered it tight, this time in line with the roofbeam, the horizon, the curve of the earth.

Tom took a deep breath and held it, let it out slow. Below

him he heard the crunch of gravel, and, turning, saw Joe Wade's Bronco pulling into his driveway. Wade was driving. Mae was sitting on the passenger's side. He could see that clear enough.

· 9 ·

He'd turned the volume way down and had only whistled sporadically as they drove the final miles to the Garvey place. His elbow hung out the window, and his left hand—the one that used to have a wedding band—frittered on the chrome strip. Mae seemed not to notice anything now but the landscape, as though she were a visitor from another planet, beamed down for a fifteen-minute ride through rich river-bottom, her duty to absorb every detail. In the back, Beth sat silently, her hands primly in her lap. The Oreos lay on the seat beside her. In the rearview, she looked as if she were sitting for a formal portrait.

As Wade turned into the driveway, he was dismayed by the ramshackle appearance of the place. Mae's pride was such that it probably pained her to have him see it. She was suddenly all bustle and motion, rearranging the shoulder strap of her handbag, straightening an imaginary crease in her jeans, telling Beth what to do as soon as they got the groceries inside. Wade pulled the Bronco as close to the door as he could, ejected the Beethoven, and turned off the ignition. He looked up as he stepped out of the car and saw Tom Garvey, perched on the top of the barn like a huge demonic weather vane. The boy was up there too. Maybe it was some sort of weird family ritual, some sacrifice for the fertility of the fields. He almost laughed out loud at that, but sobered himself. "How's the weather up there?" was all he could manage in the wake of his Biblical vision.

"Pretty nice," Tom Garvey said. "Higher than down there."

Wade nodded, uselessly; there were times when conversation wasn't worth the effort. Mae struggled with an armful of bags. He turned to her. "Here, let me help you," he said. He carried two bags to the back door. Mae hurried ahead of him, pushing open the kitchen door and then turning to take the sacks from him as though she wanted to keep him from entering the kitchen. When she'd put them behind her and walked out again to the Bronco, she seemed to have regained her friendliness, as though being on land that she knew gave her a power his car had sapped.

One item still lay on the front seat. Mae picked up the carefully wrapped vase, and said, "It's a nice thing you did."

Wade wished at that moment that she was right; it *had* been a nice thing he'd done, but he'd done it for Mae Garvey's opinion of him, and not for Judy Birkin's collection of heirlooms. He shrugged. "Just neighborly," he said. He faced the barn and raised his hand as though saluting a far-away general. "Tom," he said, his voice sailing up to the man on the roof.

Without waiting for a reply, he threw open the Bronco's door, pushed himself in behind the wheel, took his sunglasses from his pocket. As he turned back toward Millrock, he pushed the Beethoven back on. The orchestra was partway through the second movement now, the Allegretto, and though the key had changed from A minor to A major, and the first violins had begun their limpid cascade of triplets, he could still taste the tentative elegiac stateliness of the minor theme.

· 10 ·

Mae and Beth were putting the groceries away as Tom entered the kitchen. He'd sent Lewis out to the farm's perimeter to check the final miles of fenceposts and barbed wire; that should keep him busy for an hour or so. He'd walked once around the yard practicing different approaches, but he didn't *feel* angry, and when he tried, *You know I don't like it when you take rides from Joe Wade,* it sounded gruff and silly, and he knew Mae would see through it in a second. He wanted to say the right thing, and he didn't want to fumble, as he sometimes did when the moment seemed important and his feelings were full. He was bothered by Joe Wade, always had been, by his money, which bought him fancier clothes and cars, and tickets to the Grand Old Opry and to the Louisville Symphony; and bothered by the self-confidence his money and family had given him. Wade had been to college, he'd seen the world. What Garvey knew, he'd seen on television, or in the movies, or in a magazine. He'd never even been to St. Louis. Hell, he never *wanted* to go to St. Louis, but still. . . .

Wade knew big words and fancy ways of talking, and he had married Milford Leutz's only daughter, and now, with the old man failing, Leutzcorp would soon be his. Not a good man to have as an enemy, though he'd never felt Wade disliked him, never felt that way at all. And Mae was all mixed up in the middle of it. He knew only that Wade was a threat—with Mae, and most especially with the farm. But now Garvey felt embarrassed and ashamed. He said it as straight as he knew how. "I'm sorry, Mae. The roof took longer than I thought."

As always, she surprised him. "What's wrong with it?"

"Old age," he said. "Same thing's wrong with me."

"That so?" Mae said. She reached to put a box of Raisin Bran up high, and Tom came over to help her, took it out of her hand and put it in the cabinet for her. She was close to him now, close enough for him to see the little half-moon of freckles on her right shoulder. He bent down and kissed it, and then slipped his arms around her waist and pulled her close. Mae turned to where Beth stood and gently pushed at Tom's waist with her palms.

"Well," she said brightly, as though she were dusting her hands against each other. "That just about finishes things in here, sweetie. Thanks for all your help in town. Now why don't you go feed the chickens?" Tom hadn't unlocked his fingers behind her, and she wrestled to get some sunlight between them while she spoke to her daughter.

"I fed them this morning," Beth said, the beginnings of a pout showing on her face. A year ago Tom would have picked her up, kicking and screaming, and taken her right to her room for a nap.

"Why not feed them again?" Mae said sweetly.

Something in her tone appeared to convince Beth, although Tom suspected it was the knife blade under the sweetness. His wife, too, had a way with words. When he tried to pull her to him, she jabbed him in the ribs with her index finger. "It's three o'clock on a Saturday afternoon," she said.

"So what?" Tom said. He moved to kiss her neck, but she squirmed away.

"You didn't have time to come get me in town," she said. "And what about the fields?"

"You mad at me?"

"But you have time for this. Are you sure this doesn't have more to do with how I got home than with how irresistible I look, all sweaty and covered with Millrock?"

"Honey," Tom said. Sometimes she made his head spin.

"You know I love you." He moved to kiss her neck again, and this time she let him. Her hands were on his back now, her open palms warm as sunlight on thin cotton. He could feel the pressure of each individual finger. He kissed her chin, her lips. He snuck a glance. Her eyes were closed. "We got to be quiet," she whispered. He kissed her again. "I sent Lewis to check on the fenceposts," he said. "I been meaning to do that all week."

"Beth's pretty fast with the chickens," Mae said. "Come on."

· 11 ·

It was almost Memorial Day, and, as Tom had predicted, the land was about ready for a second planting. The water had been gone two weeks, the trash cleared and the silt leveled, and most of the acres had been disked and sprayed with herbicide. But with the six-row planter gone and the antiquated two-row all he had to work with, Tom's head reverberated with the sayings his father had put there: *For every day past the first of May, you lose a bushel of corn an acre. At planting, a farmer's worth a hundred dollars an hour*. Tom knew the first pronouncement was a little dire, but still, here it was almost the last of May and one full day of disking still ahead. Tomorrow—Sunday—he'd start planting.

With the six-row he could put a hundred-fifty acres of corn in the ground in a very long day; with the two-row, if he were lucky, it would take him most of a week to plant the farm again, into the first week of June. Time was money, suddenly, in a very real sense.

They had macaroni and cheese for dinner, one of Tom's favorites. He knew it wasn't sophisticated fare, but that didn't bother him. The cheese sauce was thick and the pale gold of champagne, and the crust on top was mottled brown, with a slight crunch; if he weren't so exhausted and tense, he'd be one of the happiest men on earth.

After dinner the four of them went to the corral beyond the cattle pens for Beth's riding lesson, the only break of the day. All last year she'd been frightened of horses, would cry when Mae lifted her up in the saddle before her. But this year was different. This year Beth would touch Bram the bull; she fed the chickens without any help, and if one of them pecked at her hand, she'd hit it sharply on the head and watch its comb flush with blood. Now she rode smartly, leaning forward slightly, the reins held loosely in her hands, her feet high in the stirrups, her knees pressed correctly against the horse's flanks. She stared ahead of her, concentrating on relaxing, and every now and then forgetting to concentrate, and relaxing. Lewis walked beside her, holding the bridle, taking the horse in a circle past his parents, who sat like a rodeo audience.

As he watched, Tom became aware of a liquidity to Beth's body; the stiffness was gone from her neck, and the supple muscles of the horse's haunches seemed to ripple upwards through the girl's small body. Lewis sensed it too and he glanced at his father, waiting for the signal. Tom motioned for Lewis to let go, and he did, though he walked alongside as though nothing had changed. And then he stopped walking and Beth rode on, as she had, but suddenly aware she was on her own. There was the crucial moment when her neck tensed again, and Tom tightened his hands on the corral's rails should she panic and slip, but she kept on riding, and when she came around again her face was wreathed in jubilation. Tom turned to Mae, and she was laughing, and Lewis climbed up beside his father and the three of them burst into applause and Lewis even let loose a whoop as Beth, riding alone,went around and around the ring, proud as if she'd invented horses.

It was getting toward dark, near nine o'clock, she thought. She hit the hydraulic lever. "Hold tight, now. Here we go," Mae said to her daughter, sleepy on her lap. The hydraulic strained, and the disk and harrow rose from the earth they'd been mauling. Mae turned the tractor in a wide arc, and brought it back in line. She hit the lever again, and the disk and harrow lowered into the ground. The shiny metal plates churned up the earth, and the tines of the harrow slashed through the thick clumps of dirt, breaking them up. As she moved down the field, the earth turning over violently in her wake, a flock of birds feasted on the earthworms exposed by the disking.

Tomorrow was Sunday and she was looking forward to church, seeing the neighbors, finding out how the Tessleys's chickens were laying, if Smoot's mother had thrown any china this visit. She was looking forward to giving Judy Birkin her crystal vase back. Mae tried to think of a hymn to hum, but none came to mind. As you sow, so shall you reap, she thought. As you plow, so shall you turn over earthworms. Behind her, it seemed, all the sparrows and grackles in the world were shrieking.

Tom hunkered down and sighted along his thumb as he'd seen a sidewalk painter in a smock do once; he was only half-fooling, although Lewis thought it was very funny. He was checking on the straightness of the row of stakes his son had put into the ground. Not only did the line require the rigidity of a taut string, but the intervals between the stakes had to be exact as well: then the rows of corn would be exact, and all the work which followed—cultivating, harvesting—would be easier. He stood, satisfied, and put his hand on his son's shoulder. In the distance he could see the tractor belch black smoke as Mae finished the fields. "That's good work, Lewis," Tom said. "You got your Grandad's eyes. That's a real straight row."

Lewis grinned at his father, then picked up a rock the harrow had unearthed and flung it as far as he could. "You got your father's arm, too," Tom said. "That's a good long throw. Comes in handy if you ever have to play the outfield." He stooped, scrabbled in the dirt, picked up a rock about the size of a softball, and heaved it in his wife's direction, watched as it rose high, higher, cutting across the thin cirrus brushed with orange. It reached the top of its parabola, and plummeted toward the ground. Sometimes he felt like that, pulled down just when he thought he'd broken free. He couldn't tell where the rock hit, as it merged with the line of scrub on the horizon.

Garvey picked up another. "Here," he said, flipping it to Lewis. "What's that look like to you?"

"A potato," Lewis said, "only bigger."

"Rocks are a lot like potatoes," Tom said. "Each one sprouts about ten more. This field's been plowed a hundred times and the ground keeps spitting them up." He took it back and flung it as well, this time for distance.

"You and Grandad used to do this, didn't you, Dad?"

"Throw rocks?"

"You know," Lewis said.

"Sure did." Tom said. "You know how to juggle yet?" Tom picked up three stones, which soon moved through the air as though wired to the rounds of an invisible pretzel.

"Not yet," Lewis said.

"Well, remind me to teach you," Tom said. "You're gonna be twelve in another month, and a man shouldn't get to be twelve without knowing how to juggle."

"This is where he hurt his leg, isn't it?" Lewis asked.

Garvey let the rocks drop to the earth, one, two, three. He stared off at the horizon. Mae had better bring that tractor in soon or she'd get lost and drive it clear into another state in the dark. "How'd you know that?" he asked.

"Mom."

"Got real tough for him after that," Tom said, "His leg hurt him real bad. He wanted me to do something else, go to school or work on cars. 'It's too hard on a man's family,' he told me. What he meant was he should never have fallen off the tractor."

"How'd it happen?" Lewis asked.

"Who knows?" Tom said. "He never much talked about anything."

"Are you glad you didn't work on cars?" Lewis asked.

"I work on cars," Tom said. "Practically every weekend. That pickup's always needing something."

"You know."

"Yeah, I'm glad," Tom said. He didn't feel so glad tonight, but he knew it was just tiredness. He took a deep breath, filled his lungs with the rich river-scented air. "Sure," he said. "What in the world's better than being a farmer?" He sighed, larger than he'd intended. "After the accident we had to move to Memphis, you know. I was too young to farm it by myself, even with the old man badgering me day and night. Besides, I was finishing high school, and they got rules about that. *'If you're bossed, you're lost.'*" He stopped and laughed, remembering the tone of the old man's voice wondering if Lewis heard now what he'd heard then. "He used to say that when he came home from that factory. He hated it. Knew it would kill him."

Garvey stood awkwardly, not knowing where to take the conversation now, knowing only that he wanted it to be over. Where was Mae? She should be getting back. He turned and saw she'd come around upwind so the diesel smell and the sound of the motor had gotten blown away. "There's your Mom," he said. The single beam of the tractor's headlights swept the side of the barn. "Come on," he said. "I'll race you."

· 12 ·

Lewis, dressed in a blue serge suit already a little too small for him, a bright red polyester tie tight as a noose around his neck, sat sullenly against the window, staring out at the passing fields. Beth sat between Lewis and Mae, happy to be going to church. She loved to sing, even if she couldn't carry a tune to the sink and back, and she was yelping tonelessly as Mae tried to remember "Amazing Grace" and drive at the same time.

Mae felt only a little shabby this morning. How could anyone feel anything but wonderful, with the air as clean as freshly bleached sheets, and the sky cloudless and windless? The sun through the windshield of the pickup struck the tops of her knees; she'd pulled the flouncy hem of her best skirt up, and the movement of air in the truck, the bright glancing sun, all conspired to lift her heart in perfect tune. Her voice, like her daughter's, was something else.

Lewis looked over at the two of them in scorn and stuck his fingers in his ears; Mae broke off in the middle of *How precious did that grace appear* to laugh. Sometimes Lewis acted so much older than his age, and sometimes, like today, pouting because he hadn't gotten to stay home with his father, he acted like a baby.

Beth stopped singing too, and looked from her mother to her brother, whose face was growing red. "Lewis Garvey, you take your fingers out of your ears before they get stuck there," Mae said.

Lewis did what he was told. With nowhere to put his hands, he hit the dashboard. A thin cloud of dust rose from the padded vinyl. "It's not fair," he said. "I disked it. I staked it. I should be planting it."

"There'll be plenty left to plant when we get back," Mae said. "Your father may be fast, but if he can get more than fifteen acres planted with a two-row while we're gone, my name is Jack Robinson."

"Who's he?" Beth asked.

"You don't know anything," Lewis said.

"Never mind, sweetheart," Mae said. Lewis slouched still further in the seat; his tie and collar strained against his neck, and Mae was afraid he might strangle himself before he'd relent and sit up straight.

Enormous drillings rigs, as high as towers, were being erected in the fields they were passing. The land was well fenced and posted; from every few ticks flashed a small metal sign, black letters on yellow, LEUTZCORP. Mae was used to seeing the name of a new strain of corn posted as advertising, and she even remembered the old Burma Shave signs. But Leutz was the only man around vain enough—rich enough, maybe—to plaster the roadside with his own name. She didn't need any reminding. She knew whose land this was.

They'd driven north to Millrock and turned east on US 53; the church was several miles away, and all this land was Leutz's. Leutz's and Wade's, of course. And none of it bordered the river. She knew the trouble they were having with water, and she smiled. The smile faded as they passed a new bright green and yellow John Deere pulling an eight-row cultivator, its cab so high off the earth the driver could probably see Kansas City. Their corn, away from the river, had been up almost three weeks.

In the distance a huge irrigation rig drooped on spindly metal legs, a mutant praying mantis from a Japanese horror movie. To Mae it seemed the rig was large enough to water acres in a single sweep. Everything about Leutzcorp was oversized, especially its arrogance.

Beth pointed out the window at the new water pumps dotting the landscape, at the drilling rigs, poised in their search for water, higher than the highest tree.

"What are those?" Beth asked.

"Deep drilling rigs," Lewis said. Mae was surprised he'd roused himself enough to answer.

"For what?"

"Water," Lewis said.

"Mr. Leutz is running low, Beth," Mae said, by way of explanation.

"Is all that Mr. Leutz's?" Lewis asked.

"Mr. Leutz's and Mr. Wade's," she answered. "Eleven thousand acres."

Beth's face almost flew around from looking out the window to staring at her mother. "Eleven thousand? Wow . . . that's more than . . . how many times does three hundred go into eleven thousand?"

"More that thirty," Mae said. "I can tell you that much. Hard to believe he wants more."

· 13 ·

As much as Joe Wade hated this water expert sent by some fancy firm in Arkansas to do his father-in-law's bidding, he wanted the information the man had to give. He wished he could remember the man's name; that would make it easier to talk to him. The man peered through his steel-rimmed bifocals at the field hands pulling hundreds of feet of pipe out of the ground. Wade couldn't believe it was as simple as that: you sent this drill bit down into the earth, and kept adding sections of pipe as you went deeper and deeper, and that old drill bit just kept spitting the earth back up until you hit water.

But this was ridiculous. The men kept pulling pipe until it seemed that when they got to the end it would have Chinese characters on it. Harve Stanley chewed gum and stared at the horizon, his arms crossed on his chest. The water expert stabbed the steel-rimmed spectacles further up his nose; that meant they were getting close.

As the final section of pipe was pulled, an ugly mixture of sand, rock, and mud oozed from the drilling bit. The water expert wrinkled his lip in distaste, as though the mud in Arkansas were infinitely preferable. "Your aquifer's about gone, Joe," the man said. "You're gonna have to find some way to get to the river. How else you gonna use all this equipment your father-in-law bought?" Joe Wade shook his head. Sonofabitch. He wasn't sure what annoyed him more, the lack of water or this jerk.

"I've got a way to get to the river," he said. "It's just gonna make some people pretty unhappy."

"Well, Joe," the man said. "You have to break some eggs to make an omelet."

· 14 ·

The interior of the Millrock Baptist Church was hot, even though the transoms above the stained glass windows had been opened with a long wooden pole by Rod Tessley, a deacon in the church. He wasn't much good as a farmer, but Mae had to hand it to him: he was terrific at opening transoms. She fanned herself with the Order of Service and shifted in her seat. The minister was droning on about God's mercy and God's charity. It wasn't that she didn't believe in those things. It was more that she thought they weren't as simple-minded as Reverend Burchill made them out to be. His sermons were excruciating, and this one was no exception. Around her, the other members of the congregation sat in various modes of attention. Judy and Dave Birkin were looking down at their laps; Dave had been known to do crossword puzzles in church, and today Mae wouldn't have been surprised if Judy was helping him. Sally Tessley sat at strict attention, as though the airplane she was on were about to crash and she was listening to instructions which would save her life. Beth and Lewis were being unbelievably good, but then their eyes were closed: maybe they were asleep.

Reverend Burchill's voice grew louder, and Mae understood by this that the sermon was almost over. Both Beth and Lewis opened their eyes as though stuck by hot needles. "He is the bringer of sunshine and rain," said Burchill, "and the force behind the miracle of life itself. Perhaps the water was a test, a test of our faith in him. Let us turn now to hymn eighty-six."

The room exploded in a riot of coughing and scratching and page turning; the organist bore down on her opening chords, the congregation leapt to its feet and began to sing "A Mighty Fortress Is Our God." Mae loved it for its grandeur and its sternness, although Reverend Burchill had undoubtedly chosen it for its mention of *flood*.

A mighty fortress is our God
A bulwark never failing,
Our helper He amid the flood
Of mortal ills prevailing.

As she sang, Mae thought of Tom, working with outmoded equipment on his small share of God's green earth. *The earth is the Lord's and the fullness thereof.* All he wanted was his shot at living his life according to his rules. Was that so bad? She could see him running down the row of stakes he and Lewis had so carefully planted, knocking them over with the dual front wheels of the ancient tractor. He might as well have been out there with his water buffalo and ploughshare, she thought. And Joe Wade raised and lowered a hand, and men whose names he didn't even know turned the ignitions on new John Deeres.

And still our ancient foe
Doth seek to work us woe
His craft and power are great
And armed with cruel hate
On earth is not his equal.

She could see Tom squinting into the sun, pulling his cap down to shade his eyes, his thick black hair matted, and sweat running down his chest. Behind the tractor an old two-row planter dropped seeds into the ground. The six-row planter could put in the entire crop in two days, but if they hadn't sold it, there'd be no second crop. The final organ chords rattled the transoms, and the congregation, delighted that the service was almost over, boomed out its "Amen."

"Let us pray," Reverend Burchill said, and every neck jerked down.

Outside was a flood of brightness. Mae ushered Beth and Lewis through the line of post-service wellwishers, and she too shook the Reverend's hand and thanked him, and meant it. She may not have admired the sermon, but the service always did her good. She liked the prayers, and the singing, and now, especially, the fellowship.

Everyone lingered in the parking lot, moving toward their cars and then away, as they saw one more friend to say hello to, thought of one more person to inquire after, found one more reason to keep from going home to work. Lewis edged away from Beth and Mae, and soon was talking to Lisa Tessley, his eyes on the ground. Mae kept Beth's hand in hers and caught up with Judy Birkin. Dave was nowhere to be seen.

"Judy, wait a minute," Mae said. "I have something for you." She hurried to the truck and took out a package wrapped in tissue paper, whispered to Beth, and then the two of them walked over to Judy Birkin and handed it to her.

Judy knit her brows together, clamped her pocketbook under her elbow and unwrapped the tissue paper. Her mouth opened as she saw what it was, and her eyes flew back and forth between the vase and Mae's face.

"Mae, I can't take this," she said.

"Joe Wade bought it and asked me to give it to you," Mae said. "Sorry it didn't get to you sooner."

Judy's eyes snapped. "That man is full of surprises," she said. "He wants to buy our farm."

"We got a letter, too," Mae said. "So did the Tessleys."

The anger subsided a little. Judy Birkin shook her head

so her hair bounced. "Offering good money, too, considering," she said, and blushed. Here was a woman who didn't know her own mind, Mae thought. But then, did any of them? Wasn't there something in all of them wishing for an easier life than this? "You thinking of selling?" Judy asked.

"Tom wants the land for Lewis and Beth," Mae said. But did Lewis and Beth want the land? Had he asked himself that?

"It's getting hard to hang on, Mae," Judy said, her voice rueful.

"I know," Mae said. "But you hang on to that vase now, you hear?"

Judy smiled. "Yes," she said. "I will. Thank you."

Mae stood and watched her go. She felt a hand on her arm, and, turning, looked into the kind face of Rod Tessley. Now that the service was over and his deaconship put away for another week, he was back to his good-natured self.

"Howdy, Mae. You sure do look pretty." He blushed. "But then you always do. Where's Tom?"

"Hi, Rod," Mae said. "Thanks for opening all those windows in there. If you hadn't been on the job, we'd all have died in the fiery furnace." She paused and looked at Lewis, who stood now, his hands beside him, his feet still, staring straight into the eyes of Tessley's daughter. "Tom's home working," she said. "You know we sold the six-row. He's planting the whole farm with his father's old two-row. He'll be at it for days."

· 15 ·

It was late afternoon, but the sun's intensity hadn't diminished. Tom was still bucking the tractor up and down the staked rows, dragging the planter behind him, but now Lewis was helping. He'd run into trouble while they were away at church; the planter kept jamming, and he'd wasted precious time, having to idle the tractor while he jumped down to fiddle with the sprockets. He cursed his bad luck, his lack of money, his having to work so hard each year with so little to show for it. At one point he'd thrown a fit, came perilously close to bashing his fist against the side of the tractor, a move that might have felt good for the small spot of time between his decision and the impact of flesh on steel. Then he would have regretted it, he felt fairly certain. Now Lewis trudged alongside, a wrench in his hand, his eyes fastened on the corn being dropped by the planter.

Tom's shirt was soaked with sweat and streaked with dirt. He wore a Leutzcorp cap to shade his face, but his neck was sunburnt. His beard was heavy—he hadn't shaved all weekend. He tried to hide his tension and anxiety as the afternoon wore on, but he was exhausted, and each pair of rows he planted reminded him of how many more there were to go. The river might just have finished him this time.

He'd gone through the small talk, asking about church, laughing at his son's impersonation of the Reverend's handshaking, listening attentively to Lewis's halting sentences about the Tessley girl. Now he rode, his eyes straight ahead, muttering his own kind of silent prayer.

"Wait, Dad," Lewis said. "It's jammed again."

He threw the tractor into neutral, disengaging the gears, and looked down. Lewis reached behind one of the seed bins with the wrench and joggled the chain, tightened a nut, rechecked the tension of the oiled links. Without looking up, he said, "Okay, try it."

Tom put the tractor into drive and moved on. He looked down at Lewis and was about to yell, "Good work," when they got to the end of the row, and he suddenly had too many levers to switch and wheels to turn. He hit the hydraulic, lifting the planter to turn it, when he heard a gnashing of metal. He turned in time to see oil spurt from the hydraulic. He could feel his heart clench, and his blood pressure rise, in blind fury.

"God . . . *bless* it!" Tom said. "Now what?" He suddenly understood God's wisdom in creating children—their real function was to prevent adults from doing and saying what they might otherwise do were there not children present. Had he been alone, he might have thrown himself upon the machine as if it were a dangerous animal in need of subduing. Lewis ran to the tractor as Tom turned the ignition off and jumped down. The boy reached in and pulled out a hose, oil-covered and split, and handed it to his father. Poor Lewis. Tom watched the boy's face crumple. Tom realized his lips had curled, and he was breathing in short bursts through clenched teeth. He didn't have to rip apart a piece of machinery; there were human beings he could rip apart. "Come on," he said. "We're going to town. I just bought that hose!" He ran for the farmhouse and driveway where the pickup was parked, feeling in his pocket for his keys as he went. Lewis was right behind him.

He said nothing to Mae; she'd find out about it sooner or later, and if he knew her, she'd try to talk him out of it, or try at least to cool him down and clean him up. But there was something satisfying in being covered with sweat and grease and dirt, in having oil in his hair and on his lips, in having his own hard-won earth on his hands—he looked like a wild man, and he felt like one. Lewis sat with one arm out the window, testing the wind. Garvey kept both hands on the wheel, wrapped hard around the plastic grips. He glanced at the speedometer, which registered sixty-seven, as fast as the truck had gone in over a year. Behind him, white smoke hung in the air like a ground fog.

· 16 ·

"Hi, Ruthie. Sorry to bother you on a Sunday. This is Joe Wade. Is the Senator around?" Wade lounged against the cheaply paneled wall of Bob's Pool Room, talking into the black plastic receiver of the wall phone. His back was turned to the crowd, all of them just in from the fast-pitch softball game they'd played. It was the first real exercise Wade had had in a while; the Ben-Gay he'd bought would come in handy.

While he waited for Neiswinder's voice, he turned, cupped the phone and yelled to Stanley, the team catcher, who was standing at the bar, his hands wrapped around a thick chilled mug. "Gimme a beer, will you, Harve?" The Leutzcorp team looked sharp in their yellow shirts with black pinstripes and the company name scrawled in fancy script across their backs. These were class outfits; Wade had driven to Nashville personally to supervise their design. They were like the Pittsburgh Pirates' uniforms, and they looked professional.

Everyone was drinking beer. Stanley handed Wade a cold

mug, and turned to the other team's members. He was heady with victory, slightly drunk, and his red face glistened. "Trouble with you boys is you're all musclebound from rustling all that cow shit out the barn door," he said. Wade had to hand it to Stanley; the man was a real wit. Maybe it hadn't occurred to him that the opposing team was made up largely of men who had things to do other than practice. They had been outclassed—Wade tried to imagine how dispiriting it would have been to take the field against a smartly outfitted team when you were wearing old cut-offs, t-shirts, sweat shirts: and that first inning, with its over-thrown balls, poorly fielded grounders, well, it had been an embarrassment. It was good of these men to come in and have a beer, even if it was on the house. Had it been him, he'd have gone home and pulled the shades. Where was Neiswinder, anyway? Waiting for the next commercial?

Ruth Neiswinder came back on, her voice more like that of a secretary than a wife. It was the classic office run-around, the one he'd never gotten used to, even when his own secretary did it for him: *I'm not sure, let me check, no I'm sorry he's not in,* while the guy sat there shaking his head and making weird motions with his fingers. At least Ruth Neiswinder didn't try that line; Wade couldn't really be expected to believe she didn't know if her own husband were home.

"He can't come to the phone right now, Joe," she said. "Can he call you later?"

"If he calls this evening, he could get me at home," Wade said. What was Neiswinder doing? Watching the Braves? "Otherwise he could get me tomorrow morning at the office."

"I'll tell him, Joe," Ruth said. "By the way, how are you?"

"Hot and sweaty," Wade said. "Just won a softball game fourteen to three. My pitching arm's coming back, I think. I'm considering a career change."

"Same old Joe Wade," Ruth said. "It's been nice speaking to you. I'll have Ed call." She hung up. Wade held the phone away from his ear and stared at it. Same old Joe Wade? She didn't even know him.

He hung up, refilled his beer, walked over to the green rectangle of the pool table, where Jim Harley was sighting down his stick. They were playing Eight Ball Rotation, a peculiar game Harley had made up one night when he was drunk. There were too many rules for Wade to remember, and it was a tribute to the force of Harley's economic status—he owned a combination Gulf Station, repair shop, and John Deere dealership—that anyone bothered to play with him. The cue slipped through Harley's fingers, and the cue ball gently nudged the seven into the side pocket. Harley straightened up, walked over to where Harve Stanley stood fingering a square of blue chalk. "Let's give 'em a rematch next Sunday, Harve. They wasn't ready for Joe's pitching arm." The compliment was one thing; Harley's delivering it was another. Wade turned away.

Through the window of the pool room Wade saw Tom Garvey's blue pickup coming at the building too fast for comfort. There was a screech of old brakes, and a cloud of dust billowed against the window, blocking out the truck. The door flew open and Garvey stalked in, shutting the door behind him. Good theatrical effect, Wade thought. A touch of dust had entered with him.

"Hey, Tom," Wade said, walking over toward him. He was accompanied by a chorus of greetings from the farmers. "You should have gotten here earlier, been out there with us today. Your buddies could have used you."

Garvey walked past Wade without answering, heading for the pool table. Jim Harley was bent over again, ready to take another shot. Garvey held a sooty snake in his right hand.

"Harley," he said. "I need a hose. I'm planting."

Harley took the shot. There was a racket on the table; if Wade was seeing properly, only the six went in. "See what you made me do?" Harley said. "If you hadn't broke my concentration, I woulda got the five too."

Garvey brandished the oily hose, a short section of the

whip he'd left outside. "You made me drive all the way in from the farm. I just bought this."

Harley considered Garvey's point for a minute, then turned away. "It's Sunday," he said. "I ain't open on Sunday."

"I'm not telling you to 'open,'" Garvey said. "Just drive down there and dig me out a new one."

Harley bent over the table again, as though Tom were a slight buzz from an obnoxious blue-bottle. "And I'm telling you I'm a Christian and there ain't no way I'm opening up on Sunday." He pulled the cue back, smoothed it several times against the crook of his thumb, and just as he was about to let go, Garvey grabbed the fat end of the stick. Harley almost fell onto the table with the force of the accumulated motion. He stood up fast and turned on Garvey, his fists ready.

"Harley," Tom Garvey said, his voice very quiet. "If I don't have a new hose in my hands in five minutes you're gonna have a Christian burial."

Now this was getting good, Wade thought. The bar had gone absolutely silent. Garvey was a real scrapper; Joe didn't know anyone who'd gladly mess with him. And Harley was the kind of man who couldn't back down, not through courage but through a lack of imagination.

Earl Smoot cleared his throat. "See you, Harley," he said.

It was the kind of line Wade wished had been his; the tension dispelled as though someone had fired a .38 through a balloon. Everyone laughed, too loud, turned back to the bar, too quickly. Harley was grinning, bewildered, wondering if everyone were laughing at him, or just laughing. Garvey's shoulders drooped. Oh well, Wade thought. There'd be a fight another day. In the meantime he was consumed by a minor-league depression, probably due to the watered-down beer.

· 17 ·

When Lewis asked him what had happened inside the pool room, Tom said, "I asked a man for a hose."

"Which man?" Lewis asked. He looked skeptical.

"That one," Tom said. He pointed to the door of Bob's. Harley came out and walked slowly toward his pickup parked several spaces away. "Jim Harley."

"You mean the John Deere place," Lewis said.

"That's what I mean," Tom said. He waited for Harley to back up the truck and start moving, and then he followed, close, as in a parade. Harley was doing it, but he wasn't going to give Tom full satisfaction, so he dawdled his way along, and it was all Tom could do to keep reminding himself he'd won, and without a fight. Smoot would tell Berta, and the phone would ring, and Mae would know everything. He was glad she'd know he hadn't swung his fists.

They drove through Millrock so slowly Tom had time to see every crack in the sidewalk, every broken pane of glass. Trash blew through the streets, deserted except for an old Chevy parked before the Woolworth's building. A pair of boots, toes up, stuck through the open window of the back seat. God, the place depressed him. He never could understand why people wanted to live so close together, one building after another with just a strip of grass between, sometimes not even that much space. He almost leaned on the horn to get Harley moving, but pounded the wheel lightly with his fist instead.

"He plays for the Leutzcorp team?"

"Who?" Tom said. "Harley? Yeah. They had a game this afternoon."

"You're not playing this year, huh," Lewis said.

"Too much work," Tom said. "You know that."

"Yeah," Lewis said, and turned to look out the window.

Why did that make him feel guilty? Lewis sounded disappointed, as though he'd been let down. The boy was old enough to know the difference between work and play. He knew how many things needed doing around the farm. It would be something else if the first crop were on its way as it should have been. They were a month late now, no time for smacking a leather-covered ball of string around.

But it would be nice, Tom thought, to take an afternoon off. He could almost smell the oiled leather of the gloves, clean sweet oil, not like the kind that speckled his pants and shirt. They pulled into the asphalt apron of Harley's Garage. A big banner, holes punched in it to let the wind through, hung across its front. INTEREST DEFERRED—CASH REBATES—LET'S TALK. Over in the dirt to the side, the newest model tractors sat proudly, their paint gleaming, their glass-enclosed cabs glistening, looking as though they were about to take off for the moon. God, what he'd do with one of those.

"What's a rebate?" Lewis asked.

"It's a scam they have," Tom said. "You give them money and they give you some of it back."

"Why don't they just ask for less money?" Lewis wanted to know.

"Beats me," Tom said. By now Harley had managed to let himself down out of the pickup—if he moved any slower, Tom thought, he'd be in reverse—and Tom opened his door and jumped down.

"Dad," Lewis said, beside him. "Is it okay if I . . ."

Tom knew what his son wanted; it was what *he* wanted. "Ask the man, Lewis, don't ask me."

"Is it okay if I sit in one of those tractors?" Lewis asked.

"Yeah," Harley said. "Just don't go pulling any levers or pushing any buttons, hear?"

"Yessir," Lewis said. He was inside a cab before the two men had entered the garage. He'd chosen one of the few that looked as though weather had touched it. A sign across its hood read REDUCED—EASY PAYMENTS.

Harley let them in through the office, past the aluminum chairs covered with green vinyl, the formica desk with the NCR adding machine, into the garage itself. It was dark in there. Dirt, years old, clouded the few windows, and everything was black—rubber tires, oil-stained cement, lacquered metal. Harley unlocked the door of one of the bays, hit a switch, and the door rose, folding back on itself, letting in some light and air. He scratched his crotch and moved toward the far end where a series of boxes jutted from the wall. "Let's see," he muttered, almost to himself, looking at the piece of hose Garvey had handed him. He stood before the boxes, running through them as though they were keys to distant kingdoms and he the only king. "T-seventy-eight-ninety-nine-thirty—'B'—'N' . . . nah . . ."

Tom heard the revving of a large engine, and turned to see Joe Wade pull up to Harley's gas pumps in his Bronco. Wade jumped out and stuck his head inside the bay's door, just enough to fall into shadow for a second, and then jumped back into the sunlight as though the darkness stained. "Harley, long as you're open on Sunday, I'm gonna pump myself some gas." Harley reached into his pocket, took out the set of keys he'd opened the office with, and flung them to Wade. Joe Wade caught them easily, as though the batter had just popped a short line drive into the infield. "Thanks," he said. "Put it on my tab."

Harley turned back to Garvey. "Hell of a thing, Tom," he said. "Nobody stocks parts for that old hunk of junk you drive. Why don't you let me sell you a new tractor? Listen to this for a deal . . ."

Garvey crossed his arms on his chest. "Just get the hose, Harley. Then I'll buy the Brooklyn Bridge."

· 18 ·

He *had* needed gas, and Harley's was on his way home. But still Joe Wade was uncertain as to what had pulled him here, following Garvey. Perhaps it was simply his disappointment at there not having been a fight, but he hoped his atavism wasn't that extreme.

"Harley, long as you're open, I'm gonna pump myself some gas," he yelled through the open bay into the darkness. He could see two figures against the back wall, silhouetted by the filtered light of a grime-covered window. One of the men turned and with an underarm pitch tossed something out at him. He stepped back out of the darkness he'd dipped into and caught the keys.

As he walked back to his Bronco, a movement to his left caught his attention, and, turning, he saw the Garvey kid high in an '82 John Deere. Wade figured the boy was twice as old as his sister, and probably twice as practiced in the Garvey manner: *Don't talk to strangers, especially strangers called Joe Wade*. Still, the kid looked entranced up there, and this time it seemed to Wade the tables were turned: Beth had wanted to keep the Oreos to herself; the boy wanted something he'd never have—in the world he currently inhabited—and something Wade had access to. He pocketed Harley's keys and walked nonchalantly over to the tractor. He lifted a foot and placed it on the huge cleated rubber wheel, leaned forward, his arms propped on his knee, and said, "Nice machine, huh?"

Lewis looked down at him; now, without any glass between them, Wade could see the Garvey trademarks in the face—a hardness to the eyes, as though they were polished stones. The face was rough rather than fine-boned, and he could see where the jowls would develop, the chin square.

"I'm Joe Wade," he said. "You know me?"

"Yeah," Lewis said. "I know who you are." Wade had a wild impulse to say, *Your mother ever talk about me?* Instead, he repeated his previous question. "Sweetheart of a tractor, no?"

"It's okay," Lewis said, as if he'd seen better, and in fact was sitting in this one simply to get out of the sun.

"You and your father shopping for a new one?" Wade asked.

The boy stared at him, trying to gauge the man's motivation, and failing. He wasn't fully trained yet; he still could be intimidated, humiliated. Wade was suddenly mortified. What was it about these people? Either they made him feel ashamed, or they infuriated him.

"No," Lewis said, "not today. We're planting."

Wade turned and looked at the sky, as though he hadn't before noticed the weather.

"Good day for it," he said.

"Yeah."

"Anyone ever shown you all the fancy gadgets on one of these?"

"No," Lewis said. Wade could see he was repressing his interest mightily, but a slight color rose to the boy's cheeks, and Wade pulled himself up into the cab and hovered behind Lewis. "This here's the lever which closes the cab off . . ."

"That man told me not to touch anything," Lewis said.

"Okay," Wade said. "I'm not touching, I'm just showing. Anyway, that closes the cab, and this turns on the air conditioner. And in the late fall, if you push the lever this way, you'd get heat."

"I can read," Lewis said.

"And this is the tape deck. You can plow a field and listen to your favorite cassette." He looked up in time to see Tom Garvey striding over, a hose in his hand, and knew it was time for him to quit.

· 19 ·

When Tom saw Wade approach his son, he had the impulse to forget the hose entirely, and get out there. There was nothing the man could do to the boy—he just didn't like Wade, was all. He could feel his heart pick up its tempo. "Come on, Harley," he said. "I don't want to be planting at midnight."

Harley pulled a hose out of a box, one he'd been looking around in previously, and handed it to Tom. "That looks right to me," he said. "Here, try this one. That'll be four dollars."

Tom spun on Harley so fast the other man backed away, his palms flat between them. He grinned. "Forget it," he said. "I don't do business on Sunday."

"That's what I thought you said," Tom growled. "Thanks, Harley." He took the hose, turned back to the light of day, and walked as quickly as he could toward where Joe Wade and Lewis were talking.

"You can plow a field and listen to your favorite cassette," Wade was saying as Garvey drew close.

"Let's go, Lewis," Tom said. Immediately the boy rose,

and let himself out of the cab. "What's this man been telling you?" he asked.

"Oh, nothing," Lewis said.

"I was just showing him the tractor, Tom," Joe Wade said. "I didn't think I was doing any harm."

"Probably not," Tom said. "Come on, son. See you, Joe." He turned back toward the pickup when Wade's voice stopped him.

"How come you don't play ball anymore, Tom?" Wade asked. "We miss you out there on the field."

"I didn't know you still played," Tom said. "Pitching?"

"Yeah," Wade said. "Just started again, it feels good."

"I don't have time," Garvey said. He suddenly felt suffocated, in need of moving, as though Wade were using up all the oxygen.

"Too bad," Wade said. "There's a fast-pitch game next Sunday. Doesn't seem to be anybody in the valley can touch me." And then he smiled.

Later, when he considered it, he thought he might have stayed out of the way of temptation had Wade not smiled, that large lollipop-sucking smile of his, that smile that made Tom Garvey want to insert his fingers in its edges and pull. On the other hand, maybe it was Lewis's fault, the way the boy had stood there looking at him.

"I don't know," Tom said gruffly. "I'll have to see." Wade nodded once, as though he took this as assent, and of course it was, though Tom wasn't even admitting it to himself at the moment.

In the truck on the way home, he and Lewis talked about other things—how many acres still needed planting, how much that John Deere had cost—$27,000!—how ridiculous it was for a farmer to own a tractor with air-conditioning and a tape deck, although he hadn't sounded totally convinced, even to himself.

Just before they got home, his son asked the question he'd been popping with all the way from Millrock. "You're gonna play next Sunday, aren't you, Dad?"

And though Tom Garvey tried to keep his voice gruff as before, he wasn't successful. "I don't know," he said. "I told the man I'd have to see." Which, of course, meant *yes*. Any fool could see that plain as day.

· 20 ·

The week that followed was crammed with work and school, but Lewis felt it slip through his fingers like water, so securely were his sights fastened on the following Sunday. The mornings were filled with chores—Jessica seemed better Monday and allowed him to milk her; on Memorial Day she shuffled and lowed and edged away from him when he tried to place the stool close—and then he helped his father plant, or he and Beth ran to catch the bus, off to Millrock, another day at school. But the exports of Venezuela were lost on Lewis as he sat, his chin on his hand, staring out at the baseball diamond and wooden bleachers where the game was to be played.

It had been two years since his father had played regularly. Lewis reassured himself by remembering how explosive his father's bat had been, how quick his fielding glove, and these *after* his semi-retirement from the summer leagues after high school (or so he'd been told). Lewis resolved to make his father practice—if not with Mr. Tessley or Mr. Smoot, then with him.

The planting wasn't finished until Thursday, five backbreaking eighteen-hour days, and his father only let him stay home once to help. They'd worked until after dark on Sunday and then had stumbled together, exhausted, to the house. Beth was already asleep, but Mae sat in the kitchen in the glare of the electric light with a pad of paper and a bunch of envelopes and small stubs. She was working on bills again and in the light, when she looked up, her face was pale and stern, not at all as it had been that morning at church. As he lay in bed he heard his parents' voices rising and falling, mesmerizing, rocking him to sleep, except for the insistent refrain from his mother: *But Tom we don't have*.

It was that time of month again. It had happened for as long as Lewis could remember. All the places wanted money at once—Tennessee Public Service, Southern Bell, Millrock Oil Service, Leutzcorp, the General Store, Sears—and every month about this time his mother got very quiet and scared, and his father's mouth became set, and the two of them glared at one another, as though they were angry. Which they were. But Lewis didn't think they were angry at each other.

Lewis knew they were supposed to be poor, but since he'd never known life to be different, he wasn't sure how to feel about that. There'd always been enough food on the table, and he'd always had clothes to wear; the few times life had gotten a little pinched hadn't seemed the worst of all possible situations. He was very aware of the kids at school who came from wealthier familes, and mostly he hated them, not because they had flashy metal Mr. T lunchboxes, and certainly not because of their unscuffed brown tie shoes. They seemed aloof to him, cocky; they shot their mouths off in class; and when it came time for the class members to show off their projects, the rich kids always had the fancy dioramas with little glass mirrors for lakes or the models of castles their fathers had built, with drawbridges and moats and make-believe trees. And this is what got Lewis the most—*they never admitted their parents had made them*. His were sloppy, thrown-together things: *his* parents had more pressing things to do than make clouds out of cotton and turrets out of toilet paper rolls. But Gretchen Simpson had sniffed in condescension when Lewis and Peter Hinkle had examined the doll dress she brought to school, like the one Helen of Troy was supposed to have worn, and declared it a fraud.

"Your mom made that," Peter had said.

"She did not," Gretchen said. "I made it myself on my very own machine."

Lewis turned his mouth into an upside-down smile, and minced through Gretchen's words again in a wheedling falsetto.

"Stop it," Gretchen said, "or I'll tell Miz Farmer. I'll tell my *father,*" she said, her eyes suddenly wide.

"What's he going to do?" Lewis said. "Beat me up?"

Peter pulled his arm, and made him walk across the playground away from Gretchen Simpson. "Maybe we better not mess with her," Peter said. "My dad said the other day that old man Simpson had him by the balls."

"Your dad said *that?*"

"Naw, he said something else. I asked Mom and she explained it to me. My dad meant by the balls."

So they left Gretchen Simpson alone, and the other girls she hung around with—Betty Jean Catton, whose father owned the General Store, and Edith Sabol, and Lucinda Baker. They hung around with Box Mumford, from the other side of the river ("Where'd you get a name like Box?" Lewis had asked once. "I dunno," Box had said), and with Larry Gaddis, Dennis Smoot, and Freddie Cheevers, the other kids who came from farms and were good at baseball.

If they had a lot of money, their life would change, Lewis knew. But how? They wouldn't have this hard time each month. The house would get repainted, and his mom might get a new refrigerator or something like that. But he didn't want new brown shoes, or fancy pants. He liked jeans and denim jackets and the things he had. The best stuff would be that they wouldn't owe the bank so much money. And maybe they could get one of those new tractors, like the one he'd dreamed about.

In his dream the tractor wasn't green and yellow, but silver, with red flames shooting out the back, and the seat wasn't contoured Naugahyde like the one he'd sat on: it was covered with sheepskin. And it could fly, of course, so after the disking and harrowing were done, after the other attachment was used, the one that turned the rocks to powder and made everything perfectly level, the tractor took off, right into the air, and sprayed the farm with a fine seed rain which began growing immediately. It was a great machine.

Friday night, the planting finished at last, Lewis and his father stood outside in the thickening air and tossed a softball back and forth. He watched how his father threw, from the shoulder, his elbow cocking at just the right moment, the liquid rhythm of the muscles bunching and releasing, and tried his best to copy it. When he stood against the barn waiting for his father's pitch, he tried to set his feet as his father had, tried to swing with the same steadiness, the same violent explosion of power. His father seemed to approve of his efforts, and that made him happy, because his father was the best ballplayer he'd ever seen, except on television. And those were the pros.

In the house his mother was baking another batch of bread—she'd taken to delivering a dozen loaves to the General Store to sell, to augment their money—and she must have taken them out of the oven at just that moment, for the smell of crusty oven-fresh bread drifted across the field. And the high looping fungoes his father hit had him running, stumbling all over, slipping on week-old cowpies and falling so wildly that his father screamed with laughter, another time falling with glove outstretched only to hear the satisfying smack of leather on leather and, in the distance, his father's whoops and applause.

The balls seemed to drop from the air, and Lewis was so tired he could barely walk when they went to the house—their arms around each other. They sat in the kitchen, each with a glass of milk and a piece of Mae's bread dripping with butter and her own blueberry jam. He didn't know about Gretchen Simpson, Edith Sabol, the rest of them. He liked it here. And after tonight, after he saw his father's long rangy style come back into action, he was no longer tense about Sunday. His father, Tom Garvey, would be ready: he'd show Joe Wade who could hit his fast ball.

· 21 ·

At church on Sunday Lewis couldn't sit still. The sermon, or what he heard of it, seemed a dreary go-round of *God's will,* and even that made Lewis think about baseball. Surely it was God's will that his father's team should win today, and when Reverend Burchill said, finally, "Let us pray," Lewis knew what to pray for.

His father had accompanied them to church this morning, and afterwards in the parking lot, Lewis watched him talking with other men, grinning, planning, remembering old games. Lewis wanted to get home, to get ready, to get to the school.

So he was astounded when his mother announced she wasn't coming. His father seemed to know this and approve of it, but Lewis couldn't believe it. He tried to argue with her, but his father kept saying, "Son," and his mother reminded him about last week, how his father hadn't gone to church, how *someone* had to keep the farm going, and she had a batch of bread due at the General Store in the morning. She packed a small basket with some Oreos, bananas, and a tall cold thermos of homemade lemonade, and sent the three of them off to play ball.

All the way to Millrock, Lewis was afraid they'd be late, that his father's team would have to start without him, but of course they were there in plenty of time. His father was wearing old jeans, with a patch on one knee and a tear in the other. "That's my sliding knee," he told the children. "Why bother patching it if it's just gonna get ripped open again?" But he wore a faded St. Louis Cardinals t-shirt he'd found in a bottom drawer, and a good all-cotton baseball cap with a felt rim, not that nylon kind with the plastic webbing in the back. In honor of the weekend, he hadn't shaved, and from where Lewis and Beth settled in the stands, the bottom half of his face seemed shadowed. He waved at them and grinned; he was chewing a wad of Copenhagen and spitting, and he rubbed his hands on the backs of his legs, picked up some powdery dirt and massaged it into his skin, and, in Lewis's eyes, began to lose the simplicity of *father* for something more mythical.

Lisa Tessley was there with her mother in the stands, but Lewis wasn't interested this afternoon. A few of his friends were there to watch their dads—he saw and waved to Dennis Smoot and Box Mumford—and there were some kids whose fathers played on the other team, like Charley Stanley who was pretty stupid, but a genius next to his father, and some whose parents weren't playing. Lewis saw Gretchen Simpson sitting with her father and felt disdain mingle with a superior sort of satisfaction in his gut. He nudged Beth and whispered to her, pointing to the Simpsons, reminding his sister of the day they'd all walked into the bank single-file, playing the game their mother had asked them to play: *Now look as sad as you can.*

By three o'clock the stands were almost full, and the dust from the arriving pickups, filled with families and lawn chairs, coolers of beer and bags of pretzels, had begun to settle. The other team was dressed in its Leutzcorp uniforms—and Lewis had to admit they looked snazzy, even if the colors were ridiculous. But someone had spread the word among the farmers, so that they *matched* somehow, even if not exactly: from the waist up they wore shades of red, and their usual jeans were different colors of faded. They all chewed gum or tobacco, and they looked confident and happy, to be playing so fine and abstract a game on a Sunday afternoon. All over America groups of men were wiping their sweaty foreheads on the arms of their shirts, and their wives were sitting and cheering.

Earl Smoot was this year's captain and he walked out to flip a coin with Joe Wade; Smoot won with *heads,* and chose to be the home team, so the game began with the farmers grabbing their gloves and hooting and racing out into the field. They talked up a storm, kicking at the dust with their sneakers; little explosions leapt from the infield at their feet. Tom Garvey was playing shortstop, his old high school position, though in the summer leagues he'd become famous for his blistering accurate throws from left field. Smoot acted as coach as well, hitting fungoes to the men in the outfield, bashing a few grounders to the men on the bases, and softballs were flying everywhere, lots of them over the heads of the people being thrown to, but by the end of the five-minute warmup, the team seemed to have come to a rhythmical understanding. Everything happened for Lewis in great gulps of time—that evening, when questioned by his mother, he'd only be able to remember specific moments, but those in excruciating detail—and what was most central to him was the moment when his father would pick up a Louisville slugger and walk to the plate for the first time, to face Joe Wade.

By the bottom of the sixth, Wade's mocking taunt of the week before had long been proven empty. During the bottom of the first, Tom Garvey had hit a clean single right past the Leutzcorp pitcher, catching the first baseman off guard. By the time it hopped into the left fielder's glove, Lewis was on his feet screaming and waving his arms, his father stood smugly at first, not even breathing hard, and the home team was leading one to nothing. Rod Tessley walking across the plate from his previous place on third.

From there the game had see-sawed, and by the time his father, two for two, stood at the plate again during the bottom of the sixth, the score was tied at three-three, and the free and easy tobacco-spitting mood of earlier had grown more tense. Lewis watched as his father hoisted the bat from his shoulder and moved it so its fat end did that little circle dance he liked so much. His shoulders hunched, his entire body tensed and twisted to the right, ready to move against the small white sphere about to come hurtling toward it. Wade scratched at the rubber with the tip of his cleated toe, the ritual pitcher's gesture before he began his windup; he took off his yellow and black cap, rubbed his forehead, then gave an odd little flip of the cap toward Lewis's father. He stood sideways, glaring down the pipe at Harve Stanley's glove, a grotesquely swollen leather hand still holding the indentation of a ball. Lewis stood; people around him were beginning to yell now, encouragement to Wade on the mound or his father at the plate. He blocked out as much sound as he could, cupped his mouth and screamed, "Come on, Dad, make it three for three." At his side Beth said, "Yeah, three and three." "Don't you know *any*thing?" he asked. Beth shrugged and turned back to the diamond.

Wade wound up, and let it fly, and Lewis watched as the ball moved in its inexorable trajectory. He watched as his father dropped the bat, crumpled his knees, scrambled in the dirt, out of the way of the ball. The stands were filled with catcalls, obscenities, whistles. Lewis watched as his father stood, carefully slapped the dirt from his jeans, picked up his bat, and rearranged his hat. Harley, the man whose tractor he'd sat in, stood behind Charley Stanley's father and shouted "Ball one." The men in the stands hooted and screamed, pointed at Harley and shouted: *Way to go, Harl, what an eye, let's hear it for the ump*. Harley turned to the stands and made a mincing bow from the vicinity of his waist. "You gents can kindly shut your traps," he said.

Someone yelled something back, and Harley started to walk over, but Lewis's eyes were fastened on his father. At his side, Beth pulled on his sleeve.

"Why'd Daddy fall down?" she asked.

"He didn't want to get hit in the head, stupid. Didn't you see where that ball was going?"

"Who are you calling stupid?" Beth said.

Lewis ignored her. "Go get him, Dad. Knock it in his mouth."

"I'm telling," Beth said.

"Just *watch,*" Lewis said.

Joe Wade spat in the dirt, wiped his hands around the ball, wound up, a long elaborate beautiful set of moves, and let it fly. It was his fast ball, but to Lewis it traveled as in a dream, the way it might look if an outlaw shot at you, and you were the sheriff and time slowed down. He saw it crawl through the air, tracing as if on an invisible wire the same path it had traveled before.

"Watch out, Dad," Lewis screamed, but his father already had. He crumpled again, the ball whizzing past where his head had been, a freight train, a rocket instead of a baseball. This time Garvey was up and toward the pitcher's mound in a single move, not worrying about the dust on his clothes, and only the quick arm of Harley on his shoulder slowed him down. Now Lewis's heart was making a racket in his chest, and he didn't even hear the questions his sister was asking: he wanted a fight, bad, he wanted to see Joe Wade's dark blood in the dirt.

Tom Garvey didn't know what he'd do when he got to the pitcher's mound; he vaguely thought he'd swing at Joe Wade's head with his bat, but the bat lay in the dirt behind him and he wasn't going to lose momentum to turn around and retrieve it. Then Harley grabbed his shoulder and stopped him, and he had a chance to breathe, to relieve the tightness in his chest, and the world came back into focus.

"I'll talk to him, Tom," Harley said. "He don't mean any harm."

Garvey stared at Harley and slowly it became clear that Harley was speaking the truth. What Wade was trying to do was simple: he wanted to throw his fast ball inside, where it would be hardest to hit. And that was his job, after all, to keep the batter from hitting. It wasn't personal. Still, he wanted to calm himself down, to do *something*. "No," he said to Harley and touched his arm to let him know there'd be only words on the mound. "I'll talk to him. It's *my* head he's aiming at."

Harley let him go. Garvey walked slowly toward Wade, watching the man become bigger. Like a cloud of mosquitoes surrounding him, he could hear the crowd's humming. The noise quieted as he reached the mound. And by that time, he had managed to see Wade not as an enemy: it was a *game* they were playing. Wade didn't want to kill him anymore than he wanted to kill Wade. Did he want to kill Wade? Better not to ask that question now.

Wade's face was impassive; he didn't look frightened of Garvey, nor did he look apologetic. Garvey made every effort to do the same with his face—this was a contest of wills, and he wanted to win. But could he tell the man he wouldn't take kindly to being hit in the head? Mostly, how to get what he wanted, a ball he could make sing with the happiness of having taken flight?

He looked into Wade's eyes. Nothing there for him to read. "You having a little control problem, Joe?" he asked. He took off his hat now, as though it were his last defense and he were in favor of total vulnerability.

Wade spit, adding to the brown tobacco stain in the dust. He bunched up the bottom part of his face, as if in consternation. "Guess so," he said.

"Well," Tom said. "My advice is to get hold of yourself. Brain surgery's expensive. And if you can manage it, put one right about here and see what happens." With his hands he captured an imaginary ball in mid-flight, right at the spot his bat wanted to meet it. To his surprise, Joe Wade smiled, and Garvey smiled back and turned, walking slowly toward home.

The crowd resumed its yelling as he regained his stance. He took the bat off his shoulder for a moment, and rolled his head to loosen his muscles. He wiped the wad of Copenhagen from under his lip with his finger, flung it to the ground, and spit the last bit of chew. With his right hand he touched his right eyebrow in a jaunty salute to Wade.

And then the bat returned to its spot above his right shoulder, making little circles in the air, and he bent slightly from the waist, he shuffled his sneakers until his stance felt right, he thought of miles and miles of rolling cornfields, he watched as Wade coiled, released, and as the ball came rushing at him, blazing toward his chin, he stepped back from the plate, swung, and during the follow-through he let his hands savor it—splendid, absolutely solid, better than an axe splitting oak in one chop. That ball was headed for the sunset.

The noise that suddenly came from Lewis Garvey's mouth surprised him more than it did his sister. It was a scream both so loud and so high-pitched, he thought he'd snapped a vocal cord. Once on *Hillbilly* a guitar player had broken a string, and it had swung loose and sung like that, a sound like broken china or a wet finger rubbing the rim of a thin glass. All around him people were waving their arms, trying frantically to leave the earth behind. He watched as the ball sailed over the left fielder's head and came to rest in the meadow grass beyond the farthest spot the janitor's mower reached.

The left fielder was running for it; the stands were either imploring his father to move faster, faster—*come on, come on*—or screaming for the other team to employ magic, to hurry the ball in its journey from grass to fielder's hand to air to home plate. For that's where Garvey was headed.

Beth was jumping up and down now with both her feet, like a pogo stick, making the thin plank on which she stood thrum like a rubber band. Her dad was rounding second, on his way to third, slipping and sliding in the dirt. Then the fielder had the ball, was picking it up, arching his back, and the ball rocketed from his arm, everyone screaming louder, more frantically, the sun surprised in the sky by all the commotion as Garvey rounded third, making an arc toward home, the ball falling now toward Harve Stanley's outstretched glove, Garvey's teammates screaming, and Lewis Garvey screaming most of all, feeling what voice he had left leave him and float out over the field like a white cloud of pure excitement, his father's sneakers beating through the powdered dirt now toward that pentangle of rubber called home, the ball looming larger as it lost altitude, landing in Stanley's glove, but Tom Garvey was already on his side, sliding, bringing a tornado with him, dust everywhere as Stanley planted himself and turned in time to have Garvey thunder into him, sneakers hitting his calves, and he capitulated, his legs flying out from under him, the yellow striped seat of his pants landing in a jumble of Tom Garvey, leather, rubber, and dust.

Harley began to move—but instead of both arms, only one was moving, a hand, a thumb, jerked up and over his right shoulder. "Yerrout!" he yelled, and the crowd—everyone it seemed, even those who wanted this to happen—was yelling, throwing garbage, wadded up wax paper, pop cans, beer bottles, screaming, as though they'd been robbed of their paltry savings by the bank's collapse, as though they'd just discovered their best friend all these years had been merely a shadow in the mirror, as though their lives had lost their small capacity to still believe in justice. Lewis Garvey's face was redder than the Cardinals t-shirt from screaming, and as he caught his breath, the late afternoon air scalded his lungs.

22

Tom Garvey drove slowly on the way home, or rather slowly for him; he was tired from all the running and all the screaming, and he didn't need any of the spine-jolting leaps from the road his driving often achieved. Beside him on the seat, Beth and Lewis sat, like models of good children. Lewis's head was turned to the right, toward the passing levee, its banks no longer muddy and scarred, but covered as they were each year with bluegrass, cornflowers, wild mustard, the result of windblown seed. The kids had been this way pretty much since leaving Millrock, not sullen exactly, but locked inside their skulls, mysterious to him.

"Well," he said. "I didn't do too bad for an old man, did I?"

Neither Beth nor Lewis said anything, though Beth looked up at him and he could see that her eyes were slightly red. Had she been crying?

"I mean two-for-three is *great,* and we *won,* didn't we?" There had been that consolation—a quick rally in the bottom of the seventh, a single by Zemke, followed by a single by Otto, which brought Zemke to third, and after Tessley's long pop to center, Zemke had tagged up and practically waltzed across the plate—but somehow the score, even those large black numbers swinging against the white paint of the scoreboard, wasn't enough to wash the bad taste from everyone's mouth, and so when they lingered by the pickups in the parking lot, after lifting the plastic flip-top coolers and nylon-webbed chairs into the bed, after placing the children and wives in the cab, they'd decided simply to go home rather than meet for a pitcher of beer, a game of eight ball at Bob's. He hadn't counted on it hitting the children this hard.

"Hey, come *on,*" he said.

"It's not fair," Beth said stolidly. Lewis remained silent.

"That's right," he said. "It wasn't fair. Harley made a mistake."

That brought Lewis to fumbling life, his words tripping over each other in their rush from his mouth.

"It wasn't a mistake," he said. "He was on the other team's side."

"Now we don't know that for sure," Tom said, not believing it himself. "But the important thing to remember is that life isn't always fair."

He could see his children weren't in the mood for Dad's Truths About Life, and so they drove in silence for the remainder of the way home.

It was dusk when they pulled off the highway and into the driveway. Huddled near the sunny side of the house, Mae's few peonies were almost finished. He thought how good the Stroh's would taste going down, and wondered what Mae had managed to put together for dinner, something special in case he'd won, to cheer him up in case he'd lost. Lewis got out of the cab with the nonchalance of a teenager suddenly home, but Beth was still six, and she had news to tell her mother. She tumbled ahead of them to the door, and through it into the kitchen, and Tom smiled as he heard her voice raised in sing-song. "Mo-om, we're ho-ome," Beth repeated. Mae was evidently not in the kitchen.

He pulled open the screen and stepped inside. Although it was getting dark, Mae hadn't bothered to turn on a light, and the refrigerator stood in the corner like a large rectangular ghost. The smell of burnt bread was heavy in the air;

on the counter, four loaves hulked on their sides. The bottoms were dark, partially blackened, and the oven door hung open. Tom walked over and flipped the oven shut.

"Smells funny in here," Lewis said. Beth had run up the hall to peer in bedrooms, and now she returned. "Mom's not in here."

Tom looked out the kitchen window toward the barn and saw a dim light burning inside. "Come on," he said. "Your mom's in the barn, probably doing all your chores for you."

"What's for dinner?" Lewis asked. "I'm starving."

"Let's find your mother first," Tom said. He didn't know what was for dinner. Aside from the burnt bread, there was no evidence of there being anything for dinner.

When he swung open the barn door to peer inside, his children clustered behind him, and he wondered if what he saw cut them as deeply as him. Mae sat on the straw-covered ground in the light of a kerosene lantern, the soft orange glow a prelude to fire rather than romance. She was wearing an old housedress pulled above the knees, and her arms were folded over her kneecaps, her cheek resting on one sleeve. She might have been resting had she not been heaving soundlessly, had not the body of Jessica been lying so dead a little way beside her. The barn was preternaturally quiet, as though the sow, the piglets, the chickens, were all joined in silence for the dead cow.

At the sound of the door creaking, she looked up. Tom could see her face was splotched from crying; a black smear crossed one eyebrow. There was something in her face he'd never seen before: in fact, he hardly recognized her. The kerosene glow made her freckles look like the pale marks of some disease, brought on by a life both too strenuous and too bereft of simple necessities. But it was her eyes which seemed most uncharacteristic. They were the eyes of the men in Millrock, the ones who stood before the old Woolworth's as if waiting for a call they knew would never come.

Instead of running to her mother as she normally would

have done, Beth clung to the leg of his jeans, and Lewis had temporarily forgotten the afternoon's indignity. Mae rose, uncertainly, as they walked toward her, and her voice was husky, disjointed, the voice of someone found wandering in the desert, no food or water for days. "I burnt the bread," she said, her hand moving distractedly at her dress. "I was here when it was done. I just forgot, I guess. So many things . . ." Beth ran to her and Mae hunched down and pulled her close. "I'm sorry, Beth, I tried. I should have called the vet, but we owe him so much money, I just couldn't face him. I'm sorry." She let go, and Beth stepped away, toward the body of the dead cow. Mae stood up and moved past them out of the barn.

"Is Jessica dead?" Beth asked, her voice filled with something close to wonder.

"Yes, sweetheart," Tom said. "Go in the house with Lewis, now."

"I have to say goodbye to her," Beth said.

Tom stood, not knowing what to do. He needed to go and find Mae, to reassure himself. Her reaction to the cow's death brought home for him, as nothing else had, how close to danger they were, like a spindly stick drifting lazily downriver, never knowing what was coming, despite the slowly building roar, until it teetered on the brink of the dam. He nodded at his son, who understood to stay with his sister, and then with that small task accomplished, Tom Garvey walked out into the night to find his wife.

The house was dark. He let himself in through the kitchen door, and he held his own breath and listened, hoping to hear her breathing, her crying, the familiar noise of her moving through the house. Nothing. He threw the switch, remembered how weeks ago during the middle of the night he had done all this in reverse, the night the rain had kept him awake, and it was Mae who had found him, brought him back to bed. In the pitiless glare of the light, he could see the seams and cracks in the ruined bread. "Mae," he called softly, then walked down the hall. Slowly, he eased open the door of the bedroom, expecting to find her collapsed among the rumpled bedclothes, another task neither of them had gotten to that day. But the room was empty; on the bed was the plastic wrapper in which she'd kept her grandmother's quilt.

In the kitchen he grabbed a flashlight. Outside he swung the beam crazily, raking the side of the barn, the yard around the house, the electric poles set at intervals down the road. This time he yelled her name, heard its soft echo along with the faint whooing of a mourning dove. She could be anywhere. Three hundred acres, at a time like this, was a lot of land.

He thought of other times—when Lewis had scarlet fever, when she had heard of her father's death in the lumber mill—she'd been afraid. Where had she gone? He put the flashlight in his pocket, walked down the driveway and crossed the road. The macadam was still warm; he could feel the slight heat rising. He climbed the levee, calling her name, and found her, as he thought he might, sitting, her knees tucked under her, staring at the river. The moon wasn't up yet, and the surface of the water reflected no light. He stood, her small body between him and the water. She looked like something brought here and deposited by the flood. He knelt down next to her, didn't touch her.

She started speaking almost at once, as if she'd been preparing her words, waiting for him to find her. Her voice trembled on the edge of exhaustion. "I don't know what to do about Sears," Mae said. "I guess we've been their customers long enough. I don't think they'll come and try to take anything away." He wanted to interrupt, to tell her to hush, but she had a terrible list to enumerate and he knew he'd better let her finish. "I sold the quilt, and I can't get over how little that woman gave me for it. It wasn't her family, though, I guess. I paid the FHA. The power company sent a final notice but I have a money order for that. I found an old pair of sneakers that Lewis outgrew, I can give those to Beth. But I don't know what to do about Sears."

He had the sense his life was sifting through his fingers and he was powerless to stop it. If he could reach in his pocket and pull out some cash, enough to pay off Sears, he might still salvage everything. *Oh, is that all?* he would say. *Here*. And she would turn to him and laugh, and that would be that. SEARS. Home Customer Service. Catalogues of blue jeans and washing machines and vacuum cleaners, lamps, carpets, the good life, only as far away as your mailbox. How they promised you and kept you from getting, how they tantalized you, mesmerized you with their smiling models who looked just like the kids you went to high school with, *were* the kids you went to high school with, but never bothered to tell you the rest. "Read the small print," his father had always said, and hadn't meant the writing. Well, it had happened to his father, and now it was his turn.

"The corn will be ready to cut by mid-October," he said. "Can you hold on 'til then?" He said it carefully, as though the days before them were so many steps and they were only that far from an oasis. One foot in front of the other. He thought of drought, cutworms, problems with machinery. He closed his eyes.

"I don't know," Mae said. He put his arms around her and buried his face in her neck, breathed deeply of the smell he'd miss more than the smells of river, earth, pollinating corn. She let go of her knees, reached back and stroked his head. Then she grabbed a handful of earth and threw it into the river. There was a soft splash, the sort a frog would make slipping off a log. "We got nothing left to sell," she said. "Except the land."

He looked at her. She was staring out across the water's surface as though she saw a signal on the other bank, a sign which told her what to do next, how to get by. What was she saying? What did she want?

A slight breeze wafted toward them, chill and damp. To Tom Garvey it felt like the wind a fast ball makes coming too close to your skull.

PART THREE

· 1 ·

Garvey would remember staring at the water that evening as the fulcrum of the year, the moment he himself knew how important his land was to him, important enough for him to leave it for a while in order to protect it, keep it. With Mae's head on his shoulder, he saw that the river contained nothing but water, that water was always clear as winter air before you breathed and spoiled the view; what got into it made it change color.

He and Mae wrote everything down in the morning—what they could expect from the crop when it came in, both a cautious figure and an optimistic one. They wrote down what they owed, and the latest they could pay it. They stretched their sense of credit until it broke. And then Tom called his cousin in Birmingham.

Roy Garvey was his father's brother's only son, and like his father—Tom's Uncle Frank—Roy was born for neon lights and jukeboxes, barroom brawls, cracked sidewalks, women with tight jeans and reddened cheeks and hair that didn't move in the wind. Tom wondered how his grandfather could have had such different sons, and his father always explained it this way: his brother had been in the Navy, and once you've seen that much water, you can't have much to do with fields of slowly ripening corn. A top wind, one that simply ruffled the silk, was enough to make his brother seasick again.

Roy was a jittery guy, a year younger than Tom, and he lived with a woman named Ida who worked as a cocktail waitress and wore satin high-heeled shoes and had a habit of snapping her fingers which made Tom crazy. Still, the man was family, and he'd made a lot of money working in that steel mill.

Roy couldn't promise anything—in fact, he was out of work himself—but there was this thing opening up at an iron fabrication plant on the outskirts of Birmingham, and if Tom got himself down there right away, Roy would see what he could do. Good money? Tom asked. Good enough, Roy said. Times being what they were and all, lot of people out of work. Tom knew.

The morning he left, he left before dawn; he'd said his goodbyes the night before, when he kissed his children good-night, when he lay against his wife's warm back and touched his lips to the nape of her neck. He left before he could see the farm in daylight—he wanted to remember the darkness, the flat sides of things, not their textured richness. Before he left, he ripped a peony from its stem and placed it in an empty Coke bottle. He took a handful of dirt from outside the back door and left it on the kitchen table next to the peony. He took a Magic Marker and wrote the word OURS on a small lunch bag, and propped the bag against the Coke bottle. Then he left before he did anything more stupid.

It was almost seven hours to Birmingham, but Tom Garvey smelled the city for a half hour before he reached it. Other peoples' noses were less sensitive, he thought; his was just accustomed to the smells of hay and cow manure and fertilizer. This dirty rag which hung in the air was composed of rubber and automobile exhaust, gasoline, burning plastic. It suddenly struck him that oil was responsible for cities—petroleum and its products—while water was responsible for country such as his. Black gold, white gold, take your choice. He turned on the pickup's radio, and there it was: bone-jangling city music.

He crossed the Locust Fork of the Warrior River north of Birmingham and the steel supports flipped by *fwup, fwup, fwup, fwup,* where trees had been before. Below him the water seemed unreal blue sludge in the afternoon light; as he looked ahead to Birmingham, the office buildings rose like aluminum shoeboxes, and he thought he could see a film of soot begin to accumulate on his windshield.

The next morning, his head hurt from the beer he'd drunk the night before. Roy had taken him to the place where Ida waitressed and then was sorry he had, so he'd ordered a lot of beer, four pitchers if Tom remembered correctly. Tom rubbed his eyes and looked at his watch. Five a.m. God, what a time to start a new life.

Roy had been right about the jobs opening up, and yesterday he'd gotten one for himself—that was the celebration of the night before, the natural impulse to spend your money before you made it. Tom fumbled around in Roy's ancient bathroom, splashing water in his face. His reflection in the mirror had a crack down the middle. Roy looked in on Ida to say goodbye, but she was asleep, and then they were off without breakfast, without even coffee.

The morning was chilly for early June; Tom's denim jacket wasn't quite enough to ward off the cold. The streetlights were still on, and as they walked from one thin pool to the next, down the sidewalks toward the scrapyard where the hiring was being done, Tom saw his hands were blue in the city's light.

A chain-link fence surrounded the scrapyard, the kind Tom thought of as protecting the enclaves of the very rich, the kind that held back Dobermans or German Shepherds. He shook his head in amazement. A crowd of men, maybe as many as two hundred, had gotten there before them: there was no chance for him, none at all. The men stood in a long line before two tables made of plywood sheets hurriedly thrown on sawhorses. Beyond the sawhorses the men separated into those who'd been picked, and those who'd been turned aside. The unlucky ones formed ugly little groups, and large men with night sticks pushed them on, out of the scrapyard's other end.

Fires had been lit in trashcans; men clustered around them, their hands thrust over the flames. Their faces were gaunt, unshaven, rough. They looked like men who'd been through a lot, who had little to lose, and next to them Tom felt suddenly vulnerable: he had a lot to lose. Around them in heaps, as though gigantic clocks had been taken apart and never reassembled, lay gears, their ragged teeth bigger than a man's arm, bent shafts, odd pieces of metal that could have come from the fuselage of an airplane or the hull of a destroyer. Segments of steel girders, the crushed remains of an old DeSoto, the gaping metal jaws of a crane, everything metal and damaged or useless had come here to rust. From this side of the fence, the world was now divided into a grid of angular diamonds; this was another kind of diamond mine, another kind of apartheid. Beyond the scrapyard, abandoned factories stood, their windows broken into the empty blackness within; their machines—lathes, presses, whatever—now lay disassembled around the men who stood in line.

Tom moved toward the final hopeless stragglers, but Roy took his elbow and hustled him along, headed for the plywood tables. "Hey, fellas," one of the guys behind them said.

"What are you doing?" Tom asked.

"We're going to talk to a friend of mine; shut up and walk. You want to work or play patty cake? Don't mess now, Tom. This is real hard ball."

"Hey assholes," someone else said. Roy tightened his grip on Tom's arm and kept walking. Tom could see the men behind the tables now; they wore shirts and ties under their jackets, and they wrote with pens on official-looking pieces of paper. "June, you'd think it would warm up, wouldn't you?" Roy said. "The city gets colder every year, every year, I'm telling you." He wiped his nose on the back of his hand. "I guess you noticed last night it's not so good between Ida and me. Now that I'm working, maybe she'll get off my case. That's the guy, Swick. He's the crew boss."

The man they were approaching stood to the side of one of the tables, but seemed more in command than the guys who sat behind the tables with pens. He stood in the classic male attitude of super-erogation, his feet spread the distance of his shoulders, his arms crossed on his chest, his head low on his neck as though it could be retracted into its shell.

Tom could hear more grunts and obscenities from the men they were passing. "Take your hat off," Roy said. "Tell him you're good." Roy's voice changed from peremptory to fawning in a second. "Hiya, Swick. This is the guy I told you about, my cousin, Tom Garvey. Listen, he really needs the work."

Tom understood what it felt like to be a steer at auction. "Hey, Swick," one of the men yelled. "What'd these guys do, go down on your mama?"

"Fuck you," Swick said. "One more word and you're out of here. Got that?" The man shut up. Swick turned to Garvey. He tilted his head back until he seemed to be looking across his nose, almost horizontally, at Tom. "What can you handle?"

Roy had briefed him on the work, and he'd put together what he'd done in the past on the farm with what he thought he could learn from watching. He tried to match Swick's tone. If he was right about the man, Swick was the sort who'd like a fight. "Whatever you've got," Tom said. "I can cut and weld both oxy and arc. I do layout. I can template. I can braze."

Roy's face shifted slightly as he realized he wasn't going to have to take care of Tom. "I'm telling you, Swick, he's my cousin, he's good." Swick looked at him as though he'd just seen him; why should he take this clown's word for anything? Behind Tom the noise of the men in line grew harsher, more direct. He couldn't hear individual voices. It seemed to him that whomever had yelled before had stepped back into the crowd and its threatening rumble.

Even Swick realized it wouldn't be long before violence

broke out—the conditions were as close to perfect as they could ever get: take hundreds of desperate men, put them in a dark place where they wanted something they weren't sure they could get, put pieces of metal within easy reach. Tell all the cops to stay in bed. Swick peered around them at the others. He lowered his voice. Tom had the wild impulse to wheel around, as though he were about to be attacked from behind.

"Okay, he's on," Swick said to Roy. Roy smiled widely, showing his gold-capped molars. "But he fucking better be good." Swick turned back to him. "You get eight-fifty an hour. You work a good fifty-hour week. And you get a flop. Got it? Okay, step aside before you lose your legs." Tom and Roy were hustled sharply to the right, toward the other men who'd been selected, by a gorilla dressed entirely in red nylon. Although it was still dark, it was as though he'd stepped into the sunlight. That was over four hundred dollars a week. He couldn't wait to get a phone to call Mae. "What does he mean by a flop?" he asked Roy.

Roy looked down, then up at the sky. "It's nothing," he said. He slapped Tom on the shoulder. "*You* know. It's an on-site job. We sleep there. You'll see. Hey listen, you want the work, right?" He started walking away, toward a trash can fire. Tom stood silently for a moment, trying to breathe the air. "Come on," Roy said. "This isn't the farm. We got to stick together." He put his arm around Tom's shoulder and pulled him along.

When the whistles started blowing, everything happened at once, as though the high blasting shriek of steam was the signal for life to begin a new tempo. Tom followed Roy, hoping his cousin knew what was happening. The air filled with the shouts of men, the scraping of metal. Some of the toughs strained against large iron handles and slowly the metal gates began to move apart at the far end of the yard. Men still in line began pushing and struggling forward as though carried along by an underground swell; the men at the tables stood up, turned around; for a moment it looked as though they, their sawhorses and plywood, their pens and papers were going to topple over in the wave of frantic men. Those already picked, Roy and Tom among them, surged toward the gates.

And through them a small convoy of trucks rolled, army green, unlettered, sinister in their anonymity. They bounced across the cattle guard at the entrance and as they hit the rutted dirt of the yard's interior, their headlights swung crazily, flashing like strobes across the men coming toward them. Tom saw the faces of those he'd be working with, and for a moment he was afraid, if not of these men, then of the possibility that he'd be mistaken for one of them. Their faces were scarred with deprivation. Agitated, nervous, their cheeks sucked in, the men moved forward with a purpose born more of desperation than solidarity: this was a mob, and it might end up working in a steel mill or ripping apart a department store. Tom was uneasy with strangers, and it made it worse that there were so many *kinds* of people, kinds he'd never really known. There were blacks in the crowd with him, and dark-skinned Hispanics; others who carried the hunted look of immigrants from the beginning of the century, Poles, Italians, Jews. Before him a foreman was shouting, "Load up. Come on, you want to work, load your asses." He was gesturing to the trucks which had lowered their tailgates now, and the men were scrabbling upward, grabbing a handhold wherever they could. Some were turning around and offering a hand to the others, pulling them up. "Load up," the foreman screamed. "Come on, hurry up, load your asses."

Tom reached up, and someone grabbed his hand, and before he had time to react his feet left the ground. For a sickening moment he was hanging in air, kicking out for a purchase. Then the man to his left was gone, and Tom hit the side of the truck; his foot grabbed a cleat of truck tire, his free hand looped over the side of the bed, and he was up and over, jostled with the other men. He felt a hand grab the back of his neck; he turned, and it was Roy, his face bleached, wide-eyed, breathing hard. "Load up," the foreman yelled. Now there were whistles blowing again, hand-held, in the mouths of the men in white shirts. The tables were down, the men who hadn't gotten jobs were being held back by a cordon of men in red nylon.

Under him, Tom felt the wrenching of gears as the driver managed to put the truck in first, and then the slow application of gas. Still, at the trucks' first move, its entire human cargo swayed precariously. Tom was hemmed in, men breathing down his neck, a harsh unwashed smell, cheap hair grease, after-shave lotion, garlic, fish. One after another, like bulls breaking loose from their pens, the trucks jolted forward into the street.

· 2 ·

On the farm, there would be light by now: it was illogical, he knew, but it seemed right. Here the sky was washed by the faintest hint of grey, and as the trucks began to move through steel-town, Tom could see only its vaguest outlines. Headlights sliced the heavy steel fences surrounding abandoned mills, black with soot, like remnants of the nineteenth century, slag piles, slurry pipes and conduits, everything bright in the flash of the truck's passing, and then subsumed in blackness. The rumble of the truck's engine filled the air, along with the rattles and screeches of the wooden slats Tom and the other men pressed against. They all were grimly silent. The lights that had once burned inside these plants were cold now; the only evidence they once had been filled with noise was found in the carbon covering everything. The air seemed full of it still; it might take centuries for all of it to filter down.

No one lived here, no one ever had. There were no houses, no bars, no groceries or cigar stores. This was where men had worked, their faces sweat- and soot-streaked in the orange glow of the fires, and then they'd taken the money they'd made and spent it elsewhere. Without men, the weight of the buildings was bone-crushing.

The roads themselves seemed abandoned; the trucks hit potholes so large they were like craters on the moon, and the men held on, white-knuckled, as the truck took a sickening plunge and then climbed the incline on the other side. Trying to avoid the potholes, the truck careened from one side of the road to the other.

Every building was fronted by a chain-link fence like the one around the scrapyard, and behind the fences Tom could see rusted iron sheds studded with bolts, windowless warehouses with galvanized roofs. Signs everywhere: CLOSED NO TRESPASSING NO JOBS STAY OUT. How long had those signs been posted? From the look of the area, it had been abandoned decades before, cordoned off and left to the slow rotting of metal and asphalt. Whoever had come after had left their mark with red splashed swastikas and graffiti. Someone had written FUCK THE EYEATOLLAH in foot-high letters with black spray paint. Someone else had scrawled SOLIDARNOSC. The signs made Tom homesick; he longed for a billboard advertising fertilizer or herbicide. Above him, the empty smokestacks crowded out what little light the morning was beginning to generate.

It was happening everywhere. This was just like the iron works outside Millrock, but on a scale which made that emptiness seem like nothing. Where there should have been great yellow billowing clouds of smoke, there was nothing but black sky, easier to breath, but doing nothing for the empty pockets of the recently out-of-work. "It's all shut down," Tom said to his cousin. "It's all gone to hell," Roy agreed, his voice weary.

Suddenly the trucks took a left turn down a wide concrete

slab street, at the end of which stood a vast complex of blackened and rusted buildings, much like the ones they'd been passing. It, too, was surrounded by tall fences and thick studded gates. In green block letters on plywood the name appeared: ALLIED IRON FABRICATION.

It seemed to be the place where the city ended. Beyond it was marshland, isolated scrub oaks, hummocks of swamp grass. It looked as though the ironworks had taken the quickest route possible to dispose of its wastes: they'd opened their windows and thrown it out. If any life were generated in that chemical ooze, Tom thought, he wouldn't want to meet it.

A gang of about a hundred and fifty men moiled before the gates to Allied Iron. As the trucks approached, the men became a solid mass. Above them placards waved, hand-lettered signs. Tom strained to see, pushing against the others around him, but he was pressed against the slatted sides, was coming at the mob sideways. "What is this?" Tom yelled to Roy. "Did you know about this? That's a strike! We're scabbing."

Now above the engines and the rattle of metal, Tom heard the strikers yelling. As a group they began to rush the trucks, and once they'd moved away from the metal gates, Tom could see a smaller group of men who stood inside. That group was uniformed and armed; holsters decorated their hips, the plasticine hat brims of security guards were pulled low over their foreheads. Somehow, without killing anyone, the trucks had to get through those gates. But a hundred and fifty men was a lot of men.

The drivers leaned on their horns, and the uninterrupted blare stabbed through the other noises. The security guards began to open the gates, pushing them outwards toward the trucks. Some of them held nightsticks; others had pulled their pistols.

The union men were running now, swinging their placards, picking up stones, bricks, strips of metal, bottles, chains, whatever was handy. A hail of rock started falling over the men in the trucks. Tom put his elbows before his face, tried to duck behind the wooden siding. All around him the other men were doing the same, screaming at the truck drivers to *move it, run them down*. Some of the guards had moved through the gates, attacking the strikers from behind. Toughs among the men on the trucks leaned over the wooden sides, striking down with their blackjacks and nightsticks. Tom saw a blow land squarely on the head of a man wearing a baseball cap; the hat slid sloppily sideways, and blood leapt from his scalp. He lost his handhold on the top of the siding and fell backwards into the crowd.

Somehow the trucks kept moving, though the union men flung themselves on the truck's hood and were crawling to cover the windshield, block the driver's view. One of them swung, leaving a crazy spiderweb on the glass with a baseball bat. As men tried to climb over the sides, Tom grabbed their hands and flung them backwards. They were screaming now—*scabs, scabs, scabs*—and hurling obscenities with the bricks. Everyone was panting, grunting, heaving himself against the trucks or against the men trying to climb the trucks, and the drivers, their windows shut, their doors locked, kept driving forward. When they were close enough, the security guards cracked the gates a truck's width open, and the trucks began to roll to safety. The gates swung shut; the guards pushed the straining union men back. One guard swung with a nightstick and smashed the knuckles of a man mounting the fence, his fingers wrapped around the diamond mesh as he climbed. He howled and fell backwards.

The crowd massed again now, bloody, unsuccessful, fiercer than ever. The rain of stones continued, broken glass, scrap metal, and the hail of insults as well. From the first truck, Swick jumped down, and motioned the men off. "Come on," Swick yelled, turning toward the factory, a huge building before him. Garvey looked at the stream of men following Swick, as the crowd pressed against the wire fence, chanting, shaking their fists.

"Come *on,* Tom, we gotta go," Roy hissed in his ear, pulling at his arm.

"We're taking their jobs," Tom said. "Do you know what

leverage the union has then?"

"You want that money?" Roy said. "Tom, it's the only jobs there are."

Roy's face was pinched and haggard in the grey light. There was blood on his chin, and a scrape above his left eyebrow. His eyes usually registered nothing, but now they were urgent, intense. He turned to join the crowd; Tom followed. Bricks shattered around them.

· 3 ·

They left behind one kind of noise for another. As they entered the building, Tom was swallowed by the huge hum of machines working together, the high-pitched keening of metal lathes. Massed in the scrapyard, the crowd of new men had seemed large, but it was dwarfed by the four-story factory, its iron superstructure, its catwalks and girders, webbing the area a hundred feet above Tom's head. Pale yellow light was beginning to filter down through soot-smeared clerestory windows. It reminded him of the interior of Harley's shop, the same blacks and greys, acres of concrete so deeply stained with oil they would always be slippery, the same light—as though the lens of the day's eye had been clicked almost shut. Men were already at work inside the factory, machine-tooling long cylinders of steel on the lathes, hammering at benches half the length of a football field, riveting. At the far end of the factory, a quarter-mile away, he could see the sparks of welders.

Swick was screaming now, bellowing above the machinery, and Tom nudged closer in order to hear. "Tool crib's down there," Swick yelled, pointing toward the far end of the building. Tom squinted, trying to see. Too far away. Swick kept walking and talking, and the group of men bunched around him, starting and stopping in tune to Swick's rhythms. "You get number tags," Swick said. "Don't lose 'em." What for? Tom wondered, but the men were all nodding as though they understood, and Tom kept his mouth shut. "You break a tool, you pay for it," Swick said. "You ruin the work, you pay. We don't got room for your fuck-ups, understand?"

The men at the lathes had pulled down their plastic visors and turned back to their work. "Piss call is ten minutes every two hours. Don't drink so much, you won't need to piss more often than that." With every new command Tom felt his teeth tightening. *If you're bossed, you're lost.* When was the last time he pissed when someone told him to? "You get hurt, tough shit," Swick said. "You get Band-Aids and baling wire." They passed a smelter, and a goggled worker pulled a flaming wooden rake across its blistered surface, removing slag from the molten metal.

Swick kept walking, faster now. His early speech was clearly over, and they were simply moving. Around them, Tom was beginning to hear the differences in the noises the machines made. The lathes screamed, the scrape of metal on metal, like the magnified sound of a key ripping the length of a new Impala. The presses and pulleys clanged, spitting out noise in chunks. The riveters barked in bursts and then were silent. And underneath, the bass to all this treble, the constant spin of the rollers as they carried large heavy steel plates across the center of the shed.

They were nearing an ell. "You get a cot and bedding," Swick continued. "You eat what's in the canteen." He paused and turned, leering at the men. "No booze, no dope." Catcalls from the back of the crowd. "Shut up," Swick said. "Don't let me catch you." Tom looked around, the other men grinning now at the company line. "You stay here all week," Swick said. "You want out before Saturday noon, you go through that picket line on your fucking own. Got it?" *You get a flop. It's an on-site job.* Now he got it. The thought of staying in this metal-skinned shed for a solid week, the only sunlight he'd see this jaundiced version of sun, no sky at all but what could be seen from the yard, Jesus, he guessed he could do it, but *Jesus!*

He looked down at the welders, where he'd wind up. If it hadn't been for all the old junky machinery on the farm he'd never have known how to weld. He thought momentarily of Joe Wade, always with enough money to buy it new, to have someone else fix it if it went wrong. In a situation like this, where would Joe Wade be? He didn't know how to weld. But he'd never need to know: he'd never be in a situation like this. The torches arced in brilliant flashes, oddly beautiful, spilling their load of sparks to the concrete floor. The *rat-a-tat* of riveters filled the air, like bursts of machine gun fire; farther down the line they were studding oddly shaped girders with the dime-sized heads of steel rivets.

Swick was pushing his arms before him now, as if he were doing the breaststroke, separating the men into their work groups. "All right, let's get into your workclothes. Pick up goggles at the tool crib, and sign out for 'em. You fitters over there, shapers and finishers, you go on. Welders to the right, go on, goddammit, *move.*"

The large group dispersed now, following Swick's instructions, and Tom and Roy moved off with the other welders, toward the crackling arcs of fire. God, he would hate this. He closed his eyes and reminded himself why: it was seven-thirty, and Beth and Lewis were already on the bus for Millrock. Mae would have been up for hours now, collecting the eggs, swilling the hogs.

He had to get the truck back home; he'd driven it down because he hadn't been sure about getting work. But Mae would need it. It was seven hours each way, at least, and he had thirty-six hours on the weekend. Mae would have to meet him in Decatur or Corinth, and he'd have to turn right around on a bus for Birmingham.

Another couple of days and she'd be out on the tractor, cultivating. He'd have money to give her next Saturday, though, over four hundred dollars. That would keep the Sears people happy. A welder before him pushed the blue core of the flame close to the weld, and the shower of sparks reminded Tom of the Fourth of July, when the corn's first tassels usually appeared, weeks of shitwork away.

Already he hated the helmet. He was used to nothing but the sun and wind on his face; this metal band with its flip-back, see-through plastic shield was worse than a harness. Gloves, an asbestos apron to keep from turning to flame, all in the name of safety. If he'd had to run for it, he'd get three steps before falling. Men already on the job had their backs to Tom and Roy, working on large metal plates, the pieces for which came rumbling from the shed's far end, down the steel rollers.

The welding foreman was black, a bull-necked man named Truck, who looked like he had an alternate job picking up small houses and moving them for people. Tom wouldn't want to be in a fight with that man. Truck's face was lined and bitter; he looked like he'd spent his whole life working at jobs like this, and obviously doing as well as a man could to rise to this position. "You gotta pay attention," Truck was saying. "These plates come rolling down here, see, and we got to put them together. Five welds; you got to do it right, or you pay for the steel. Swick told you, I'm sure, it's his favorite part. You tack here, same here. Then you go back. Got to be sound, Jim, because they magneflux."

"Name's Tom," Garvey said.

"Nice to meet you, Jim," Truck said. "So you go easy in the beginning 'til you learn that pattern by heart, then you *go*."

"What're we making?" Roy asked. Truck looked at him

as though he were crazy. "What the hell do I know? They don't pay me to know stuff like that. They pay me to hold a torch. You too. Could be a boiler for a ship, a power plant. It's work, it pays. That's all I know. All you need to know."

Roy nodded, as though this made perfect sense. Tom thought fleetingly of farming, of how the whole place was his, from beginning to end, the dirt which he plowed, disked, fertilized, harrowed, the corn which he planted, cultivated, harvested, all part of one long process which was his, not this bullshit where everyone did one small thing and didn't have any idea where his work was going. Oh, shit, what did it matter, he'd be back there soon.

He pulled the plastic shield down; he'd stay behind it. He knew how to keep to himself. He struck the arc and watched as the acetylene burned brilliant orange, roaring, with a thin blue heart. He turned the gas down until all that remained was the blue flame, thinner and longer now, a spearhead, a burning arrow. He touched it to the metal, and a burst of sparks flew around him. All right; time to focus, to pay attention. He'd do a good job for these people, whoever they were. If they treated him fair, he'd give them their money's worth. He brought the flame close, melting the steel to make the weld. Under his careful touch, it pooled and rippled, turned molten as sunlight on water, blindingly bright.

· 4 ·

The long drawn-out blare of the horn broke the stillness. Lady, lying nearby, began barking. Mae stood up, almost knocking over the pail she was milking into. "There's the bus. Go on. Hurry up," she said. Lewis and Beth were in the midst of milking too, and they looked at her uncertainly. "Go on," she said. "I'll finish up."

Her son looked at her with those steady brown eyes. His tone was the kind you'd take with a lunatic. "Mom, there's too much to do. Lemme stay home."

"Lewis," she said. "It's the last week of school. You'll be home for the whole summer. Get moving or that bus will leave." Lewis shrugged and moved toward the door; Beth followed. Lewis had been trying every morning to stay home and help with the chores. And she could have used him. But she knew if she gave in, he'd be out for the rest of the year. Both of them had been wonderful since Tom had gone to Birmingham, especially good around the house, picking up their clothes, making their beds. Had she let him, Lewis would have taken over most of the barn chores, and the field chores too.

The two of them picked up their books and slipped through the door, and Mae heard Lewis's voice raised in a shout. "Beth! Come on!" He'd been so good with Beth, taking care of her when Mae went to get the pickup. Mae looked up to see her daughter come rushing back into the barn.

"What is it?" she asked. Beth pulled her mother's face down and gave her a kiss on the cheek. There was the horn again. Beth ran out, herded by Lady.

Mae stood up now and went to the door. Outside the sky was the clear blue of colored glass. She'd have to apologize to the bus driver; he'd been more than patient. Lewis stood at the bottom of the steps, yelling at his sister to hurry. Then both kids were on in a flurry of books and legs, and she waved in a wide, even sweep. They hung out the window calling to her and waving, as the no-nonsense yellow of the school bus began moving away.

They were good kids; they were very good kids. She was proud of them.

What a morning! For a week now, she'd awakened to a cool breeze slipping under the bottom rail of the bedroom window. Although she missed Tom more than she cared to admit, she loved having the whole bed to herself, and she rolled around in it, flopping like a freshly landed fish. And after wrapping herself in her robe and walking barefoot to the kitchen, she'd thrown open the door to the faint smell of wisteria, the trees spreading their green leaves, the translucent blue sky, and that smell—better than anything she knew—of grass and dirt and a fresh wind from the west, just a hint of darkness as it smoothed itself against her cheek. Tom's decision to go to the city had depressed her at first, but now, with the specter of foreclosure fading, she felt fine, she felt great. Out in the fields to the east, the young fingers of corn rose into the morning light. As the sky brightened with the rising sun, the long shadows shortened.

Soon she'd be out there, cultivating on the old tractor, a job she loved, and found she loved more, with Tom away. She could move at her own pace, raking over the packed earth between rows, listening to the *whip, whip* as the young supple stalks passed under the cultivator's iron arms. But first there was the barn work, another hour.

She finished milking the cows, and carried the pails to the separator, and then into the house and the refrigerator.

Later, maybe, she'd make it to Millrock with the extra milk and the loaves of bread she'd baked the night before. With Tom at the factory, the money she made with the bread was probably unnecessary, a strain on her energy, but she liked to do her part.

She returned to the yard to feed the chickens, slop the hogs. And then back to the house. She wiped the crumbs from the kitchen table, emptied the egg shells and bread crusts into the slop bucket, washed the few dishes there were—no one in her family could much stomach breakfast, though she was a firm believer in soft boiled eggs for the children, possibly because she'd been forced to eat one every morning of her childhood. In her bedroom, she threw the blankets back, smoothed out the sheet, snapping it smartly, and then replaced the blankets, plumped the pillows, and threw open the window wide to air the room.

The cows looked dazed as they lowered their heads into their hay. It was time for them to air and eat outside, and she called to them by name, then took a switch to them when they refused to move. Finally she got them going, and then it was just a matter of keeping them going until they were through the pasture gate, and she'd closed it behind her.

Now to the sheep. And then the tractor. And then, same as every morning since he'd gone, it happened. She thought she saw something moving out of the corner of her eye, and turned to what she knew would be him, his large familiar body, his faded blue workshirt buttoned over his cotton underwear, the coarse black hair he continually pushed back with his spread fingers, the lines in his forehead and cheeks. But he wasn't there, and with a rush, the morning wind was punched out of her with the strength of his absence. The day looked longer now, and harder. It would be eight hours before that yellow bus pulled up and her children ran down to meet her, and until then she'd be alone on this three hundred acres. She knew she'd be fine, there was nothing to worry about. But still . . . there was a lot of work on a farm this size, and she was alone with two children, and the reason he'd gone in the first place was they couldn't make it pay. Sometimes it scared the daylights right out of her. She took a deep breath and started moving.

· 5 ·

The henhouse was streaked with morning light slanting through the eastern-facing window. Mae had shooed the chickens into the barnyard, where they strutted and clucked and pecked at the ground. She carefully placed the eggs, some of them still warm, in her mother's old wire basket. She heard the whishing sound of tires, and thought it was simply another car on the road, until the gravel of her driveway crackled, and she heard a car door slam. Who could it be? She heard her name called—"Mae"—and then she knew. Joe Wade would have heard from someone that Tom was gone. What was that Everly Brothers song? *Hey, bird dog, get away from my quail. . . .* She picked up the last of the eggs and walked outside, where the full light hit her.

Wade's Bronco glared in the sun, the chrome trumpeting its newly polished highlights. Wade stood in chinos and a short-sleeved sports shirt, searching the barnyard. Around his feet the chickens pecked and clucked.

"Tom's not here," Mae said.

Joe Wade glanced down at the ground where the toe of his penny loafers made a small circle in the dirt. "I heard," he said. He put his hands on his hips, took an exaggerated breath of good country air, and then pointed out to the fields. "Our crop looks pretty good. You've done a mighty good job. But I wouldn't wait for rain. I'd irrigate, if I were you. Want me to send someone to help?"

Mae remembered him driving up that day she and the children had sat before the bank. *Anything I can do?* he'd said, his silver sunglasses glinting. She'd said *no* then; she could say it again.

"I can handle it," Mae said.

And then she smelled the smoke. The bread was burning; she'd put it in after the kids had left for school, and forgotten all about it. "Not again," she said, already on her way. It distressed her beyond words, being forgetful like that, and it upset her, reminded her of the night Tom had decided to leave. By the time she was even with Wade, she was moving fast, too fast for eggs. "Here," she said, thrusting the wire basket at him, and, leaving it balanced in his outthrust arms, she ran for the kitchen door.

Inside, she could tell it was already way too late. Smoke seeped from the corners of the door, up through the vents where the burners were. She pulled open the oven, and the cloud of smoke blinded her. She reached up for a potholder, groped inside for the eight loaves lined up like coffins in a crematorium. She stuck her fingers in her mouth to wet them, then tried to pull the loaves out to balance on the oven door, but she was in too much of a hurry and she burned herself twice. The pain was almost welcome, that first sharp sear of a good first-degree burn, but the defeat of the bread was too much for her to bear, especially with this man coming in the kitchen now, cradling her extra eggs.

She burst into tears and sat down at the kitchen table. It wasn't the good cry she'd have had if Wade hadn't been there, but the tears helped wash out the smoke, and the simple act of release was enough to make her feel a little better. Wade stood in the doorway, bewildered.

"You opening a bakery?" he asked. His face was blank

as a stone, except for those crinkles by his eyes.

"I sell them to Mavis at the store," she said. "If I don't burn them."

"Is there good money in that?"

"So far it's cost me a fortune." Mae said. "That's my last batch."

Wade laughed, and walked over to the table. "Where do you want these?"

"Anywhere," she said. "Toss them against the wall if you want. I feel in the mood to join you." She reached for a potholder and began wiping her eyes, but he was next to her with a clean handkerchief he pressed into her hands. "Here," he said. "Use this."

She took it.

"Nice looking eggs," he said.

Mae wiped her eyes and blew her nose. With her face still in the handkerchief she asked, "Want to buy a dozen?"

"If you cook them," Wade said. "I'm so hungry I could eat them all."

"Cook them yourself," she said. "I'm busy crying."

· 6 ·

He wasn't sure why he'd come out to the Garvey place this morning; he certainly could have eaten more efficiently in Millrock. But a fresh wind had swept in overnight, bringing the smell of corn and hay instead of the old familiar smell of mud and water; and, to be honest, he had heard that Tom Garvey had gone to work in a factory down south to make some quick money. Now he'd stumbled into this petty tragedy—a housewife, alone, her kids at school, her husband at work, burning the bread. He liked it, the way he'd had a handkerchief ready, the way she'd taken it from him.

Well, he *was* hungry, that hadn't been a lie, and he decided to take Mae up on her offer. He picked up two large brown eggs and revolved them in his palm. The shells were thick and speckled with bumps, real eggs, not the kind the supermarket chains had manufactured. "Want some?" he asked.

She shook her head and sat back, slumped in the chair, as though his question had taken away her last remaining wind. She picked up a serrated knife from the wooden table and disconsolately stabbed at the ruined loaves. She'd stopped crying now, although he would hardly have called it crying. Just a few sniffles and a few wet lines on her freckled cheeks. Emily had been a cryer, a wailer even, but he felt terribly disloyal to think that. She'd been in absolute pain near the end, and the chemo had made her lose her hair, her biggest vanity. And she was only thirty-two years olds.

He remembered coming home from Peace Corps training, his future suddenly nothing Jimmy the Greek would bet on, and there she was, the only child of Milford Leutz, the only heir to all that money. It had made her more attractive than she truly was, for she'd grown up spoiled and whiny, having everything she wanted and no place to show it off. The irony was that it was probably more difficult to be wealthy in Millrock than it was to be poor, since the status quo was definitely in favor of the latter. She was tall and angular, and she played tennis as well as professional lessons could make her. She pounded out "Clair de Lune," could do the box step and rhumba years after all the kids at Millrock High had ever known they existed. She was a debutante in search of a debutante party, but her father was still Prussian enough to refuse to transport her to Memphis or Louisville for those festivities, occurring as they would among total strangers.

Then there'd been her mother's death, and the ruination

of her ambitions to go to school in the east, to escape this banality, to leave everything behind but her father's money. And he had failed so suddenly after his wife's death that Emily Leutz had realized she had two choices: escape the confines of her pillared home of Penney Avenue, fly to a place where the rhumba and white gloves would come in handy, and be poor; or stay, shuttered behind dusty venetian blinds, caring for a man dying slowly of grief, the only heir to a fortune made in grain and the sweat of other men. She chose the money; and Joe Wade chose her. He didn't know at the time that the cancer was already blooming within her.

He turned to the eggs. "Want some?" he asked. Mae was watching him now, staring at him, as though his face had become a secret code she was trying to decipher. When he didn't look away, she rose and walked to the sink, and bent over, splashing water into her face, and slowly drying it off with his handkerchief. It looked dark now, permanently stained. When she sat back down again, not moving toward the cast iron skillet hanging on the wall, he knew he'd have to take her at her word.

He took it down, examined its surface, smooth as a baby's skin, from years of oil and butter lovingly wiped on and off, until the grease had melded with the iron, the perfect frying tool. He put some margarine on it, watched as the yellow square skittled across the black circle, cracked some eggs into the pan and watched with satisfaction as the transparent eggwhite began to cloud over.

Above the stove two pictures hung, one of each of the children, the kind kids brought home from school. Behind Beth and Lewis the same pleated blue curtain hung; they sat on the same hidden stool, and their bodies were amputated just below the curve of shoulder. Both of them grinned madly at some tired joke the photographer had made; both were dressed in bright cheap clothes, freshly washed and ironed. They were clear-eyed, happy, beautiful children. He thought of his encounters with each of them, the Oreos and tractor, and shook his head, wondering at how life replicated itself so haphazardly, so perfectly.

He took down the picture of Beth and held it before him as though it were an icon, then put it back. "Great kids," he said. "You and Tom are doing a fine job." In the pan, the twin yolks stared at him, the edges of the whites browning slightly. He adjusted the heat. "Emily wanted kids so bad, you know. We shouldn't have waited. She would have been a terrific mother. On the other hand, well, you know. She wouldn't have been a terrific mother for long. Now that she's gone, I'll end up leaving everything to my sister." He reached for the spatula, thought better of it. He grabbed a potholder and then the slim handle of the skillet. "I hate my sister," he said. With a quick shake to loosen the eggs and a backwards pull, he flipped them into the air and caught them so skillfully, so tenderly, the yolks didn't break. He turned around to make sure Mae had seen him. She had, and he grinned broadly at her.

"Pretty slick," she said.

"The fastest skillet at the campus Steak N' Beer," he said. "Did you know I worked for a living while I was in college?" He slid the eggs onto a plate, sprinkled some salt and pepper over the yolks as though the condiments were rare and magical ingredients, and sat at the table.

"Your secret's safe with me," Mae said. "Wouldn't want it to get around you ever did anything but make money in your basement."

"Sure you won't have a bite?" Joe said.

She shook her head no, slightly, just a quick movement from the neck. She looked flushed and very beautiful. All the outside work had tanned her, and her freckles were less noticeable. Her eyes were still as pale, as undefended as they'd ever been, and it seemed her left hand trembled a bit as it lay on the table. Wade reached across and put one of his hands on top of hers to quell the trembling.

"Mae, can't you talk to Tom? Can't you help me handle him? It kills me to see you like this."

Mae's face changed as suddenly as if she'd noticed a

snake coiled under her chair. She quickly withdrew her hand, and her eyes became opaque as the eggs on his plate. She stood, pushing back the chair with her legs. "Don't come around here, Joe. It's not right." She walked out of the kitchen and into the yard. He left the eggs behind and followed. God, he had a way of blundering. Every time he thought he knew the proper things to say in the proper order, either he blew it, or one of the Garveys moved in an unpredictable direction, and left him stumped and breathless.

He caught up with her and grabbed her by the arm, but she wouldn't turn to look at him. Instead she stared out to the fields, where an ancient tractor stood.

"You'll have to excuse me. I've got a couple hundred acres to cultivate."

"Mae," Wade said. "I'm sorry. I didn't mean *handle*, it's the wrong word, it's not what I meant."

"You shouldn't be here," Mae said. "And don't bother sending us any more letters."

"I'm trying to *help* you," Wade said. Couldn't she see that? Didn't she know he was doing this partly for her?

"We don't need your help." She looked at him at last, and he felt fastened by her stare, as though the anger it contained chastised and threatened at once.

He blindly went on, trying to recapture some of the ground he felt surely slipping away from him. "Does he want more money? Is that it? Are you holding out to bargain? I'll give you another ten thousand."

"And how much is that now?" Mae asked. "All together?"

"Let's see," Joe said. "We started with ..."

"How much did Milford Leutz spend on Emily when she lay dying?" Mae asked. And all that money didn't save her, did it? You still don't understand. You know how much things cost, but you have no idea what they're worth. We'll be seeing you," she said, and turned and walked into the kitchen, slamming first the screen and then the door behind her.

He wanted to yell something obscene; he wanted to pick

up a rock and hurl it through the window. He wanted to rip her wisteria up by the roots and shake it until it screamed for mercy. His fingernails had made small halfmoon indentations in his palm. He strode to the Bronco, threw it into first and stamped on the gas, spewing gravel behind him. If he were lucky, some of it spattered against the house, like a warning.

· 7 ·

Tom Garvey lay exhausted on his cot, slowly flexing and relaxing his muscles. The last time he'd done this it had been raining, too, seemed like months ago. He tried to remember what day it was, when he'd get out of this goddamn factory for the weekend. The place was quiet now, except for snatches of song from radios scattered among the cots. A cheap transistor playing country-and-western hung near his head. He groaned and rolled on his side. If Mae were here, he'd ask her to massage his shoulders; they were the worst, hunched from all that concentration with the slowly moving acetylene, the added weight of the helmet pushing down. Next to him Roy was looking at a tattered issue of *Hustler* he'd pulled from the trash. Roy's eyes were intent, and he flipped the pages regularly. Maybe he really *was* reading.

Truck, the foreman, lay on the cot beyond Roy. His eyes were closed, and his hands folded over his huge chest, in rehearsal for his eventual death. "Hey, what you doing, Truck?" Tom asked. "Counting sheep?"

"Counting pigs," Truck said. "Sides of bacon."

Tom laughed. He liked Truck. The guy kept to himself, but wasn't a snob. He just lived his life alone, didn't seem to have any family "on the outside," as they'd come to joking about it, as though they were in prison. Tom had done a little talking about the outside, but not very much. It hurt to talk about it; it hurt not to, as well. Roy seemed happy to be away from Ida; when he spoke about her, his comments were disparaging, and the job was a perfect excuse not to be with her.

He thought about getting up and going for a walk, wandering the factory now when all the machines were quiet, and the only thing he'd notice would be the glowing furnaces, waiting for the next day's work, pulsing at the center of the operation like a multitude of hearts. And in the main four-story section, he knew the rain would be more intense, the windows washing clean. He tried to think of what the rain sounded like beating against his bedroom window at home, had to admit it sounded pretty much like this. He could walk among the growing rows of steel piping, thick as cornstalks, a dark crop sprouting from a concrete field. He could try again to guess what those huge ugly forms were he was helping build; the plates were multiplying, the welds like scabs, their strange and complex shapes like nothing he'd ever seen before. And he'd feel better out there, alone, than here with the stink of the open latrines, steaming in their dim yellow light, the stink of all these bodies and unwashed clothes and bed linen, all these unmade cots that men lay in, one after another, like a conveyer belt of sleep, leaving behind the stench of their sweat and troubled dreams.

Tom felt a stab of hunger, and groaned. How strange the body was, demanding even when the brain knew the demand was impossible to fulfill. The canteen was closed for the night, and all that remained of the food they'd managed to stuff in their mouths that day were greasy ribs and chicken bones. The tables were littered with Twinkies wrappers, styrofoam cups half-filled with automated coffee, and slick green paper, like the kind florists wrapped flowers in, sticky with mayonnaise, barbecue sauce, catsup. Across the way, he saw someone nudge the man in the next cot and surreptitiously stick a bag-wrapped bottle out from under the pillow at him.

He lay on his back again and tried to count dollar bills. That was the only thing that kept him sane, kept him from turning the torch on someone near him, kept him from holding the flame steadily as he ripped down the middle of a plate, searing it in two. How many dollars had he made since he'd started here? How much had he spent on food? What day was it?

He opened his eyes, tried to decipher a pattern in the patternless ceiling. *I want both sugar in my coffee, and some sugar in my bed,* some guy wailed in the background. *Weather report coming up,* the DJ said. Then Baines came in.

Tom had learned his name the first day, but had forgotten it. Everyone called the kid Baines. He was a farmer, the son of a farmer, like Tom; but there were differences too immense not to notice. Baines was twenty-four, married last year, and sick to death about being away from home. Everything around him was failing, or so he said—the house was falling down, his wife was sickly and now pregnant for the first time, just a little slip of a poor country girl, barely twenty years old. He was tall, and gawky, with carroty hair, and a musty air of defeat about him that made Tom alternately irritable and sympathetic. Tonight the kid looked even more hangdog than usual; he'd just come back from the phone. Baines sat down on the cot next to Tom, blocking the light from the overhead bulb, enough to be grateful for under these circumstances.

"I just talked to her," Baines said. "She don't sound good."

"Probably just lonely down there alone," Tom said. "This is your first, isn't it?" Baines swallowed and nodded.

Roy put down the *Hustler*. He hadn't been reading. "What month is she?" he asked. Tom stared at the enormous breasts of the woman who lay on the bed.

Baines didn't notice the magazine. "Seventh," he said. "I just don't like her working the farm alone. All that lifting, and riding."

Tom thought about Mae; would he have left had she been pregnant?

"Don't worry, kid," Roy said. "When nature takes over, it's smooth as silk." What did *he* know? He'd never even been married. But that didn't mean . . . Tom wondered if Roy had a child somewhere, one he kept quiet about. The idea suddenly made his cousin more interesting than he'd ever been before.

A farm report came on the radio, the cost of feed in Chicago, in Cincinnati, in Omaha, and Tom's attention was instantly back on the announcer's voice. Had he missed the weather?

Truck sat up suddenly. "Can't you get some music out of the box? I don't give a fuck what cowfeed costs, and the rest of that shit sounds like killing a cat by pulling its guts through its nose." He stood up to change the station. Tom reached over and grabbed his wrist.

"Leave it," Tom said. "The weather's next."

Truck snatched his wrist out of the handcuff of Tom's hand. "The weather's comin' in the window. It's raining. What else you need to know?"

"He's got a farm, too," Roy said.

"You working in this shithole, you can't be doing so good," Truck said. He sighed and lay back on his cot. A toilet flushed, loudly, in the humming stillness of the factory. A fat man, swinging his hips as if trying to walk around himself, left the latrine, buckling his pants as he walked.

Truck sniffed, sat up, and exploded. "Jezsus! Something must a crawled up inside you and died."

Without missing a step, the fat man said, "Maybe it was your mama."

Truck stood at that, and something in his stance let Tom know the tension coiled there waiting for release. "Jesus!"

Truck said. "I gotta get me some air. How about you, farmer? You're into air, aren't you?"

"I could use a smoke," Roy said.

Tom lay still on the cot. Getting outside sounded good; so did the idea of being alone. One of the things Garvey loved most about farming was the long uninterrupted solitude, the row after row of corn whispering in a language all its own, no need to answer.

"Sure," he said. "I'll go outside." He was surprised how much it hurt to stand, to move slowly with these other men out of the fluorescent glare of the factory, into the cool moisture of the night. The work they had him doing was exhausting him more than he knew. Baines came along, lost in his own worries.

If this were home, he'd be exulting in the thin drizzle penetrating the fields, soaking deep beyond the easy reach of the sun. Here he huddled against the dull ribbed corrugation of the shed, turning his collar up to keep out what moisture he could. Rain ran from the roof in a steady stream. Roy took out a cigarette and lit it, holding the smoke in his lungs for a full count of two before sending a jet into the air. In the distance, beyond the chain-link fence, the flickering light from barrels of fire silhouetted the barely visible forms of the strikers. Did they stay here all night? Didn't they have families, wives, beds? What good were they doing with their wet and lonely vigil?

The four of them stopped near a cyclone fence and tried to get comfortable sitting on the empty oil drums which stood against the shed, under the overhang. "Man, that's gonna kill you," Truck said to Roy, as Roy pulled again on the cigarette. Truck took out a candy bar, peeled back the wrapper and began chewing. Roy offered Tom a cigarette; Tom shook his head.

"Hey, Jim," Truck said to Tom. "How come you guys grow all that food and people are still hungry? You know about being hungry?"

"Most of the time me and my family know about it first-hand," Tom said. "I don't know. Something's wrong somewhere."

"Hey, but you're a farmer," Truck said.

"I just grow one crop," Tom said. "As much of it as I can. I got no answers. What about you, Baines?" The tall man looked at him warily, as though he were about to get committed to something. He was edgy, fidgeting with his cigarette, jumping down from the barrel he sat on, staring off toward the strikers. Christ, they were all restless: exhausted, unable to sleep, full of a kind of energy they had no release for, sexual energy, wanting to break out.

Baines moved slightly away from the group, entering a running drip of water as he did; instead of jerking back under the roof's protection, he wandered out into the night, turned his face toward the sky, let the rain wash his face. He walked, as in sleep, toward a barely exposed gate hidden behind stacks of boxes. Truck had finished his Milky Way. He jumped down from the barrel he sat on, leaned over, picked it up and pressed it over his head. He lowered it, and pressed it again, like a barbell.

"What are you? Some kind of freaking Russian weightlifter?" Roy asked.

Truck threw the barrel into the yard where it clattered across the gravel. "If I had some land," he said, "I'd make a fucking garden and feed the world." Tom laughed, at the demonstration of strength and the bravado in the claim. Truck walked over and punched him lightly on the shoulder. "What do you weigh, Jim?" he asked.

"One-sixty," Tom said.

"You?" Truck nodded at Roy.

"One-fifty-five," Roy said, clearly the lightest man around. Maybe even including Baines. Where was he? He seemed to be fumbling around in those boxes in the darkness.

Truck flexed his biceps and stood in absurd imitation of a weightlifting ad. Tom laughed again. "You mothers are staring at two-hundred-and-twenty-five pounds of USDA prime," Truck said. "Hey, Baines, how about you?"

The three of them turned their attention to Baines, who was fumbling in the dark. Tom heard the sound of a chain being pulled against metal. "One-sixty-three," Baines said. "I'm going. I got to get home." The metal cleared, and the gate swung open.

"Hey!" Truck yelled. "Get your ass back here."

Baines hadn't seen the strikers crouched on the other side of the fence, watchdogs, four or five of them. Tom's stomach clenched in a spasm of fear. They were in for it. The sentries were on Baines now; he'd been thrown to the ground by their weight, and one of them sat on his chest, pounding the kid's face. Another kicked him in the side and yelled, "Scab sonofabitch!" Tom looked at Roy, who nodded, and the two of them ran through the gate to help. Behind him, Tom heard Truck yell, "You crazy? They'll kill your asses."

Tom grabbed the jacket of the man who sat on Baines's chest and jerked; the body rose, and as it did it met Tom's right fist. Another man wrapped his arms around Tom from behind, pinning him. One of the strikers had a length of pipe and as Baines struggled to his feet, Tom saw the pipe bury itself in the kid's side. The kid grunted and fell again, trying to crawl clear. Tom wrestled in the grip of his attacker, managed to break the lock of his hands, and grabbing the man's wrists he twisted and yanked him up and over his shoulder, and flung him to the ground. He heard a crack as the man's arm hit the pavement. Now the guy with the pipe was swinging at Roy. With his back turned, engaged with another striker who circled in the darkness looking for entry, Roy caught the pipe on the shoulder. His knees buckled, and he swayed, grabbing at his shoulder with his opposite hand.

Then Tom heard Truck's voice hissing in his ears. "Dumbass farmers." Truck brought his elbow down with the pressure of both arms, on the neck of one of the strikers. He crumbled to the ground as if made of cardboard. Truck pulled off one of the guys clinging to Tom's back and sent him reeling into the cyclone fence. He had ways of fighting Tom didn't know, city-ways: and Tom dimly knew that without Truck's help, he'd be lying soon, broken in the rain. "Oh, Jesus, Tom," he heard Roy yell; the lower half of his cousin's face was covered with blood. Someone had gotten him good in the mouth, was still on him. Buoyed by Truck's thrashing arms, Tom pulled the guy off Roy, and with a rush of adrenalin he picked the man off his feet, and, staggering slightly, flung him into a stack of wooden pallets. The man twitched and lay still.

Truck had already pulled Baines back through the fence, and now Tom pulled at Roy. Truck stood before them, swinging a length of chain in a vicious circle, covering their retreat. A group of strikers watched him, ready to lunge. "Come on, motherfuckers," Truck growled. "Come mess with me." He backed through the gate, wrapped the chain around to close it. The strikers hurled themselves against the fence, and clung there.

Tom was back with the others; he was hurt the least. Roy groaned, holding his palm to his cheek. "You okay?" Tom asked.

"Yeah," Roy said. "Terrific. Know any good dentists?"

Truck stood over him now. "You crazy sonofabitch," he said. "You're really strong, ain't you? Lucky for that dude you didn't hit him."

Garvey stared back and didn't say anything. Rain mixed with blood from the cut on his eyebrow and streamed down the side of his face. He wiped at it with his hand and then stared at the crimson stain on his palm. Head wounds—they really bled. It probably wasn't so bad. Baines slumped to the side, wiping the blood off his face with an oily handkerchief. Tom was torn between anger at the kid and pity—he knew how he felt, the urge to get out, no matter what it cost. "You all right, kid?" he finally asked.

"Yeah," Baines said. He held the handkerchief against the cut on his chin. "You?"

"Yeah," Tom said. "I think so."

Baines stared at him, then at Roy and Truck. "Thanks," he said. "They woulda killed me."

Truck shrugged. "Someone else woulda got your job," he said.

"Thanks anyway," Baines said.

"Sure," Roy said. "Let's get inside."

· 8 ·

He held the phone to his ear, and could barely hear it ringing. The steady thump of machines, the clanging of presses, the thunder of rolling steel was so loud it seemed to be coming over the receiver. Sweat dripped from his scalp. His entire face was coated with it. He turned away from the factory, as though trying to shield the phone from harm. He scowled, felt the tug of the butterfly bandage covering the gash on his eyebrow. "Come on," he said, under his breath. "Come on."

When he heard the whisper of Beth's voice on the other end, he started screaming as loud as he could. "Beth? Can you hear me? Beth, Beth, it's me, Daddy. Honey, get your mother." He wanted to cover the phone, press a button and bring everything around him to a screeching halt. He heard, as underwater, the sound of the other receiver clunking against the kitchen floor, and he saw his daughter running out into the sunlight to find his wife.

When she heard her daughter's voice, its urgency almost stopped her heart. Beth came running across the barnyard, her arms waving wildly, her schooldress flapping behind her like a banner. The voice was shrill with excitement and when she finally heard the words—*Mama, Mama, it's Daddy*—she began running too, through the rows of corn, taller now, golden pollen swirling around her. Beth stopped at the edge of the field, panting, and Mae passed her, yelling back over her shoulder, "Honey, come on," in her rush for the phone. From another part of the field Lewis came running, all three of them honing in on the kitchen door, the phone, its precious words.

She heard nothing but a dull roaring at first, as though a vacuum cleaner were talking, and then she began to pick out the words—randomly—the voice of her husband darting through the wires. "Yes," she said. "Of course. Yes, yes. I love you, too." She held the receiver against her chest, hugged Beth to her. She turned to Lewis. "We're going to Birmingham to visit Daddy," she said. "Just two more days."

· 9 ·

Even the showers smelled sweet, as though they'd been scrubbed with Clorox and then sprayed with bay rum. Tom soaped himself lavishly, over and over, washing off the grit of shaved steel, the rancid smoke of cigarettes, the sour smell of bodies deprived of sunlight. He pushed his face into the fine spray from the shower, until his eyeballs ached with the pressure, enough pain to really feel clean. He toweled himself until his skin reddened, and then he dressed himself in the only clean clothes he had left, the ones he'd saved, the white western shirt with red mother-of-pearl buttons, the green wide wale cords he'd laid under the mattress last night to press. Roy was still shaving, carefully pulling the razor they shared across his cheekbone, picking his way between whisker and skin; the blade's dullness made that especially hard, and a spot of lather on Roy's chin was stained pink. Roy was singing some snatches of a Donna Summer song, moving his hips dreamily before the mirror, making love to himself. "Come on," Tom said. "Quit that bullshit humping."

"Hot stuff, baby," Roy sang, and the rest degenerated into a tuneless mumble.

Tom grabbed his jacket, slung it over his shoulder, and he and Roy strode to the door. A line of men waited to climb into the truck, subdued, even polite, not wanting to mess up their clothes. Weekend pass. Some of the men were whistling, others stood silently, all lost in a vision of the coming hours. Swick stood to the side making a megaphone with his hands.

"Meet the pickup Sunday midnight. Place we hired you. Be there sharp. You don't show, you don't get back in. Same as always. Got it?" He walked up toward the cab. "Okay, take them out the dump," he told the driver.

The trucks began to move. There were fewer of them now, it seemed to Tom. He wondered how many had left, tried to walk out like Baines; he wondered if any of them were the kind who stayed on the inside. Where *was* Baines?

He searched the truck he rode, and the one behind, couldn't see Baines anywhere; as a matter of fact, he couldn't remember seeing him since the fight. Had the kid gone home? He hoped so, although he knew that what he'd find there wouldn't solve his problems either.

The trucks bounced through potholes, over ruts and buried pipes that looked like cattle guards, but everything about this trip was more sedate. This was the seventh weekend he'd gone out; the others he'd just hung mournfully with Roy and Ida, when Ida was home. It hadn't been worth it to try to get back to the farm—he'd gotten home for Lewis's twelfth birthday, but it was just far enough so he'd had to turn around and start back hours after getting there.

He'd gotten used to the rhythm of the weekend trips. Sunday midnight, dark, tense, everyone packed cussing, drunk, ready to rip throats and gouge eyes, keyed with the expectation of another week: but Saturday afternoon, their hair slicked, smelling of deodorant and cologne, the men could have been a group of Rotarians on their way to a fish fry.

The back gates opened onto the chemical dump and the marsh beyond. Who dumped here Tom didn't know, but it was worse than ugly. What oozed and burbled in the tire tracks was the stuff the papers had been full of for years now—the place called the Love Canal, that town in Missouri that the federal government had had to *buy:* it was right here, too, and no one seemed to notice it. It splashed to either side of the truck as the tires rolled, and it smelled like burnt rubber and singed hair and old molding socks. Some of it was slag and oil, and some of it must be the shit they poured in the smelting pots. But some of it looked like it had seeped up from hell—iridescent purple and fluorescent orange, more flamboyant than nature's wildest colors.

The strikers knew the trucks took this way out, but only the real fanatics wanted to muck in the marsh. Three of them stood ready with rocks, yelling; still they kept an eye on the ground should it heave open to grab them.

"Scab sonsabitches!" they yelled, but their hearts weren't in it; their rocks were heaved high and clattered against the wooden siding. The men Tom worked with treated them with good-natured contempt, as though it were part of a too-familiar ritual they all wished would end. The truck ground past them onto a twisting dirt road skirting the edge of the marsh.

There was something definitely spooky about the place, and each week Tom waited for an enormous alligator, spawned here and fed on the radioactive muck of the dump, to rise out of the water and swallow the truck. He'd told Roy about his fantasy, and his cousin had told him a story he hadn't wanted to hear, about some movie he'd seen on TV where an alligator came right up through the sidewalk in New York City, right through the cement. A truck would be nothing.

The surface of the water here was never placid; bubbles blistered its skin, continuous streams of them. Hummocks interrupted the flatness, big enough to hide behind. And beyond the marsh, almost rising out of it, was a stand of trees large enough to be called a woods. The trees were stunted, mostly swamp maples and locusts, junk trees, suckers, but enough to form a refuge. Deer lived there. Lots of them, too many. Last week he'd heard the heavy thuds of gunfire as the truck rolled past, and when he asked Roy, he'd been told about the white-tails who lived there and were being steadily hunted down.

"Twelve-gauge," Roy had said. "Poachers been in there all summer. Everybody's hungry." His eyes had narrowed, and he pointed. "Look," he said. Tom followed his finger. Sure enough, a pair of small deer gingerly skirted the marsh, their tails high, skittish and frightened. The wind shifted, they heard the approach of the truck, and flicking their tails, they bounded into the woods. "They been getting on the highways. City's set up a special two-week season end of the month," Roy said. "Ida sure could use the meat. What do you say?"

"I bet it's poisoned," Tom said. "I bet everything around here glows in the dark."

"Shit," Roy said. "Meat's meat, ain't it? A venison stew would sure taste good after that plastic-wrapped crap we eat at the factory."

Tom nodded. Roy was right. And you died of something, sooner or later. Still, it wasn't the same. That marsh had once been clean enough to drink from and the deer had been sweet as the first berries of summer. Still, he'd always loved to hunt. Maybe he could even bring Lewis. He stared into the woods, trying to see what was there. The truck lurched on, and he fumbled on his feet, knocking into Roy. From the woods, three separate shots echoed off the tree trunks. Sure, he'd have the kid come down during that two-week season. Hell of a spot to hunt, but better than sitting around in a tenement waiting for Sunday midnight.

· 10 ·

They'd had cheeseburgers and fries and Cokes all around at McDonald's, except Ida who'd had Chicken McNuggets. They always looked to Tom like batter-fried styrofoam. Ida ate them daintily, holding her pinky up as if it were high tea, and dipping them in some kind of mustard sauce.

Now they were standing in line to see a movie called *Splash*, about a mermaid with legs. Mae had read about it. It was supposed to be good. There was a car chase for Lewis and the mermaid for Tom, and if it got too raunchy, Mae would put her hands over Beth's eyes and ears.

"What's in it for Beth?" he'd asked.

"She likes my hands," Mae said.

"Maybe *I'll* find parts of it too dirty."

"I doubt it," Mae said. "Besides, it's close by."

It was one of those warm summer evenings when even the city seemed romantic. Tom looked at the teenaged couples waiting in line. One girl was wearing a white cotton dress, and she leaned against the brick of the building next to the theatre, her legs slightly apart. Her date, a tall earnest young man, with a crewcut, stood before her, his knee between her legs. As he talked, he rocked forward and back, and Tom wondered if they knew what they were doing. From the slow smile on the girl's face, he thought they probably did.

And there were families, none as handsome as his. There were kids as little as Beth who whined and hung on their parents' arms as though they were at the playground, and others who looked pale and sickly. Beth stood with Ida now, displaying her new sneakers. Yeah, she was stuck-up, but she was good with Beth, and that counted for a lot. She was listening seriously now, as Beth turned the sneaker over to illuminate the secret of its sole.

Tom squeezed Mae's hand and bent down to Lewis's ear. "I'm hunting with Roy in a couple of weeks. There's a place near where I work where there's a herd of white-tails, and they opened a special two week season. Want to come?" Lewis had been listening attentively, but the last question clearly astonished him.

"I can, Dad?" he said, his voice rising.

"Yes."

"I can?"

"I said yes."

Tom wasn't sure if Mae or Lewis had the bigger smile. Lewis couldn't hold in the good news. He leaned forward to where Beth was demonstrating shoelaces to an entranced Ida. "Did you hear that? I'm going hunting with Dad and Roy."

"That's nice, honey," Ida said. "Am I invited?"

"I don't know," Lewis said. "You'll have to ask my dad."

Tom laughed. "You're welcome, Ida. Have to buy yourself something other than those spike shoes."

Mae stood close now, as close as the boy and girl had stood before. Sobered by how near they were to the ticket booth, those two now stood like West Point cadets. But Mae and Tom were still far enough away. His palm was moist; Mae was tracing the vein in the crook of his arm with her nail; she had turned so that she almost faced him, and he felt the slight pressure of her knee through her skirt as it grazed the inside of his thigh. She moistened her lips, put both arms around him and hugged. This time her knee moved higher, and her lips brushed the side of his neck. Beyond the theatre, he saw the neon lights of the Sleep Well Motel, the red outline of a bed blinking on and off in lazy rhythm. He tightened his arms around her back, crushing her to him. "The kids can stay with Ida and Roy for the night," he said. "I already checked."

· 11 ·

The Huntington Hotel was shabby but genteel, the sort of place that had been nice forty years ago, before everyone started going to motels. The lobby needed painting, but the horsehair plaster was cool to the touch, and ornamental filigree surrounded the modest chandelier. The desk clerk smoked BelAirs and asked no question other than "Name?"

The curtains were thin cotton instead of gauzy nylon, and they blew in the window as Tom creaked open the door to take a first peek. The double bed sagged a bit in the middle, but the coverlet was dotted with tiny pompons, white against the pale blue fabric, and it streaked with blues and reds as the city's neon filtered through the window. There were two water glasses upturned on paper doilies on the unvarnished bureau, a thin white strip of paper circling the toilet seat. Tom snapped it, smiled, and threw it away. Mae stood behind him, looking at herself in the bathroom mirror. "Darling," he said, "let's buy it," and she laughed.

• • •

He was soaked with sweat. It ran from some point he couldn't quite locate, between his shoulderblades, down his back, across his buttocks, sheening his sides until the places his skin met hers were slick and slippery. She'd walked naked from the bathroom, moving to him with an air of self-assurance both lascivious and threatening. She seemed new, foreign; her freckles had disappeared in her tan, her hair was almost the white of cornsilk, and the concentrated paleness of her eyes was like the power of a dime catching the full weight of the sun. He was ashamed of the dirt beneath his fingernails, a different dirt from any she'd seen him wear. He wondered if she smelled the factory on him; she smelled of hay and sunlight. He kissed her again, struggled against her, massaged her breasts, tried to concentrate. But the weeks between them rose up, the acres of concrete his feet had walked, the dirt under hers, the fluorescent tubing above his head, the sky above hers.

"Tom?" she said, softly. He opened his eyes, and saw her—first red, then blue. Her nails gently scratched his back, and he closed his eyes and moved his mouth to her breast. But it was no use; all he could see was cornstalks, Swick, barrel fires, eggs, the faces of his children. He couldn't get hard, not even when he'd taken himself in his own hand. He rolled off her and flung his elbow over the edge. "I'm sorry," he said. "I can't. Oh, God, I don't know. Maybe I want you too bad."

"I know," Mae said. "Me too."

"Really?"

"Yeah," Mae said. "Couldn't you tell?"

"I guess not," Tom said. "I was paying too much attention to myself."

She laughed, and he laughed too, and the tension coiling in his chest dissolved. "What's your hurry?" she said. "You sleepy? We got all night."

She sat up, and the lovely rope of her spine knotted along her back's tanned expanse. She grabbed a corner of the sheet, pulled it over them, turned on her side, supporting her head on her hand. With the other she grazed his nipples. Then she saw the burn on his arm, the one he'd gotten when he'd walked too close to a lathe. She touched it gently, bent to kiss it. "How'd you get that?" she asked.

"The machinery's hot."

She rose up and kissed the butterfly bandage on his eyebrow. "And this?"

"People aren't so neighborly in there."

She shrugged as she sometimes did when he answered her questions this way, as though each word were expensive and he very poor. She kissed his lips once and then pointed to a red welt on his neck, which she seemed proud of. "I know where you got that," she said. "I gave it to you. Want another?"

"Maybe later," he said. "I'm still recovering from the first."

She lay back, and the sheet settled slowly over them, casting their bodies in percale. They were breathing in unison, and he saw with satisfaction the edges of their ribcages, the flat plains of their bellies. Mae had a foolish little belly button, an "outie," as she called it, and the small lump it made under the sheet was silly and touching. Her hands were folded on the turned-back edge, and her breasts were just visible in the soft neon flares. Outside on the street a horn blared; beneath their window, and several stories down, another couple walked by, their voices rising and falling, their words lost. From the next room, a snore rose and fell. They'd joked about it before, had forgotten it. Now, as they lay still, it was impossible to ignore, sonorous as the ocean.

"The snore that ate Birmingham," Mae said.

"Youi ought to hear the barracks at three in the morning," Tom said. "Sounds like a saw mill."

Mae laughed, then was still. Tom felt his heart clench; now he rose up to look at her. The questions he'd had before flooded out.

"Crop's okay?"

"It's doing fine."

"Can you take care of it all?"

"I can handle it," she said.

Something crossed her face, a darker shadow. He knew he'd have to ask, but didn't want to. He trusted her, yes, with his life, but he had to ask. He couldn't go another week without knowing. He reached over and touched her face, drew his index finger under her nose, an imaginary moustache, trailed it across one cheek and grabbed her ear-lobe. Her face turned toward him.

"Anything wrong?" he asked.

"No," she said.

"Wade been around?"

"No."

It was a lie, and he knew it. But it gave him the information he needed. It meant *no* in a way he understood.

"You don't always tell me everything," he said.

Mae looked away and then back, and the calmness of her face was disturbed. "Want me to make something up? We got weevils in the corn? Snow White won't suckle?" Now she covered her breasts with the sheet, a little girl home sick from school, in a pout. "You don't tell me everything either," she said.

True enough. She'd asked him before about his burn, about his cut, and he'd said nothing. Outside, another siren wailed. All over this city people were in trouble. Thank God he was where he was.

"The plant's noisy," he said. "I don't know. It's hot. There's lots of strange men—some don't even speak English. It's hard to breathe sometimes. The ceiling's four stories high, but the air's all trapped and sometimes I think that air's been in there since they built the place." He took the sheet and mopped the sweat from his forehead; it was burning his eyes. "And then when I go *out* for air, I see the strikers. And I know I've got their job and that they have families like me. Even when I can't see them, I know they're there."

Mae held a finger up to his lips. He took a deep breath,

and she bent over and gave him a kiss so full of understanding and desire it brought tears to his eyes. Her hand ran down his chest now, tangled in the dark hair by his navel, moved up again, greased by his sweat.

"I can't sleep," he said. "And if I do. . . . Last night I dreamed about the river. Only it wasn't a river. It was a snake, and I couldn't find the head or tail. It was endless and it kept moving, and the more I tried the harder it squeezed. It had me wrapped so hard I couldn't breathe."

Her hand had moved below his navel now, had brushed his penis and gone beyond. Her fingernails were slowly scratching the inside of his thigh, and he moaned, feeling himself get hard. His heart began beating faster. She had him in her hand now, gently pulling, and this time his moan was like a growl. She bent to his ear, nibbled, whispered, "Some nights I miss you so bad. I ache for you so bad." He reached down, took her hand away, placed it on his chest. She drew a line from his navel to his left nipple and took the right one in her mouth. Now her breasts hung down and he kissed each one in turn, then sat up and put his arms around her.

"He stopped," he said, in wonder. And it was true. The man next door, the hotel, the city now seemed absolutely quiet, poised on the verge of tumult. "Let's wake him up," Tom said. He lay back down, pulled Mae on top of him, squeezed all the breath right out of her until he pressed his lips to hers, filled her with air again.

· 12 ·

The three weeks between his return from the city and his trip back were torture for Lewis. He moved through each day, milking, cultivating, working around the farm, but with a new purpose. His mother lost count of the times he took the deer rifle from its corner of the front closet beside the L.C. Smith twelve-gauge and polished its stock, oiled and rubbed its barrel, until the blue-black metal seemed luminous. He pored through old magazines until he found a small ad for a sporting goods mail order house in Memphis, and, carefully, with his mother's sewing scissors, he snipped a stamp-sized picture of a deer and taped it over the Saturday in late August he was hunting with his dad.

They'd shot at cans and bottles together, and his father had set up target after target in front of bales of hay; they'd shot skeet in Millrock, and for the last two years since he'd turned ten he'd entered the junior division of the Kiwanis Turkey Shoot in November. They'd flushed quail and pheasant from the brush along the river. But this was his first deer, the first time his father had planned it special. Just him, and his dad's cousin Roy.

When he told Scott Mabrey at church, Scott said, "Wow!" And that was something: usually Scott had heard it before, the joke, the story, the new unimaginable sexual detail. But he was impressed: Lewis Garvey was going to Birmingham in August to shoot a deer.

• • •

Lewis was up before the first light cracked the eastern horizon; in fact, he wasn't sure he'd slept. But he felt fine, rested, ready. Outside he wanted to yell, but his mother's window was right there, and she'd tan his hide. He milked the cows, scattered seed for the chickens. He walked the fields, between the rows of corn, as the sky moved from black to grey. Another six weeks and the crop would be ready for harvest, his dad would be home for good. The combine already stood in the fields, waiting.

When he pulled open the screen door, it creaked on his hinges, and he was quiet for a moment to see what damage he'd done. From his mother's room he thought he heard a muffled snoring. The refrigerator jerked on, its faint humming unnaturally loud in the stillness. A mouse nibbled at the plaster. One foot after the other, he crept down the hall to his room.

Everything was ready. He'd laid out all his gear the night before. Now he took off his farm clothes, with their barnyard stink and deep dirt stains, and carefully put on his hunting clothes. His shirt was red cotton, freshly washed and neatly pressed; his pants were the green khaki ones he sometimes wore to school. Though he had no need of it now, he put on the fluorescent orange cap and looked at himself in the mirror, then lowered the brim so his eyes were almost invisible. He took the cap off, put on his boots and tied the laces with the care he'd have given to knots intended to save his life. Then he gathered up the rest of his gear; he hung the already-filled canteen from its strap around his neck, he put his belt through the sheath of his hunting knife and that through the loops of his pants. He checked the contents of his small knapsack: compass, waterproof matches. He felt a little silly, really. After all, he wasn't going off to the wilderness. He really should be packing spare change, bus tokens, a can of Mace. The smell of bacon reached his room, and he picked up all his stuff and went down the hall to the kitchen.

His mother's hair was disheveled, and she wore her frowsiest brown bathrobe, but she was whistling as she poured the pancake batter on the skillet. She was different with him now; when his dad was home he was still a kid, but in the months his dad had been away, his mom had depended on him more and more. Her tone was different, softer, fuller. She turned and smiled when she heard him, made no comment about the paraphernalia festooning his chest. "Morning, Lewis," she said, as though it were any morning.

She turned back to the pancakes, and he said, "Mom?"

She nodded, knowing what he meant, and said, "You know where it is." She flipped the cakes, turned and watched him as he went to the front closet and got out the deer rifle. He looked up to see her smile as he pulled the bolt, checked the action, carefully sequestered it in its canvas case. He looked at her triumphantly, and she said, "I'm still your mother. Come eat your breakfast."

He watched her waving goodbye in Millrock as the bus pulled alway, growing smaller through the dirty glass, as though he were off to war. The bus was almost empty, though he knew it would crowd as they neared Birmingham. An elderly man and woman sat directly behind the driver, and a man, younger than Lewis's father, sat in the middle of the right hand-side. Over him, rolling on the slick aluminum bars, was a brown-speckled suitcase tied with rope. He stared vacantly out the window, as though his neck were stuck.

Lewis had picked a seat near the back. His knapsack occupied the space beside him. He, too, stared out the window as the bus wove south through farmland, past fields of corn, soybeans, alfalfa, not a single deer.

At noon he ate the chicken sandwich and the orange his mother had packed.

He'd fallen asleep long before the bus reached the city, and he woke to motor oil, gas fumes, the rich petroleum stink of bus stations. It was almost dark. In a panic he looked above him; the canvas case with the gun was where he'd left it, and his knapsack was safe on his lap. Out the window, he saw the clean-shaven face of his father smiling at him, safe harbor on the other end.

· 13 ·

His father moved cautiously through the misty woods, and Lewis stayed close behind him, watching where his father stepped, placing his feet in the same silent places. Roy was ahead of them, looking for a good stand. All three wore orange hunting hats, special licenses and tags pinned to them, but that didn't make Lewis feel safe. Not even his father's presence calmed him this morning.

In the distance, a gun fired. Almost in response, there were five closer blasts, each distinct, booming in the morning's stillness. His father froze at the first shot, didn't move during the answering five. Each boom seemed louder than the one before it, causing Lewis's heart to knock more loudly against his ribs.

He'd hated the chemical dump they'd passed through, didn't trust his father's answers to his questions. They meant, as they always did, that his father wasn't telling him everything. Not even the dump in Millrock smelled as bad as that sludge they'd crossed. And even here, on this island of trees and moss, something was wrong. Lewis wasn't sure if the odor in his nose wafted in from the swamp or seeped out of the ground.

The shots echoed away, and they walked on. Lewis cradled his rifle carefully, making sure the barrel pointed left and toward the ground, and the safety was on. Last year's leaves still littered the earth. An aluminum can gleamed among the leaves, and then a small cache of them, Old Milwaukee in silver and red on the shiny cylinders. A few steps farther and they came upon the torn-off haunch of a deer. Lewis stared at it; who would do a thing like that? If he hadn't seen a deer before he'd never have known what it was. It lay there, ragged and bloody, and it made him flinch.

More beer cans, and the remains of a fire. Blackened rocks had been scattered with a stick, and the firepit lay uncovered. Roy turned back and shook his head at Lewis's father. "Pretty ugly," Roy said.

"Take a look at that," Tom said. He motioned with his head and Lewis saw what he'd missed before; someone had taken the deer's head and propped it on a rock overhang above where the fire was. The stub of a cigar protruded obscenely from the bloody muzzle.

"Jesus Christ," Roy said. "Friggin' freaks."

"Hush," Tom said. "The boy."

But Lewis almost hadn't heard. It was as though he'd fallen past all his dreams of what this day would be like into a nightmare beyond reckoning. Just past the campfire, they found the latrine, a rude hole kicked out of the dirt, littered with the smeared pages of a glossy magazine. They'd eaten and drunk here then, and bowed before the bloody head, kept warm at the fire until they'd had their fill, then stumbled over there to purge themselves. It sickened Lewis, and it frightened him. He wished he'd stayed on the farm; he hadn't known that men like these existed.

The woods were quiet for most of the morning; Lewis, his father, and Roy had taken stands about ten feet off the ground in the crotches of swamp maples. No one had spoken for an hour, or longer. Lewis didn't know. He'd lost all track of time. From this height, the woods seemed more peaceful, unmarred by the ugliness of those who'd tromped through, spewing their garbage. His mind wandered, distracted by the underbuzz of insects, the sweat running down his back. It was hot, the sun high in the sky.

Then he heard his father whisper urgently, "There," and Lewis watched in amazement as a buck moved toward them through the brush. Its brown eyes searched the underbrush placidly; it moved with a liquid grace that made Lewis's heart catch in his throat. "It's yours," his father said. "Take it."

Lewis's finger tightened on the trigger; he could feel his father's eyes on him. He drew a breath, held it, sighted, found the buck's chest and fired. When the bullet hit, the deer's head twitched up as though on a rope, and a bright splash of red appeared over its right leg. Its eyes flew wide, its legs buckled, but it reared and stumbled off, crashing through the underbrush. "Careful with your gun now," his father said, and Lewis put the safety on, and handed it down to his father, who was already on the ground with Roy. Then he jumped down, took his gun back, and the three of them, Lewis ahead, ran after the wounded deer. Branches whipped his face, and his breath was harsh in his lungs.

Suddenly there was a barrage of shots, loud, close by. Lewis jerked to a stop. In the clearing ahead he could see the fallen deer, and four men running toward it. They were pushing and stumbling, their guns wildly bucking; they clutched at one another, trying to slow one another down.

"It's mine," one of them screamed. "Goddamn you, it's mine."

"It's my kill," another said. "Shit."

"Get away, it's mine."

Their knives were already out; for a bewildering moment Lewis thought they were going to kill each other, but then they fell upon the deer, cut its throat, and watched the blood pouring onto the ground.

Lewis felt his face flame; the words rose through his throat, no thought of being stopped. "It's mine," he yelled. "I shot it."

"Lewis," his father said.

"I shot it," Lewis yelled. "Get away."

One of the men stood. There was blood on his face, and on his jacket. The knife pointed toward Lewis, his father, and Roy. "You want to take it, kid?"

"Come on," Roy said. "They're crazy. They're animals. Let's get out of here."

· 14 ·

Roy was driving. Lewis sat wedged between Roy and his father, and he felt the casual weight of his father's palm on his shoulder. He knew the arm was resting on the seatback as it always did when his father wasn't driving, but the tentative touch of those oil-blackened fingers annoyed him. He scowled over at his father, who was staring out the windshield at the chemical dump.

Hardly moving his mouth, Roy said, "I think they live there. Like wild men."

Tom nodded, and turned away. The boy felt caught between them, unsure of what to think, of what they thought. Those men lived there? He was beginning to get a picture from scraps of conversation, things he'd seen in Millrock, or on the news. He didn't understand, but all across America there were people who had no jobs, no food, no place to live.

"Why'd they do it, Dad?" he finally asked. "It was my deer."

His father shrugged. "They were hungry," he said. "It was probably all they had."

"So why do they do stuff like put cigars in its mouth and mess everything up?"

"I don't know, Lewis. I wish I could tell you."

"It's still wrong, isn't it?"

"Yeah," his father said. "It's still wrong."

They were bouncing through the last of the potholes now. The swirls of cirrus in the sky were delicate mare's tails, white as milkweed fluff; in the afternoon light, the chemical dump became a mirror, giving back the world's real colors, not the manufactured colors of poison.

Then they were skirting the chain-link fence surrounding the Allied Iron Fabrication plant. Only a few more hours now and the weekend would be another memory; he'd be on the bus heading home, sleeping, jostling in the seat, and his father would be back with the other men.

"That where you work, Dad?" he asked. They'd talked about it on the way out here, but other questions troubled him, questions about the men who stood before the gates, holding hand-lettered signs, cigarettes hanging loosely from their lips, their caps pulled low.

"Yes," his father said.

"They're striking," Lewis said.

"They want more money, better conditions. They say their labor is the most valuable thing they have."

"Where'd you hear that, professor?" Roy asked.

"Talking to some of the strikers. You know. Through the fence, late at night. Sometimes I can't sleep. Everyone's too tired to fight."

"You been listening to the Marxist crap?" Roy said. "Boy, I'd steer clear of that, Tom."

"It makes sense," Tom said. "Or it would if we weren't scabbing."

"How do you get in?" Lewis asked. He remembered the hooded look in the men's eyes, the way they'd followed the wavering movement of the truck. They were unshaven, mean.

"They drive us in the back way."

"Are they right to strike?" Lewis asked.

"I don't know," Tom said. "They get paid pretty good already, seems to me. I don't know if it's wrong for a man to want more. Do you think it's wrong for me to take their jobs?"

"I don't know," Lewis said.

"Well," Roy said. "I've heard about enough of that shit."

"Roy," his father said. "I told you not to."

"Sorry," Roy said. Then he let a hand fall from the steering wheel and slapped Lewis's knee. "Ida'll get you on the bus early, Lewis. It's a long trip back."

His father's hand came down now too, no longer casual, and gripped his shoulder. "You be sure and tell your mom and sister I love them," he said. "You be sure to do that. And I know you'll go on taking care of the place. It won't be long now. How long you figure until the corn's ready?"

"Don't know," Lewis mumbled. Tears blurred his eyes, and he wanted badly to keep them from spilling over. "You know. Mid-October."

"Well, I'll be back for good in about six weeks then. And I'll see you before that. You all just hold on till then. Okay?"

"Okay," Lewis said. "We will." He let his head fall back and to the side until it touched his father's hand. And the palm turned, the fingers touched his cheek, then tangled in his hair.

· 15 ·

They met the truck at midnight. Tom wore his coveralls again, and he held tight to the small canvas bag with his razor, toothbrush, his outside clothes. Some of the men were drunk; all were sullen, quiet. They swayed together as the truck turned corners in the darkness, immigrants up from steerage staring at the ocean's molten surface. By the time they entered the quiet factory lot a fine drizzle had begun to fall. Tom thought of Lewis and the long bus ride home, the driver staring at the solid white line while the wipers slicked the falling mist from the glass.

His hair was damp; he could feel the mist in his bones. The men grumbled as they stripped and lay down in the darkness of the factory barracks. The first snorts started, men drifting into interior landscapes. With his eyes open the world was black, when he shut them, the world was red. Black, red; black, red. The sun was red, the strikers' fires were red, Old Milwaukee cans, deer's blood, his son's hunting shirt.

A young buck moves through dappled light and shadow as in the woods, but the trees are jutting from concrete, and the shadows and sun fall on iron walls. It's a white-tail, its pelt ticked with grey, its muzzle black. Above his eyes, dilated with fear, the first buds of antlers are visible. All this in silence; and then, as through a suddenly opened door, the thunder of the metal works. The buck's pointed ears prick; he scans the gravel he stands on, looking for a path, but the only one leads toward the liquid noise, the red noise of steel pouring into molds, hammered sheets of it rolling steeply down like rain. In the distance, alien forms hunch over, and from their hands lightning zigzags, the air around them streaming with pungent smoke. Thunder, lightning, smoke, deafening noise.

Go back, he wants to say, but he is asleep, and the deer cannot hear him.

The buck's hooves click on the worn cement, bone on rock, slowing down, rounding a corner; suddenly it's in the thick of the factory. He's in his own dream, of course. When he sees it, he says "Hey" softly, in wonder and surprise, as he might have said to a lover, or to his own face suddenly glimpsed in a mirror, the apparition so familiar and foreign it makes his heart beat faster. He is one of the men with lightning at his fingers, but he puts down his torch, watching the buck approach. He knows it is coming to him: it will speak: *it will tell him a secret.*

The deer slips between great steel lathes lying idle, under conveyers bearing wide steel sheets. Men begin to follow it, and he realizes they can see it too. Roy and Truck are beside him, and he needs to tell them to leave now, the buck is coming to him, but he cannot speak. "What the hell is it?" Roy asks. "It's a goddamn deer," Truck says. Tom says nothing, but the words skitter in his head, click like hooves on cement.

It begins to run, slipping on the oiled cement. The workshed elongates, and the deer is running full out now, its back bowing in the middle of full stride so its hind and front legs seem interlocked, already a trophy on someone's pickup, and then it stretches, hits the ground and leaps. There are swamp maples around it, and its hide is covered with sunlight, and it's being pursued by a pack of dogs with the faces of men in the factory.

The dogs are coming from everywhere now, closing in, a vast perimeter of howling. The deer wheels and skitters, turning in ever-narrowing circles. *He* is the deer, now, of course, knows the secret it was coming to tell him. He runs through the fields of iron piping, barrows of black steel plate. There is a river, but it's glowing metal, rolling slowly down one side of the factory. Dogs leap it in one slick stride. His hooves snap in curls of smoke.

Under the rumble of machinery, he hears the rasp of air in the thin tube of his throat, he hears the roar of water. Pipe clatters, the dogs leap to the shiny tops of workbenches, their canines bared. They bark and growl; their ears are pressed flat.

The circle has closed now, and the ring of dogs has turned to men again, their workclothes wet with sweat, their faces flushed. He is inside their circle, and trapped; he shakes, his legs splay, he urinates in terror.

As though that is a signal, the world falls into a grey leaded silence, a fine mist falling from the sky. The men's faces slacken, as he grows still. His muzzle droops; his tongue hangs flecked with pale foam. His eyes are dull, exhausted, resigned. Everything has stopped: the river grows cold in its banks, the machines halt, the iron piping no longer sprouts branches, leaves. He looks around him at the rigid men. They stare at the circle of oiled cement where he stands: their faces are wild with terror. They pant, they flinch, they cannot move.

His heart pounds terribly, the only noise in the factory, bong, bong, bong, bong.

Tom opened his eyes on the darkness, his heart pounding, the bell of St. Stephen's Ukranian Catholic Church tolling the hours. He looked at his watch. It was five o'clock, and the men around him were sleeping stealthily, snoring.

What if a deer did cross the chemical sludge from the woods and enter the factory? What if it did begin to run, its hooves clicking like dice thrown harshly down, a final gamble? What would he do?

The men in the woods would rip it to pieces, turn its head to a buzzing trophy. Tom hoped that he would be different, that he and Roy and the others would see that it meant no harm, had fallen as if through a hole in its world into theirs, that it, no more than they, wanted sunlight, water, a place to run.

He closed his eyes and willed an ending to his dream. In the redness the men crushed forward and lifted the terrified deer, they held it tenderly, and it was unafraid. They raised it above their heads and moved down the long sweeping hollow center of the factory to the small back gate that opened to the marshland. When they reached the gate, they lowered the deer, stood back. It shimmered for a moment, then turned and bounded away from them, toward the stand of hazy trees in the distance where the sun was rising.

· 16 ·

Lewis had been home for more than three weeks, quiet, a bit withdrawn. He'd done his chores, but since the hunting trip, his exuberance was gone. When Mae sat on the edge of his bed at night, smoothing back his hair, giving herself the luxury of her palm against his forehead, he turned away from her toward the wall and mumbled good-night. He was growing up, that was all. She hoped that was all.

He'd told her about how he'd shot a deer and followed it, only to have four other hunters claim it. He'd told how Roy and Tom had put their hands on his shoulders and walked away with him. There was something he wasn't telling, though, she knew: something he'd seen that he couldn't shake.

He and Beth were on the bus now, heading for Millrock;

school had started right after Labor Day. They probably shared a seat, Lewis moodily staring out the window while his sister sat beside him, happily talking to his shoulder.

She finished wiping the crumbs from the counter, threw the sponge in the sink. Out the kitchen window she saw the bull straining at his tether. The latch holding his pen shut was broken and he hated being tied. She'd fix that, she thought, as soon as she'd finished with the combine. Now she hefted Tom's canvas tool bag, closed the kitchen door behind her, and started toward the fields. Lord knew she wasn't the world's most mechanically-minded person, but a sprocket and pulley on the combine needed fixing, and if the machine were ready by the time Tom got home, all the better for everyone. She whistled as she moved past the drying silo, the chemical and fuel tanks, onto the banked path which ran parallel to the road for a while and then curved inward to the distant field where the combine sat waiting.

The corn formed a green wall on either side as Mae walked between rows. She loved the press of the earth beneath her feet, the rasp of the broad coarse leaves against her jeans, the blue strip of sky overhead. Cows lying low in the pasture flicked past between the corn. As she neared the end of a row, she caught glimpses of the combine, the green and yellow of its paint mirroring the corn. And then there it was cocked on a furrow in a cleared area Tom had left unplanted, space to maneuver machinery in.

She'd already unhitched the drive belt to find the problem; and the large green sheet-metal plate was swung back and away from the interior machinery. Now she put down the tool bag, unbuttoned the snaps, clattered around until she found a wrench. It wasn't a difficult task; she had to remove the octagonal nut holding the V-belt pulley in place to get behind to the gear which had slipped off its shaft. Then it was simpler: replace the cotter pin after putting the gear back on. She'd need some leverage, but it shouldn't be hard.

She heard a rustling in the corn louder than the wind, louder than anything should sound out there in the fields unless the machinery were going. The rustling turned to crashing; whatever it was came running now, though all she could see was the thick rows of green above her. She moved away from the machine, hesitantly, both wanting and fearing the knowledge.

When she saw the bull tearing through the corn, snorting, lowering his horns as he came, her first thought was, *I should have fixed that first,* though later she would marvel at the fact that she hadn't turned and run for her life. His tie-rope hung loose from his muzzle ring, and his nostrils were flecked with blood. And when she recalled the odd fact that she'd talked to him, asked him levelly how he'd managed to join her there, so far from the farmhouse, she realized she must have been already in a state of shock. She moved toward him, as though he were searching for comfort, reaching out to take the rope in her hand and lead him back. But he was coming on his own business; he lowered his horns even further and charged.

Mae sidestepped the first rush, throwing the wrench into the bull's muzzle as he left the rows of corn and joined her in the small ring. The corn blew in the wind, knocking its long green hands together. Bram thrashed past her to the edge of the field and stood there. Talking quietly to him now, she began to approach him as slowly as she could, but he turned, snorting, twisted away and plunged deep into the cornfield. All she could hear was his thrashing; after the first several yards she lost the sight of his wake in the ruined corn.

She shook her fist and yelled, "You're gonna pay for this." There was no use chasing him; she'd get him later. Now she picked up the wrench from where it had bounced off his muzzle, and turned back to the combine. She bent to the large sprocketed gear, pushing it against the chain it ran on, trying to tighten the nut with the wrench. As she pushed, she was aware of what seemed a shadow blocking the sun, and then she realized that the furrow she stood on, the one the machine rested on, was crumbling; she was sinking, and the combine tilted toward her, enough to make her slip. As the combine tilted, and the pressure she put on the gear relented, everything came together at once. Her arm moved inward as the gear moved out, and the sudden pain just above her wrist, more than a pinch, let her know her arm was pinned. It had gotten twisted somehow, stuck between the gear's large sprockets and the chain which ran the gear, and even as she wrenched her arm to free it, she knew she'd gotten in deep. The greasy edges of the sprockets were unrelenting, and they cut into her arm. "Oh, damn me," she said in a flat level voice. "Damn me."

· 17 ·

Harve Stanley wondered why Wade hadn't planned on delivering the fertilizer himself. As far as Harve could see, Wade took every opportunity to get himself down to the Garvey place. But no, not this morning; Wade had a meeting with Senator Neiswinder about the hydroelectric project to look over bids. Anyway it wasn't so bad, being out and away from Leutzcorp. Stanley drove south along the river, the company station wagon weighted down with the Garveys's order.

As he pulled into the driveway, a flurry of chickens came at him, then scattered. It was a nice place, they kept it clean; some of the other farms looked like junk yards, with old refrigerators, car parts, baling wire lying around. Here the walk curved smartly from the driveway to the kitchen door; nasturtiums and zinnias nodded in the flower beds. The yard itself looked as though it had been swept with a broom.

He leaned on his horn, one long blare followed by a couple of quick toots. He stuck his head out the window and yelled toward the house. "Mrs. Garvey. Mrs. Garvey? I got your fertilizer." No response. He leaned again.

Stanley closed his eyes and slumped against the vinyl. It *was* warm, but the sun felt good, streaming down through the windshield, flooding the tops of his thighs. He beat out the *Dragnet* theme on the horn, thought of other songs he could play with his one-toned instrument. Still nothing.

He got out of the station wagon, walked to the barn, and looked in. "Mrs. Garvey?" This wasn't working out the way he thought it would. He'd imagined a cup of coffee, sitting at the Garveys's kitchen table; he walked to the wagon, got in and backed up to the barn, and unloaded the bags of fertilizer right inside the door. If she wasn't going to tell him where to put them, he didn't care if they weren't in the right place.

It was a little weird, even in the bright sun, doing this with no one around. A light wind made the barn door creak, and there *should* have been someone there. He shrugged, unloaded the last bag, closed the barn door, bowed to the empty barnyard, got in the station wagon, and drove away.

· 18 ·

When Mae heard the distant horn, she tried to yell, but her mouth was too dry and the horn was too far away. But the noise, coming from her yard, set her to struggling again. Each time she wrenched or twisted her arm, she could feel the sprockets digging deeper into her skin, and the pain, which she'd thought would level out, had simply increased.

The sun moved overhead so slowly she knew she'd never had the time before simply to watch the earth turn. Her throat actively hurt now, and when she tried to swallow, hard, she could feel her saliva leaving whole patches of throat untouched. Well, she wouldn't die here. Sooner or later her kids would be home, and they'd come looking, or she thought they would—Lewis would know something had happened, with the truck in the driveway and no one in the house. In the meantime, if she stayed conscious, didn't swoon from dehydration or heat prostration, if she didn't lose too much blood. . . . Mae attempted to concentrate, to focus, to remember odd things: she thought of the broccoli casserole she sometimes made, one of Tom's favorites, and tried to visualize the recipe card, all the ingredients, mayonnaise, eggs, bread crumbs. She said aloud all the telephone numbers she could remember, then zip codes.

When the thrashing started again, and Bram burst from the rows into the clearing, Mae had long given up on zip codes, was becoming a little desperate, ready for radical action. What if school never ended, and the sun never moved, and she slowly cooked to death? What was terminal sunburn like? The bull stared at her, snorting. The idea was crazy, but so was her situation. If the combine had kicked over a gear by falling, maybe it could kick over another one if it moved again. She stared at the bull; he was much calmer now, wasn't in the mood to charge. She'd have to anger him.

He pawed the ground, once, twice, but it was the restless pawing of boredom. "Bram," she said. With her free hand she unlaced her boot and pulled it off. He was getting ready to turn and ramble off through the corn again when the boot hit him on the snout. His eyes opened wide, and slowly he fixed her in his gaze. By the time he'd lowered his horns and charged, Mae was ready. She twisted her legs, ducked out of the way beneath the combine to avoid Bram's horns; they struck metal and Bram roared in pain, backed off. The force of the blow clicked the gears over a notch, yanking her arm painfully, and she yelled to match his roar, but the gear's movement gave her hope. She might get out of this yet if she wasn't killed by the bull she'd enraged.

The bull bellowed, turned, charged again. The gears snapped forward. Mae cried out, squirmed as close as she could and kicked him hard with her foot. The bull whipped around and charged the combine once more. He hit the metal low, trying to gore Mae. From under the machine, she could hear it rattling over her, and she thought for a minute it would clatter down on her, crush her. She'd never been quite so aware there were so many ways to die. She looked up to see the bull's horns six inches from her arm, hooked in the metal.

He bellowed, snorted, pushed; the gear clicked over again and Mae felt her arm loosen. The pain was excruciating, and for a moment she saw pure red. And then she dove forward to where Bram's rope dangled before her, grabbed it and pulled, dragging his nose into the dirt. The bull bellowed, struggled, stood still. She wrapped the rope around the axle to hold on.

· 19 ·

It seemed to Mae, from the sun, the pain, the loss of blood, that everything moved in slow motion. The combine inched toward the farmhouse. As she cleared the final field and turned into the barnyard, Lady rounded the corner, barking furiously, her black-and-white coat gleaming in the afternoon sun. Bram followed the combine now, much subdued; he walked with his huge muzzle close to the ground, as though picking up litter with his horns. She lowered herself from the combine, overcome with weariness; she wanted to sink to the ground and lie there, simply let go. Holding her right arm tightly against her, she stumbled toward the house.

As she stood at the kitchen sink, Mae caught a glimpse of herself in the window glass, and was shocked at how dirty her face looked, how pale. Her hair was matted with sweat and dirt, and a dark smear of mud covered her left cheek. There was blood on her chin.

She ran the water, cold as she could, and stuck her forearm under it. The wound was a bad one, nothing clean about it: the gears and belt had torn the flesh, and the inside of her arm looked like raw meat. It made her stomach flip. When would the kids be home? Rinsing the wound intensified the pain: she'd hoped the cold would numb the nerves, but she'd been wrong.

She grabbed a kitchen towel, the cleanest she could find, and wrapped it around the wound to stanch the bleeding. The pain was worse now, coming in waves. She moved to the telephone, dialed the Birkins' number, listened to it ring, four times, five, six. . . . "Judy, where are you. Oh, God. . . ." With her left hand she slammed the hook down, dialed the Tessleys', waited. "Please be home," she said. She was further frightened by the sound of her own voice, quavery, cracked, the voice of someone on the edge. No answer.

With her arm clamped tightly to her side, she returned to the sink, turned on the cold faucet and threw water in her face as best she could. It was startlingly cold, and she realized she was feverish. Her feet felt unsteady, and a large cold hand passed across her face. It was shock, pretty clearly, the medical kind, and Mae realized she could be in bad trouble if she didn't get help soon. What was the treatment? Was it *lie down* or *sit up:* and then she remembered from high school—"head pale, raise the tail," and she thought of lying down on the kitchen floor, putting her feet on the seat of a chair and quietly dying. Her stomach was heaving, she could feel the contractions, reverse peristalsis. She barely made it to the phone, dialed Operator. There were times you asked for help, even from strangers.

· 20 ·

In the outer office, the telephone rang twice, shrill bursts like the yapping of a tiny dog. His secretary answered it before the third yap, and then the customary silence while he waited for her careful screening. He stared at the sheet of figures before him, and the letter he'd drafted to Leroy Butler, the contractor who'd submitted the lowest bid on the plans for the dam and hydroelectric plant, copies to go to his father-in-law and Neiswinder. He'd asked Etta not to disturb him unless the call was from the Senator's liaison in Washington. The deal would be finalized soon, and that made Joe Wade feel slick and snappy. He pushed back from the desk and folded his hands behind his head; the weather was beautiful, clear, no haze, the sky a cobalt blue they rarely saw in these parts. He wished he could be outside, supervising the dam, cutting the ribbon, hell, lying on the grass somewhere.

When the red light on his phone glowed, he picked up the receiver and said, "Yes, Etta?"

"There's a Mrs. Garvey on the line, Mr. Wade," the woman said. "I hope you don't mind the interruption. I told her I'd check. She sounds, well . . . I . . . I thought you'd want the call."

"Thank you," he said curtly, and punched the button. "Hello? Mae?"

Her voice was so weak, so pained and desperate, that he hung up before a minute had passed; he opened his drawer and shoved the letter inside, passed Etta, telling her he'd be out for the rest of the day, moved through the office down the hall, one, two, three, as though his entire life had been a rehearsal for this.

The Emergency Waiting Room of the Millrock County Hospital was painted green, and the vinyl seats were the textured brown of imitation leather. He remembered the colors; this was the hospital where Emily heard the first report, and where she stayed while the old man made arrangements for her at Sloan Kettering, Sidney Farber, the Lahey Clinic. He knew intimately the mingled smells of disinfectant, vending machine coffee, and cigarette smoke. He stood and pushed his hands deeper in his pockets, and read the pamphlets tacked to the bulletin board. *Are You Dying For A Smoke? Venereal Disease: The True Story,* oddly comforting reminders of the routine worries of others. They took your mind off the person who'd just fallen down a flight of stairs, clutched at his heart, been pulled from a twisted automobile.

Of course Mae was all right; she wasn't in danger. In fact, he'd be taking her home after the doctor was finished. After the doctors here were finished with Emily, he'd taken her home, too, but both of them knew she wouldn't be there for long: soon it would be New York and Boston, Houston and Cleveland, the health spas of the dying.

Thinking of Emily like this, in the hospital where they'd first found the nest of murderous cells, made his eyes sting with guilt. For he'd given her up without much pain, let her father fly the shuttle while he stayed and took care of

Leutzcorp. Someone had to, after all; someone still did, and it was still him.

The double doors to the Emergency Room swung in and Mae and Doctor Greenberg came out. Greenberg was frowning; Mae's face was drained of all color. Her lips, pressed together in the thinnest of smiles, looked blue in the fluorescent light. Her arm was bandaged, in a sling.

Greenberg stuck out his beefy hand and Joe took it, amazed as always that something that crude could do surgery. "Joe, how are you?" Greenberg said, and didn't wait for an answer. He turned and took Mae by the shoulders, bending his knees so he could look her in the eyes, as though he needed to impress on her his information at risk of her life. "Tell Tom to do the cooking for a couple of days—you should be off your feet." He reached in the pocket of his white smock and took out a square prescription pad. "Here, this is for pain. It'll help when the shot wears off." He ripped off a sheet, handed it to her, kept writing. "And this is an antibiotic to fight infection. You take all of these now, until they're gone." The doctors had talked to Emily like this, too; sickness made you a child again, and all doctors were, at heart, slightly disapproving parents.

"I'll be fine," Mae said. "Thank you, Doctor."

"Joe," Greenberg said. It sounded like a question, and then he was gone, back through the double doors to another emergency.

Mae turned to Wade, who stood waiting. He offered her his arm, a gesture both quixotically gallant and practical; she didn't look as though she could stand much longer. To his surprise and pleasure, she took it, and he walked with her toward the exit.

All the way to her place, Mae didn't speak, and though Joe stole glances at her, he couldn't read her face. He decided to honor her silence; after all, what she'd been through that morning was traumatic enough. He wanted to know what she was thinking, wanted to turn her thinking around so she realized who she'd called on for help, who she thought of, what it could mean. There'd be lots to work out between them, he knew it wouldn't be easy. There were the children, for one thing.

He lay her down on the living room sofa, went to the kitchen to get her a glass of water. He'd propped up her head on a pillow, and as he came back in, she followed him with her eyes, and smiled.

Mae sat up to take the pill, and Wade put his arm behind her to support her, then gently lowered her. He took the glass of water away, placed it on the end table; then he pulled up a chair and sat beside her. "Thanks, Joe," she said. "You've been real kind."

He caught her eyes, tried to understand what else she was telling him and just when he thought she might be willing to say something, she looked away, toward the wall, where a crudely painted landscape hung. He looked at it too: a waterfall, a covered bridge, a tree with orange leaves. What was a New England scene doing on her living room wall? He turned back to face her, but her eyes didn't leave the painting.

"Mae," he said.

"Don't, Joe." There, it was out: her disavowal was an avowal of sorts; by forbidding him to talk about an unspoken subject, she'd proven to him she'd been thinking it, too. The information gave him courage.

"I'm going to say it," he said.

"I don't want to hear." With difficulty, she swung her legs off the sofa cushions, put them on the floor. She steadied herself with her left hand as she rose, and began to move slowly, the shuffling walk of a sick woman, toward the hall and the stairs. "Excuse me."

Without thinking, he stood and put himself in her way. When she tried to walk around him, he moved sideways, reached out to grab her left elbow, but she took a step backwards and said, "Leave me alone." His heart was beating more quickly, knowing this was the final attempt he'd ever make. She'd be lost to him unless this afternoon he made her capitulate, unless he could make her see the foolish decisions she'd based her life upon.

"Mae, listen to me," he said.

"We don't have to do this," she said evenly. "We don't."

"You called me when you needed me," he said. "And I came." The statement brought blood flaming to his cheeks, as he realized the anger that accompanied the possibility of her refusal. To make yourself so vulnerable, to offer and be rejected again and again. . . .

"I know," Mae said, "and I thank you." She looked down at the worn carpet. "There was nobody else." But before the statement was out of her mouth, before it could register and stop him, the words came flooding out, a subterranean river.

"I can't stop thinking about you," he said. "I try, but I can't help myself. I think of all the times we spent together, of all the good times. Why can't it be like that again? Even these last few months, I know you've been thinking differently about me, I can see it in your eyes."

"It's too late, Joe. You know that. We've both made our choices." Her voice was weaker now, and she supported herself on the back of a chair. "You married Emily, you're Milford Leutz's son-in-law. Now let me go."

On the mantel was an old kerosene lantern, and he walked there swiftly now, picked it up. He wanted to dash it to the floor, but instead he shook it at her. "This kind of life is over. Can't you see that, Mae? Leutz isn't going to live forever. Think of what that could mean to your kids. Life doesn't have to be so hard."

She said nothing. A horn sounded out on the road; across the September afternoon he heard the mechanical creaking of a school bus door, the sounds of children's voices yelling *goodbye,* as though it were his own valediction.

"You'd better go now," Mae said. "My kids are home. I've got to let them know everything's okay." She tried to comb her hair with her fingers, straighten her dress, arrange the arm in its sling to look less threatening; he saw her try to rearrange her face, but it was little use. Those kids were smart; they'd know what she'd been through. And here again they'd spoiled the moment, come between him and Mae. As they always would. They were Tom Garvey's children, and she was his wife.

He nodded, curtly, turned to go. "Mom," Beth yelled in the kitchen. He heard the screen door slam, the purposeful thud of good school shoes. Then she stood in the doorway, the Oreos girl, and her face went blank, as though she'd never seen him before.

· 21 ·

Tom Garvey was wearing his helmet and asbestos apron, but he was thinking of corn. He'd gotten a letter from Mae that afternoon, and the words lingered in his mind, giving him reason to go on with this welding. Sparks flew around him in a fiery parabola; now they reminded him of tassels of cornsilk. *A good crop;* Mae had written, *ears dense as mulberries*. They'd been lucky so far: after the river flooded, anything could have finished them—drought, weevils, too much rain at planting time, an accident. He thought of Mae with her arm stuck in the combine, the bull charging across the field. Now that she was fine, he had to laugh; mostly he thought of her throwing the wrench in Bram's face. That was just like Mae; if she didn't take *his* bull, why should she take Bram's?

He concentrated now, bearing down with his torch, fixing the blue cone of fire on the weld. It wasn't just the back-breaking posture you had to assume, it was the undying monotony of the job, the same movements day after day. He would be through with it soon though, very soon; they were even ahead a bit as a result of his work. The bills were paid, the mortgage cleared for the next two months, a bumper crop in the field. He remembered when Mae had come to see him in the city again, leaving the kids with the Birkins for the weekend; it was after the accident, and she couldn't drive. He met her bus and she stepped down the narrow stairwell, carrying her overnight bag in her left hand. The right arm was still in a sling, a dirty sling now, soiled with the chores she'd done regardless of the doctor's orders. She looked thinner, and her mouth seemed pinched, but she was beautiful. She was tan, her legs slipped down those steps as if she were stripping off nylons; he saw again how her nose turned up slightly, how wide and clear her eyes were, a woman totally happy to be herself.

He shook his head, stared at the glowing steel. He'd better be careful or he'd hurt himself. Around him the rumble of machinery lessened, and he looked at his watch. Was it time for a break already? Roy was motioning him to take off his helmet. He twisted the nozzle, shutting off the acetylene, pushed back the visor. "Come on," he heard behind him, the voice harsh. He turned and there was Swick. "You're fired, all of you," Swick said. "Get your pay from the window. I want you out of here in an hour. The strike's over. It's settled. You're out." He turned, without waiting for an answer, and stalked up the cement floor of the factory; as he walked, the men drew back into their own small groups, too stunned by the sudden dismissal to feel angry yet. Tom was stunned too; he'd planned on two, maybe three more Sunday midnight rides. But he was ready. He'd go home, hell yes. He could already feel the sun on his face.

All the men stuffed their bags and satchels with dirty clothes; no one talked. They collected their final pay and stumbled into the day's light. Tom looked around for the trucks, but the lot was empty. On the other side of the chain-link fence the strikers stood. Tom was rudely pushed from behind, and when he turned he saw guards with billy clubs, the navy blue of their uniforms almost black in the glare. They were shoving at the stragglers, tightening the gang of men, pushing them toward the gates. Truck lurched forward into Tom; he yelled to Swick, who stood safely, unscathed, beyond the herding line of guards. "Swick, where are the trucks? You bastard, where are the goddamn trucks?" Tom started yelling too, and others until the yard rang with their cries, the voices tightening, rising in fear. Swick's arms were crossed on his chest. No trucks, Tom understood; the other men were getting the idea, began screaming at Swick. The guards kept pushing. No trucks. It was a part of the deal the strikers had negotiated; the scabs walked out.

Against the tide of men, guards were pulling open the gates. The strikers moved back, no trouble this time. Let them come, they were saying. *Come on*. Swick nodded for the guards to use their clubs, and the wooden truncheons began raining on the shoulders of the men. And the whole crowd moved roughly forward. Tom felt himself almost carried along; there was no way to resist. They were packed so densely he could hardly move his arms. He struggled not to fall down and be trampled under the boot heels of these men. The gates were closing behind them now, sealing off the factory, Swick, the guards.

The men stopped, massed tightly. Before them hundreds of strikers, their wives and children, appeared from the side streets and formed two lines, a gauntlet he and the others would have to run. Everyone saw at once, and the entire crowd fell silent, and contracted, the way a pupil, shocked by sunlight, would contract. The strikers stood in jeans or coveralls, John Deere and Atlanta Braves hats on their heads, their wives wore slacks or housedresses, and the kids—all concentrating on the small crowd of men bunched at the far end of the street, no way out but past them. Tom straightened his shoulders, tried to prepare himself for the certain beating he'd take. Where would it start? Would they close around him the way the men in his dream had crowded around the deer, to threaten and hurt? What did the hands they held behind them contain?

They began to move, sticking together as much as they could. The strikers and their families were strangely still; their faces were taut, wild, their eyes fierce with hatred. But they said nothing, and they took no swings, threw no rocks as the men began to file slowly by. The gauntlet narrowed and the crowd began to break up, forced through an opening not big enough to contain it.

Tom's face was red with shame; his fists clenched and unclenched at his side. Beside him, Truck muttered, "Let's get it on," and Tom had to admit he felt the same. Nothing was worse than this tension, this wondering where it would come from, when it would begin. He walked now, slowly, one foot in front of the other, keeping time with the man in front, and the one in front of him. He looked at the faces of the people he passed, and their eyes were narrow, their lips curled as though they stared at something so disgusting, so vile it took the full effort of their will to lock eyes with it. Tom found he could not look back at them, began to pray for a beating.

He lowered his head, stared at the ground disappearing beneath his feet. He could hardly bear it; and he understood that what he was suffering now was worse than any blows his body could take. He knew in a way he hadn't before how these people felt about him, what he'd done to injure their lives, even if he had meant them no personal harm. They felt toward him the way he felt toward Joe Wade, Harve Stanley, the others at Leutzcorp—the ones who worked against him for their personal gain, implacably.

Around Tom now rose a noise like wind soughing through long grass, and he had taken two more steps before he realized what it was, a hiss begun somewhere in the line, picked up and magnified by others until he could have been moving in a field of rattlesnakes, the soft buzz of their warning. Tom moved with the shuffling crowd as more and more of the men took on the hatred: their shoulders wilted under the strikers' glare, their steps became shuffles. They trudged, Tom among them, their eyes on the ground. Beside Tom, Roy trembled.

By the time the spitting began, Tom was almost ready for it. No one had ever taunted him like that before, no one had dared, and yet now he both wished for it, feeling he deserved it, and knew there was nothing he could do to retaliate. The wives and children left the ranks of the gauntlet, stepped forward to spit and curse. Coming from women's lips, the words scalded even more, and the ones who did not speak—cold level, looking straight on, with fury—let their saliva speak for them. When the young woman stepped before him, Tom didn't try to avoid her; he took her gaze as best he could, tried to memorize her face. She was pretty in a common way, her eyebrows teased to disappearing, her hair captured by a cheap blue scarf. Her teeth were bad.

She was holding a sleeping child, and that was what finally moved Tom. The kid lay lifeless in her arms, curled toward her, one leg slipping out of her grasp to dangle in the air, weighed down by its small scuffed shoe. "You scum," the woman said, to Tom, directly, and the words got through. Her lips pursed, like an adder's, and her head darted forward. Her spittle was warm on his cheek. He stared at her, at her sleeping cargo, while the other men streamed around him.

The woman stepped back, and he moved on, but her image had burned his eyes. He wanted to talk to her, to explain, to show her pictures of Beth and Lewis. He wanted to bring her eggs, to show her the nesting place of a convey of quail, to let her smell the pollen as it rose and drifted in the summer air. He wanted to crush her face with his bare palms. He wanted to disappear.

PART FOUR

· 1 ·

Years later, Lewis would still remember the day his father came home: a Thursday afternoon, early October, the sky bleached almost white by the high clouds. At school that day, in art, they'd been exposed once again to the Christopher Columbus lesson, and he'd spent a miserable forty minutes drawing the ragged explorer, hand to forehead, leaning over the blue waves in search of land. Then the clock ticked its final minute amid a flurry of papers and books, and the bus swallowed him and Beth, disgorged them on the road in front of the farm.

He'd been working on the silo every evening after dinner for a week, repairing a seam between two ribbed metal plates, and as he worked tonight he saw the strange pickup stop on the road, his father emerging from it, and he thought, *Dad's home,* as though it were any day and his father always hitchhiked home. And then he registered the pickup's absolute strangeness. He said, "Dad," almost under his breath, and began descending the ladder, his voice rising until he was yelling "Mom . . . Beth . . . Dad's home."

But they already knew, and as he streaked across the yard to where his father stood, Beth ran from the porch and into their father's arms. He stooped to pick her up, turned with the motion of her running, and swung her wildly around him as she screamed in pleasure. Lewis stood before his father, suddenly shy. Without letting go of Beth, wrapped monkey-like around him, his father reached down and shook his hand, once, hard. His mother was beside him, flushed and breathless, and his parents were hugging, and then kissing, and he and Beth stood there embarrassed and then they were in the kitchen, where sun tea was being poured into tall cool glasses.

Not ten minutes later his mother was pulling his father out the door, toward the fields. "Wait a minute," his father said. "I just got home."

"I know," his mother said.

"It's that good?" his father asked. Lewis was filled with an unreasonable excitement, unlike anything he'd felt since he'd been promised the hunting trip. Now it was just that everything was itself again, his father home, the corn tall in the fields, his mother proud of the way the crop had turned out. The four of them walked out the door, across the yard, and disappeared among the rows. His mother let her hand whip the leaves, like the pages of book after book being flipped; and his father simply walked, the smile never leaving his face. In front of his father, Lewis kept turning to watch, until Tom reached down and made to grab him, saying, "What do you think *you're* looking at?"

"This is far enough," his mother said. She watched intently as Tom bent an ear away from the stalk; Lewis delighted in the sharp crisp snap as it broke loose, and the sweet ripping as his father tugged at the husk. The kernels were bright yellow, full, in even rows. "It's a good crop," his father said. "I'm proud of you. All of you."

He stooped, dug in the earth with his hand, scooped up a handful and stood, taking a deep smell. "You don't know how I missed that," he said. "My Lord, it's good to be *home!*" He yelled the last word and Beth jumped.

"Daddy," she said.

"Come on," he said. "I'll race you back to the house."

· 2 ·

Lewis was half-asleep when he heard his bedroom door creak open, and he sat bolt upright, gasping for air. He had a recurring nightmare that went just like this: something came into his room; he sat up, and froze, unable to move as he watched it come closer, still unseeable, come closer, until he woke up. Tonight, it was only Beth. "Lewis," she whispered.

"God, Beth," he said, to mask his fear.

Without asking permission, she crawled onto his bed and put her cheek on his pillow; if he lay back down, her nose would be practically in his ear. "Move over," he said, and nudged her through the covers. She wiggled a little, and when he lay back, her head was inches away. "Did you have a nightmare?" he asked, so she wouldn't ask him first.

"They finished kissing. Now they're just talking," Beth said.

"Were you listening again?" Lewis asked. "In the hall? I'm telling."

"Daddy said a lady spit on him."

"You sure?"

"Yes," Beth said. "He said there were lots of people spitting."

"You were dreaming," Lewis said.

"Are daddies allowed to cry? Have you ever heard Dad cry?"

"You heard Dad cry?" He tried to imagine the fact, and couldn't. "From the hall?"

"He was talking to Mom and then he started to cry."

"It was probably her," Lewis said.

"It was Dad," Beth said.

There were things his father had gone through Lewis didn't understand; things at the factory Lewis would have to ask about. But his father would say, "You big Buttinsky," and that would be that. Life was full of stuff that happened to you that you didn't understand. Like those men with the deer. Like that umpire. He turned on his side and stared at his sister's open eye, practically all he could see. "It's okay," he said. "It's all right. Go back to bed."

He kissed her cheek, and she kissed him back; looking a little doubtful, she sat up, wriggled off his bed, and was gone.

· 3 ·

The corn would be ready for harvest in another week, mid-October, and Tom Garvey couldn't have been happier. He'd walked the fields, all three hundred acres. If it wasn't the best crop they'd ever raised, it was damn close. On a piece of paper in the kitchen, he scrawled the number of bushels he'd contracted for per acre—one hundred thirty—added five percent and multiplied by three dollars and forty-five cents. Hell, they were set, any way you looked at it, even after expenses.

When he called Leutzcorp with his estimations, he was passed on and on, until he was given to Harve Stanley, whose voice was guarded, low.

"Don't know, Tom," Stanley said over the phone. "Sounds awful high to me. We ain't got any estimates from around the country high as that one."

"Mae said the yield's so good down here because of those couple summer storms that got us; you know the weather's been spotty."

"Hell yes," Stanley said. "Dry summer after a wet spring. That's the way it is."

"Well, you come on down and see for yourself," Tom said. "It's a good crop, Harve." And Stanley said he'd be by just as soon as he could. He didn't know just when, but as soon as he could. Which put Tom on pins and needles; which made him watch the road.

Stanley came three days later. He was edgy and circular when Tom tried to make small talk, and he refused to look either Tom or Mae in the eye. They took a ride in the Leutzcorp pickup, back toward Millrock, along the Garveys's fields. Stanley pulled over suddenly, stopped, got out, cracked his back by putting his hands on his hips and stretching. "This okay with you folks?" he asked.

"It's fine," Tom said. "Any place is fine."

He glanced at his wife, who was trying to look nonchalant and was failing. Her earlobes were bright red, a dead giveaway. She held her hand lightly over her throat. He could feel his heart beginning to race as Stanley stepped over the culvert, walked to the edge of the field and ruffled the corn. He grabbed an ear, shucked it, smelled it, studied it. His face was grave when he looked up.

"Pretty dry, Tom. Don't weigh enough."

Now Mae's entire face was red, and she walked to the row and grabbed three ears, shucking one after another. All three were perfect, full, deep yellow. "What are you talking about?" she said; her voice had an edge like sharpened steel.

Stanley shrugged and looked at the ground. "Hey," he said, as if he meant *Don't blame me*. "Joe offered to get you some help irrigating this crop and you told him you could handle it yourself."

"I did handle it myself," Mae said. "My son and I . . ."

"Well, I don't want to stand here arguing, but . . ."

Tom's heart was pounding so hard now, he could hardly breathe. His voice was thin, pointed, his jaws tight. "We got a contract, Harve."

"If the corn's no good, neither's the contract. Two-seventy-five's the best I can do for you."

"Two-seventy-five?" Tom said. "Our contract's for three-forty-five."

"Sorry, Tom," Stanley said, looking past Garvey to where his pickup was parked, planning the getaway.

"You asking me to take a cut of seventy cents *a bushel?"*

"Two-seventy-five," Stanley said. "Take it or leave it."

"It costs more than that to grow the fucking stuff," Garvey said. "You know that. Who told you to do this? Was it Wade?"

"Next time you got a crop to raise," Stanley said, "you better do it yourself. You can keep an eye on it that way. Don't leave it to a woman." As though he'd said *good day,* Stanley made to leave. "You bastard," Mae said, and started toward him, but Tom put his hand on her shoulder, stepped forward. Stanley eyed him uncertainly, his face suddenly white under his tan. "What my wife meant," Tom said, "is this." He swung. A sharp pain jolted his hand and wrist as he belted Stanley in the jaw. The man staggered backwards and crashed down heavily against the green stalks.

"Hit him again if he gets up," he told his wife. He grabbed an ear of corn from the ground where it had fallen. "I got an errand to run." He walked to the Leutzcorp pickup, and jumped behind the wheel. Stanley had left the keys in the ignition, as he'd thought. The engine flicked on; the tires squealed as Tom floored the truck, steadied it, drove fast toward Millrock.

· 4 ·

All morning Joe Wade had been uneasy, and he didn't know why. The weather? *Unseasonably warm, humidity eighty-nine percent, winds out of the southwest, eighty percent chance of thunderstorms*. Coffee? Too many cups, admittedly. The meeting? If not exactly silken in its smoothness, it was going according to plan. Everyone was saying just what he knew they'd be saying. All that remained was applying the pressure until the final couple of farms, the Birkins, Earl Smoot, the Garveys goddammit, buckled. The project would have to hang fire until then; he'd told them all a hundred times. Neiswinder was nibbling at a doughnut, looking at his watch, making Joe look at his, eleven-forty-eight. The esteemed Senator would leave in another twelve minutes for his luncheon engagement, too full of doughnuts to eat, and once he was gone all the flunkeys would let their jaws flop open.

They stood hunched over the blueprints for the hydroelectric plant, dam, and lake, as though scrutiny would change the elevations, the sharp-edged letters and numbers only architects could draw. Those few remaining farms were outlined in black magic marker, and they irritated him; it was a masterful jigsaw puzzle, but the final triumph wouldn't be complete until the last few pieces could be assembled.

Leroy Butler, the contractor they'd settled on at Neiswinder's urging, was grumbling again about the delay. The man was a broken record, a loop tape.

"Look, all I'm saying is . . ." Butler managed before Neiswinder, the soul of good intentions, interrupted.

"Gentlemen, please, no reason for arguments. We all understand." He snuck another look at his watch. "Joe, I'm sure you have Leroy's side of this in mind. He's tied up an army of men and equipment for this job, and he turned down two highway projects he could have already begun. You've got to get that land sewed up."

"I understand," Wade said. "It'll be done, I give you my word."

When the door flew open, Wade knew what it was he'd been waiting for, ever since Stanley had left for the Garvey place. Tom hulked in the doorway, holding something in his hand. He raised his arm and to Wade's amazement threw it across the room at him. Wade caught it, an ear of corn. The men around him stepped away.

"Gentlemen," Joe Wade said. "This is Tom Garvey."

Garvey stood where he was and stared across the room at Wade, his eyes steady. "You tell me that corn's too dry."

"Tom," Wade said, as though speaking to an errant child. "We're in a meeting. This isn't the time. I'm sure my secretary . . ."

"Yes, she did. It *is* the time. Don't send some flunky down to do me in, you sonofabitch. Have the guts to do it yourself. I want to hear it from you. Now look at that corn. Slit a kernel. Tell me it's too dry."

Wade turned to the other men. "Will you excuse me for a minute, fellas?"

Neiswinder grinned and stuck out his hand to Wade. "Thanks *very* much, Joe, for the information. I'm sure everything will work out. As you know, I have a luncheon engagement."

"Senator," Wade said. "My pleasure." Neiswinder was the last one out, and closed the door behind him; the others had made a wide path around Garvey, as though he had a highly contagious disease.

"Okay bonehead," Wade said. "You want your eviction notice? You got it. Come over here." Garvey walked across the room, nothing in his hands. Wade held the ear of corn now, the secret weapon in the war between them.

With his free hand he took hold of a piece of green felt and flipped it back, revealing the scale model of the Leutz Hydroelectric Plant, its dam, its resulting lake. He admired the precision of the model, its clarity, simplicity. All the small farms bordering the river were gone, submerged, like those towns in Indiana which were flooded when they dammed the Whitewater River; in Massachusetts too, in California. The dam looked imposing, even in the model. He turned mildly to Garvey; the other man stood stunned.

"You're gonna flood the valley," Garvey said numbly.

"That's right," Wade said.

"You crazy bastard," Garvey said, with wonder. "My people are buried on that land. So are yours."

"But they're dead." Wade's voice was steady. "And Leutzcorp needs that water. I want that water. Little farms like yours don't count anymore, Tom. Can't you see that? It doesn't pay to farm small. Agribusiness is the future, and you're in the way."

"That may be so," Garvey said, his voice rising. "That may be so. But if you're the future, I don't want any part of it. You make me sick." He turned to leave. Wade flooded with fury.

"You selfish motherfucker," Wade said. "Who are you doing this for? Your dead father? Your kids? Mae? She deserves better. Have you ever asked her what she wants?"

Garvey turned, his face crimson. He walked toward Wade and Joe took a step back. But Garvey stalked past him to the table where the model sat, grabbed its edge and flung the model against the wall, smashing it. "The only way you're gonna get me off my land," he said, "is in a box." He turned and went.

Now that's a violent man, Wade thought, when the door had closed and he was alone. Why did he feel defeated when all the power was his?

· 5 ·

The rain began the tenth of October, and at first it didn't bother Garvey. Once the corn was ready, there wasn't a whole lot that would hurt it. He'd been known to wait until January and a good solid freeze to get the combine out there; sure, you lost a bunch to rodents, deer, the weather. Wind knocked ears from the stalks; ice could break a field clear down to the ground. Still, there wasn't a lot that would hurt it if the yield was good to begin with, and you could afford to wait.

Tom knew he couldn't wait long; still the rain didn't bother him.

Not until the fourth day. It hadn't rained steadily, but almost. There'd been two solid days of heavy rain, followed by clouds, then another day of rain. No sun to dry the fields, and as he walked among the rows, his boots sank deeper and deeper in mud. No way he'd get the combine in there for a while.

When the anxiety hit, like it had last spring, everything rocked: he couldn't keep his food down and he couldn't sleep. He rumbled around the house, ready to snap. That night, he sat before the television, waiting for the eleven o'clock news and weather. Mae darned socks, mended clothes, worked on a sweater she was knitting for Beth for Christmas.

"Shhh," Tom said when the show began, straining to

hear the announcer's voice. Mae was drumming her fingers on the chair arm. When he stole a quick look at her, she was sewing, and her eyebrows were raised to let him know he'd been an idiot again. It wasn't her; it was the rain on the roof interfering, the same noise he'd been hearing asleep or awake for days.

The local newscasters were folksy as could be. "We've got real heavy stuff coming down upstate," the weatherman said, "and I'm sorry to say the forecast's for more of the same. Jim, Barbara," he said, nodding his head towards the news announcers as though they were personal friends, "I wish the news was better."

"We'll worry about the news," Jim said. "You take care of the weather." Jim looked enormously pleased with himself, and Barbara laughed. If Tom ever met one of those jokers on the street, he'd murder him. The weatherman cleared his throat and stared at Tom. His voice was instantly more somber. "Flash flood warnings are in effect in the northeastern part of the state. The barometer is twenty-nine-point-twenty-four and falling, winds are out of the southwest at . . ."

Tom washed his face with his hands. "Damn," he said, turning toward Mae. She looked at him as though he hadn't finished what he'd started to say. When Beth walked in, the thought crossed his mind that she should have been in bed hours ago. What time was it, anyway? She was in her pajamas, holding out a towel. Her face was flushed, her hair wet.

"Did you just get out of the tub?" Tom asked. "I hope you left some water for someone else."

Beth ignored him and walked toward Mae. "Mommy, will you dry my hair?" she asked.

Mae gathered her in, and kissed the top of her head, then pushed her out to arm's length. "Honey, this towel is wet. Go get me another one from the . . ."

His anger had been building at the new interruption, and Tom let loose with another, "Shhhh!" Didn't they understand?

"Tom," Mae said. "That man isn't going to make the rain stop."

"There *are* no more dry ones," Beth said, her voice turning toward a whine.

"Stop it," Tom said. "Hush, the both of you." He shot Mae a glare full of reproach, was surprised to receive one.

"Come on, sweetheart," Mae said. "Let's go somewhere else."

Then he was alone. The weather didn't improve; the long-range forecast, the barometer, the river level at Tunneyburg, Vailston. . . . All the towels were wet. Everything was wet.

If the levee went, they were done for. In spring, at least, they'd had the chance to plant again, and though the first crop had been ruined, and they'd lost every penny, they'd managed to put in the second crop, only to meet the river rising again. Tom couldn't remember this happening before, two stretches of rain in the same year. It was more than a man could take. Now, if the water got loose, the corn would rot or be flattened; nothing to show for a full season's work, and Wade and Leutzcorp would have the land. He wouldn't be able to stop them. His last words to Wade came back to him, and in a superstitious way he thought maybe he'd brought this on himself.

He checked the floodpoles hourly; the floodline was marked in red at eleven feet, the height of the levee. Some jerk had marked twelve feet on the pole. If it got to there, it would already be too late. There'd be no one around to see the final line submerged. Nobody.

At eleven feet, the river would simply wash over the levee's edge, but Tom knew it didn't need to be that high. Last spring it had been near *9* when the hole in the levee opened and inundated the field. Now the river stood at eight, and the rain still slanted from the southwest, and the weather report promised more of the same. All day he'd worked with the dozer, trying to buttress the levee; and all afternoon with Lewis, bagging, walking, checking, worrying. He tried to remember the last meal he'd eaten, and couldn't. He tried to remember the last time he'd felt hungry.

Sometimes when he couldn't stand it anymore, he'd get in the pickup and drive upriver or down, to see how things were holding. Everywhere it was the same, though Roy Tessley's eyes were hollower than Tom's and Tom understood he was ready to buckle. So he talked to Rod in low tones, while Sally fed him cup after cup of coffee and the rain washed against the kitchen windows with the words, "Ssssell, sssssell."

· 6 ·

Joe Wade browsed through his library looking for his old dog-eared copy of Faulkner's *The Wild Palms*. There it was, marked in his sophomore hand with notes he'd taken in Doctor Sheffield's Modern American Fiction class, and he pulled it down and found the passage about the flood: ". . . a flat still sheet of brown water which extended into the fields beyond the pits, ravelled out into long motionless shreds in the bottom of the plow furrows and gleamed faintly in the gray light like the bars of a prone and enormous grating." He smiled, put it back, found his Bible . . . *and darkness was upon the face of the deep; and the Spirit of God was moving over the face of the waters*. It was time for bed.

· 7 ·

Tom sat in his yellow rain slicker, the same yellow as the dozer, high on the machine as its blade lowered and strained against the earth. It seemed he'd been at this since dawn, and now it was almost night. Lewis searched the side of the levee for leaks, holding tight to Beth's hand. She was practically being dragged by him, she was that tired. She and Mae had been bagging all afternoon.

When Tom heard his name, he looked straight up, as though it were being spoken from the sky, but it was Mae, standing in the mud almost to her ankles, clutching a green army-surplus poncho around her like a beach towel. He looked at her, and she stood on tiptoe, as though the extra inch would bring her voice home to him through the rain. He took his foot off the gas, disengaged the clutch, strained his ear in her direction. "What?" he yelled.

"I've got to get the kids to bed. School tomorrow."

"Leave Lewis," he yelled. "He'll have to stay with me tonight. Forget school."

"I'm taking Beth," Mae yelled. Tom nodded and watched as Mae went and took Beth's hand from Lewis. The two of them struggled through the mud toward the farmhouse. Beth stumbled and fell; Mae stopped, picked her up, and staggered on. Tom stepped on the clutch, put the dozer in first. The engine re-engaged with a heightened roar.

When he was almost sleepwalking, he called Lewis from

the task of sentry; the boy was hardly able to stand straight. Together they slipped to the top of the levee and checked the water. The flashlight beam met the swirling brown skin of the river at *9*. Two feet to go, fourth down, time running out.

· 8 ·

That night Lewis had the dream again. He woke in terror, knowing something had entered his room, but unable to find it, to see it. He sat up, pushed his back against the wall, clutching the covers around him and tried to speak, to call its name, or call for help, but his mouth wouldn't open, and no sound came out. There was a new noise, like the air leaving a bicycle tire, but when he *really* awoke, he understood it was only the rain, and the wind blowing the curtains through the gap he'd left for air.

He looked at the clock beside the bed; it was a little after five, and he'd set the alarm for five-thirty, so there was no use trying to get back to sleep. He might as well get up and start his chores. Soon enough it would be time to work with his father on the levee again. He threw back the covers and sheets, damp to the touch of his skin, like everything in the house. All his clothes were damp; his skin recoiled as he stuck his legs into his jeans, as he pulled the cotton sweatshirt over his undershirt. He carried his boots and tiptoed down the hall.

He creaked open the kitchen door and light spilled onto

his feet. His father sat at the table, his chin resting on his palms, his fingers curled over his cheeks. A mug of coffee sat before him.

"Morning, Dad," he said.

"You couldn't sleep either, huh?" his father asked.

"I had this dream," Lewis said.

"Yeah," his father said. "Want some coffee?"

"I got to get the chores done."

"The cows can wait." He got up and poured some coffee from the pot into a small cup, brought it to Lewis.

The boy picked it up in both hands, brought it close to his face, and savored the feel of the steam on his cheeks. His father stared at the salt and pepper shakers. "It'll be all right, Dad," Lewis said.

"Yeah," his father said. "I know." But he didn't look up.

It was two-thirty when Lewis returned to the house, wet, cold, hungry. His sister had gone to school, and was almost due home. The sky had lightened; maybe the rain would stop. It continued to stream out of the sky, in sheets, sometimes blown by the wind. The poncho Lewis wore was supposed to be waterproof, but he was soaked.

He opened the kitchen door, slipped in. His mother stood at the counter wrapping sandwiches. By the grey light filtering through the window she looked old and haggard, about ready to cave in. When she glanced at him, she tried to smile.

"Mom, are you okay?" he asked.

"Yes, Lewis," she said. He was suddenly aware of the puddle forming under him as the rain dripped off his poncho and hit the floor. "You warm enough?" she asked.

"Sure," he said. "Mom, we're going to get slag at the Ironworks."

"I've got sandwiches for you," she said. Outside a horn blared, followed by two short bursts.

"I've got to go, Mom. There's no time."

His mother's voice was stern. "You missed lunch, Lewis. You have to eat, and so does your father." He stood while she slapped the bread back over the top of the sandwiches, hurriedly wrapped them in waxed paper and stuck them in two bags. The horn blared again. "Damn him," his mother said. "Here."

Lewis grabbed the bags and let himself back into the day. His father sat behind the smeared windshield of the pickup. Its lights cut through the rain. He ran, splashing across the barnyard, and climbed into the cab. The noise of the rain slackened as soon as he pulled the door shut, was replaced by the dull thud on the cab's roof, the whine of the wipers.

They were almost to the road when the truck jerked; it sounded to Lewis as if someone had taken a sledge to the engine. The grinding of gear on gear, metal ripping metal, lasted only a second before the truck faltered and stopped, the generator light burning red on the dashboard, but it seemed to Lewis the final word on the subject.

"Goddammit," his father said, almost too tired to swear. He hung onto the steering wheel with both hands, brought his head down until his forehead rested against it. Lewis sat rigid, waiting for instructions. The rain kept up its steady complaint, a strange kind of hush.

In the barn, they hoisted the engine out with a block and tackle, so his father could fix the transmission. Lewis went to check on the river. He climbed the levee slowly, using a pole for extra leverage so he could bend to the slope and keep himself steady. He found the river's surface moving at a terrific speed, not much more than a foot below where he stood on the levee path. He could put his fingers in the river without kneeling. The water hit the pole at nine-and-a-half, and any fool could see it hadn't finished rising.

Supper was tense and silent. Franks and beans. The milk tasted cold, rich, thick, and Lewis drank it too fast. His mother stared openly at his father, as if she didn't know him. Beth was the only one who talked; but after a couple of sentences about how many kids were absent from school, and what the people in Millrock were saying, she was quiet too, and moved the franks and beans around, segregating the meat with her spoon. Then they sat there, their plates empty, until Tom stood up, scraping the chair's legs against the linoleum, and said it was time to get back to the truck.

"You have to?" his mother said, almost not a question.

"Yeah," his father said, and Lewis stood too, knowing it was now or not at all; if his mother had her chance at him, he wouldn't leave the house again today. Beth wanted to come as well, claiming she hadn't visited the cows in a long time, and his mother finally began clearing the dishes, her face letting them know she'd rather hurl them at the wall.

It was dark in the barn, but dry at least. Lewis held a work light for his father, shifting it as the tools were moved. It was hard to hold, and his arms ached; the zinc cage which held the bulb threw a lot of heat. But it was the only way he could really be useful. He asked a couple of questions about what his father was doing, but his heart wasn't in them, and his father didn't want to talk. Beth stood out of the ring of light, stroking the flank of her new favorite cow.

His father concentrated on the work, and when he said, "Lewis, go to the pickup and get me the other ratchet set," the boy put the light down on the fender without a question and went. He flew to the truck and was back in a minute. As he let himself in through the door he heard his father's voice raised in aggravation. "I said, Beth, come hold this light for me."

"I have to pet Alice. She's sad," Beth said.

"Get over here," his father said. Beth moved to the truck reluctantly and picked up the light. "Now shine it over here. See where I'm working?" his father said. "Hold it up high."

"Daddy, I'm tired," Beth said.

"I'm back," Lewis said. "I got the ratchets."

"I said *hold it up,*" his father said to Beth. His sister began to cry, loudly, with no warning. She dropped the light against the truck, and ran from the barn, right past him. He was torn between wanting to follow and comfort her and wanting to help his father. "Goddammit," his father said. "Bring them over here."

He slept in the barn that night. His mother had come three times and tried to get them to stop, but his father had finally said, "Mae, I can only tell you once. The river's at *10,* and I got to have this truck ready. I need slag from the Works, and I need it by morning. If you can't stop the rain, at least stop your complaining." She turned and left. Lewis was shocked. He'd never heard his father scold his mother before, in fact couldn't remember a time when things seemed so strained between them. But they'd been apart for months, and his father had just gotten home, and then that run-in with the guy from Leutzcorp, and the rain. He tried one final time. "You need me, Dad?" he asked and when his father shook his head, Lewis curled against a bale of hay, covered himself with the poncho, and was asleep.

· 9 ·

Mae slept badly. When she woke, it was the eighteenth of October, the seventh straight day of rain. She rolled over, found herself alone. The pigheaded fool she called *husband* hadn't creased the sheets. What did he think he was doing? He couldn't go days without washing, eating proper food, laying his body down. She went to her daughter's room, and stood in the doorway, watching the small body breathe under the blankets. Beth had made a corral of stuffed animals, slept safe in their magic circle. She'd let her sleep until breakfast was ready. Now it was time to get Lewis.

When she pushed open his door, she stood dumbfounded at the empty bed, its covers unrumpled, its spread pulled tight; clearly he hadn't slept in his bed that night. Who did Tom think he was? It was one thing to push himself beyond human endurance, but Lewis was just a boy. With a sense of old hurts burning within her, Mae went to the kitchen, put some wood in the stove, and lit a burner for coffee. They needed some breakfast: they needed a *big* breakfast. She'd make pancakes. First she'd make coffee.

When the coffee had brewed, and the first pancakes were warm in the oven, she put on her slicker and carried a mug of coffee to the barn, shielding the top with her hand to keep out the rain. She edged open the door; her son was asleep, jumbled in a bale of hay. Her husband turned toward her, the black pools of his eyes almost too intense, a man who hadn't slept in weeks. "Coffee," she said, as cheerfully as she could muster, and thrust the mug at him. In answer Tom slammed the hood of the truck and moved to the cab. He climbed in and turned the key. The engine coughed, twice, choked off; he tried it again. The whole truck shook as the engine sputtered, and then roared to life. He left the engine idling and swung down from the cab. He walked to her, took the coffee. She'd never seen him like this: there were days of beard on his face, so the bottom half of him was black, and the eyes were off somewhere else, seeing something she didn't see. In his eyes were desperation and animal intensity. He was thinking of nothing but the river, nothing at all.

"Thanks," he said.

"I've got pancakes warm in the oven. Come eat a real breakfast," Mae said.

"Can't," Tom said. "Wake Lewis while I drink this, will you?"

That was the end of it. The boy was only twelve. "I want to talk to you," she said.

"Not now," he said. "There's no time. I got to get that slag. Do you know how lucky we are the levee's held out this long?" He walked over to Lewis and nudged him with his boot, leaving a clot of mud on the boy's leg. "Wake up," he said. "Come on now."

Without thinking much, without needing to think, Mae pulled at Tom's slicker. "Leave him alone," she said.

Tom turned, a look of wary surprise on his face. "What?" he said.

"You heard me," she said. "You're driving him too hard. He's still a child. What's the matter with you? That's your *son,* he's not a hired hand."

Tom nudged the boy again. Lewis stirred, sat up, and rubbed his eyes. "Don't you dare," Mae said. But Tom had turned away, was walking toward the truck. "Lewis, get in," he said. The boy stood, wobbling on legs that were still asleep, and moved to follow his father. Before he got away, Mae grabbed the boy and pulled her to him. "I won't let you do this," she said. "You leave him alone. I let you keep him from school, and food, and sleep. But not anymore."

Tom's hands were on his hips, his voice filled with scorn. "Let him go, Mae. We got to save this crop. If we don't keep the river out, we're finished. You hear me?"

"Then let it in!" Mae yelled. "Let it finish us before you do!"

Tom made a grab for the boy. She was filled with unreasonable hate for him, could have easily clawed at his eyes. She stepped back, pressed Lewis more tightly to her. "You stay away from us. I mean it. I don't want to live like this anymore."

He stopped, and the look that crossed his face was a mixture of exhaustion and something like hatred as well. "Fine," he said. "I get it. Then go live in a big fancy house with Joe Wade. Just leave the boy here. At least *he* can help me."

"Joe Wade?" Mae echoed. *"He* can help you? Lewis, go outside." She couldn't remember trembling like this, not in lust or worry or pain. She watched the back of her son disappear.

As soon as Lewis had cleared the barn door, stumbling into the grey morning, Mae Garvey slapped her husband as hard as she could, savoring the swing, the sweet delicious contact her palm made with his cheek, the way his head ricocheted, the sting his face left on her hand. She seemed to have knocked some humanity back into him; he wasn't the man she loved, but she recognized him now, a bit in pain from the blow.

"I don't want to live in a fancy house with Joe Wade. I want to live here with you. But you can't beat the river with a wife and two exhausted children. Why won't you get the others to help you? You know they're struggling too. They call on us enough. We *need* them, Tom."

"I don't need them."

"You don't need anybody, do you?" Mae said. "Nobody needs anybody else. We're all put here to stumble around in the mud and make do as best we can, is that it? You stupid . . . goddamn . . ." She could feel the tears about to break loose, and the last thing she wanted to do was let him see her cry; he'd think they were tears of pain instead of rage, just the natural overflow of powerful feeling. "Give me that," she said, grabbing the mug away from him. It was half-full, and the coffee swirled and splattered her husband's chest. She didn't care. She held the mug against her as though it were the key to a locked door she needed to walk through, and she strode from the barn into the thin light of day. The rain on her burning face felt wonderful.

· 10 ·

It wasn't the slap that stung so much, but her words, which made sense. He'd always been like that, too prideful and arrogant to ask anyone for help. When his father lay dying, he'd somehow managed it all, without calling on neighbors or friends, though they'd been ready. He'd taken care of the farm *and* the old man, not even letting the scattered relatives know until the final weeks. His parents were buried on this place, and his grandfather and grandmother; and he was the only one left, the only Garvey save Lewis, who'd have the farm when Tom died. He didn't need anyone's help.

But he did; she was right. He'd been relying solely on a twelve-year-old boy, driving him until the kid practically walked on his knees, he was so tired and worn down.

He walked to the kitchen door and looked in. Mae sat at the table with her arms crossed, her lips in a thin line. Lewis sat opposite her, his head bowed low over a plate of pancakes he'd flooded with syrup. He opened the door, and stood there with the wind blowing rain past him onto the floor. Her eyes still on Lewis, Mae said, "Come on in and shut the door. There's coffee on the stove and food in the oven. Help yourself."

"Thank you," he said, and this time he meant it. After he ate, trying to catch her eyes and hold them—she was good at this and prevented him—he picked up the receiver and dialed. The first call was the hardest.

• • •

As he drove up the rain-splashed highway toward Millrock, passing their places, Birkin and Tessley pulled in behind him. At the Conover intersection Youngdall was waiting. And by the time they reached the Harkness Ironworks, there were seven trucks in all. Zemke, Wilderfoot, Smoot. Two more and they could field another softball team.

Lewis sat on the seat beside him, staring out the window at fields heavy with rain. It ran in the furrows between fully mature rows of corn, it fell in sheets, like curtains being hauled back and forth by invisible pulleys, blown by the wind which buffeted the truck as well, pushing it over to the shoulder so that Tom had to wrestle with the steering wheel to bring it back to the right of center. Seven trucks—it was hard to believe. Seven trucks would hold a lot of slag and scrap, enough to build the levee another foot for a long ways, maybe even far enough. He shook his head as he thought back to who he'd been that morning. He'd really thought he could do it himself; he'd just drive to Millrock and load up, then dump it at home, drive back to Millrock. . . . What had he been thinking?

"Are you and Mom really mad at each other?" Lewis asked, still staring out the window. Tom looked at his son's neck, its raw nakedness.

"No, Lewis," he said finally. "Don't worry. Your mother and I love each other very much: you know that." He'd have put a hand on his son's head if he hadn't needed both of them to keep the truck on the road.

"Did some lady really spit in your face?" Lewis asked. The boy's head had turned now, and Tom saw how hard he'd struggled with that question. He decided simply to answer instead of asking his own question: *How did you know that?*

"Yes," he said. "You know, I crossed a picket line." He paused. The wipers pushed the rain to the left, to the right, long sweeps. "When they worked out a way to end the strike, the union men and their families were mad. Do you understand?"

"But why did she spit at *you?*"

"It wasn't personal," Tom said. "Sometimes you get so full of anger you have to let it out. You ever feel like that?"

"Yeah," Lewis said.

"Do you think I was wrong to work in that plant?"

Lewis shrugged and squirmed in the seat, turning his face toward the window again. "*I* don't know," he said.

"Maybe I was," Tom said. "Maybe I was. But there wasn't another thing I could think of to do."

He had the radio turned to the farm station out of habit, and their whole conversation competed with news and weather: record rains, more inches since back in the late 1800's, when the first numbers were recorded. Flooding reported all over western Tennessee, Alabama, Arkansas.

They passed the trailer camp outside the Harkness Ironworks; the number of trailers there had increased, noticeably. Where were they all coming from? When did they think the Works would fire up again? He peered at children playing in the mud under the overhangs surrounding the trailers and the factory, at men huddled in groups, wearing slickers and ponchos, at women hunched over fires protected by makeshift awnings. It looked to Tom like pictures he'd seen of the Great Depression.

Past the trailers, he turned left into the Ironworks, and the other trucks followed, one, two, three, four, five, six: just like that.

Dave Birkin backed his truck into position as Tom gave him signals with his hand, and then Tom jumped behind the controls of a skip loader and raised the first shovelful from the heap of abandoned rebarred concrete and broken fire brick. He swiveled the machine, balanced the scrap, and dumped it into the bed of Birkin's truck. Birkin jumped out, his face glistening in the grey light, watching as Tom filled the bed and kept on piling until Birkin checked the wheels, saw how dangerously heavy the truck was, and signalled to Tom he had all he could take.

Tom motioned to Lewis, who started their truck and

moved it forward under the loader. He filled that truck and then the next, and Lewis stood in the rain waiting for him to finish. By noon, all seven trucks were loaded and headed south, back to do battle with the river.

· 11 ·

The idea, when Harve Stanley first suggested it, appalled Wade; it was unseemly, he thought, to drive down to the Garveys, as unseemly as it would be to hang around a sickroom waiting for someone to die. But the more he thought about the idea, the more he liked it. This rain served the Garveys right; they had it coming. He'd like to see them wriggle. Wade suggested to Stanley they take the Bronco, so there'd be no question of who was driving.

For a while on the way down the road, the two of them were silent, just the swish of the tires spraying water; Wade popped a tape of Beethoven's "Pastoral" onto the deck and scanned for the fourth movement, then thought better of it: at best it was a sick joke. But once his mind had started, it poured forth endless possibilities—The Little River Band, Credence Clearwater Revival, Jesse Winchester's "A Touch on the Rainy Side." He thought of beginning a contest with Stanley to see who could come up with the best song. Or poem! "Western wind, when wilt thou blow?" Frost's "Once By the Pacific." Then he remembered who Stanley was and kept his mouth shut.

He smiled bleakly when he thought of all the word games he and Emily had played when they drove, most of them alphabet-based—name an artist (Altdorfer, Bosch, Corot), a poet (Auden, Blake, Cummings). Now he turned on the radio instead. Rain continuing, barometer at twenty-eight-point-thirty-two, winds out of the southwest. . . .

He watched the stiff rubber of the wipers strop the windshield, sharpening themselves on the glass. He flicked on the defroster, put the back of his hand to the inside and wiped. All the hot air in the car, condensing! He cracked his window. The bits of rain that blew in felt cold on his neck.

When he saw the first crew working at the Garvey place, Wade brought the Bronco down to fifteen. "Will you look at that," he said.

Stanley craned his neck. "There's Earl Smoot," he said, "and his whole brood. That's Bill Youngdall. Are *they* wasting their time."

Wade stared at the yellow dozers lined up like rare and beautiful animals ready for a race, at the trucks and tractors, the piles of slag. "Looks like they got themselves a plan," he said. "They're trying to raise the levee."

"It's gonna get worse," Stanley said. "See that floodline?" Stanley hit his knee with an open palm, in jubilation. "Whoo-eee. They're done for. They ain't gonna make it."

As he peered through the windshield clouded with moisture, Wade felt the old antagonism with Garvey eating away at his restraint, his veneer of high-minded civility. "They might," he said. "They just might." He brought the Bronco to a skidding stop, turned, and took off for Millrock, hydroplaning.

He dropped Stanley off and drove himself home. He had a stiff Scotch, put some early Mozart on the stereo, turned it up loud, and got into the shower to take the chill out of his body. As the water pounded his back, he stood, his shoulders bent, trying to think of his own plan, a reciprocal plan. He needed that farm, and soon. If Neiswinder got more antsy the whole project could go under wraps for a year, maybe longer; Neiswinder was the key to federal funding.

Garvey going under would be the last hint of resistance; without a whimper the others would just give up and sell. And now only the river could finish off Garvey. The water had to get into those fields. And Wade could no longer count on the rain to make that happen.

He broiled himself a steak, poured another Scotch. He knew the route he'd pretty much have to take, and knew that everyone would support him in it; partly because of that, partly because it would take no more than his go-ahead, he recoiled at the whole idea. By temperament, he was not a violent man, and given his choice he would always side with finesse against brute force. But he could no longer afford to see if matters would play themselves out. He had to start controlling them.

He tried to read, tried to watch a rerun of *Bonanza*. Nothing worked. He brooded. He played solitaire. At two-twenty a.m. he called Howard Simpson, made five more calls, dressed for the weather, and left the house.

He had to wait outside the bank almost a half-hour, and he sat with the motor running, the wipers on *fast,* his headlights punching twin holes in the dark rain. He counted, slowly, methodically, out loud. By the time Simpson had pulled up behind him, and stood shivering by his door, he'd reached twelve-thousand-five-hundred-fifty-three. Simpson wore a raincoat over his pajamas, and rubbers on his feet. Wade threw open the door and stepped out into the weather. "Where the hell you been? You know how high I counted?"

"I was asleep, Joe," Simpson whined. "It's four o'clock in the morning."

"I know what time it is," Wade said. "Get your bank open." He followed Simpson up the wide concrete steps. Simpson unlocked the door, ran inside to snap on a light and disengage the alarm. The glare of white fluorescence spilled from the bank's windows onto the sidewalk and street, a surreal spot of light in the uniform darkness of Millrock.

"I need twenty thousand in hundreds," Wade said. Simpson stared at him blankly for a moment, as though those figures meant nothing to him at 4 a.m. Then he mumbled, "Okay, Joe," and turned and shuffled over to the vault. Wade paced, was on his third trip, when the sheriff's car pulled up, its light bar blinking. Wade tipped his hat to the sheriff, and to Stanley, who got out of the other side and joined them on the sidewalk in the rain.

Howard Simpson followed him, the money in a large canvas bag. "Evening, Harve, Jim Roy," Wade said.

"Joe," the sheriff said. "What can I do for you?"

"I think I've got it under control," Wade said. "Just get your men first thing in the morning and cruise down to Osborne."

"You sure you won't need me, Joe?" the sheriff asked.

"I'm sure."

"Okay." He nodded at Wade, smiled stiffly, let himself down the steps. He turned around once, as if he'd forgotten something, but the rain was slanting directly into his face, and he whipped around, opened the door, and disappeared into his cruiser. The single white bulb in the middle of the light bar came on, and the car pulled away from the curb, cleaving the long puddle. Howard Simpson was backed against the door of the bank, now dark again. He stepped forward as the sheriff drove off. "There gonna be trouble, Joe?" he asked.

Wade smiled, shook his head. "Not that I know of, Howard. Go home now. Get back to sleep. Thanks for coming out on a night like this."

Simpson slapped down the steps and into his car, pulling his raincoat tight around him. And then it was just Joe and Stanley in the dark of Millrock, four-thirty in the morning. "I wish to hell there was a diner in this town," Stanley said.

"I could use a cup of coffee."

"We can get one at my place," Wade said. "Come on. We've got an hour to kill."

· 12 ·

At dawn Wade sat behind the wheel of the Bronco while Stanley and three other Leutzcorp employees moved through the trailer camp behind the Ironworks. They'd gone around banging on the trailer doors, making a metal racket louder than the constant sound of the rain. The men came to their doors in their underwear, still asleep, ready for a fight. But Stanley had said, "Want to make some money?" and they calmed right down, went to get into their clothes.

The two flatbed trucks, in Leutzcorp colors, stood placidly in the rain, waiting to be boarded, and by six-twenty a group of thirty men huddled under their wide-brimmed hats, the only shelter. Wade watched as others joined them. Whatever differences existed among them were nothing compared to the similarities: these were men he was about to buy, and they knew it. It made them restless, eager, wanting to know what the dirtiness was. It made them bristle with violence.

At six-thirty as planned, Harve Stanley swung himself up on the back of one of the trucks, brandishing a fistful of money. He yelled above the rain, sweeping his face back and forth across the crowd as though it were a searchlight.

"A hundred dollars a man," he yelled. "How many of you want to work?"

"What you got in mind?" one of the men yelled back.

Stanley didn't answer. "A hundred dollars," he said.

"I'll take it," one of the men said, and soon the whole crowd of them had their hands in the air, the money just out of reach.

Wade got out of the Bronco, and walked toward Stanley. Their voices in the grey light of morning were as bleached and colorless as their faces, as desperate. Their eyes were narrow, their noses pinched; they looked half-starved, tight, sallow, drawn. He was horrified by them, men so down on their luck they could manufacture hatred for an invisible enemy, but he couldn't tear his eyes away, as though they knew something about being alive that he could never know. He was driven by instincts less finely honed by poverty and need.

"Load 'em up," he called, and as though they really were cattle, Stanley and the other three men began to herd them onto the trucks. They stood hunched against the rain, leaning on the slatted sides. Wade noticed one man in particular; he hung back from the others, waiting to board. He was very tall and the bright carrot hair which stuck from beneath the edges of a baseball cap was the only color in a drab scene. He was waving to a young freckle-faced woman nursing an infant, who divided her attention between the child and waving back; finally he clambered up with the other men, became one of them. Was it the freckles which made the woman remind him of Mae, years ago, before the boy was born? He walked toward her in order to see her more closely. Instinctively, she pulled the baby to her chest, turned away from him. But he'd gotten that far, and couldn't stop.

"Excuse me," he said.

The woman swung around, her eyes wide. She held the baby so tightly, it had almost disappeared. "Where are they going?" she said.

"Just down the road a couple miles," Wade said. "Some work to do on the levee."

"Will there be fighting?" she asked.

"I don't think so," Wade said. "That's a mighty young baby, isn't it?"

"Two months," the woman said. "He was born on the homeplace in Kentucky, but we had to leave when the bank foreclosed. My husband's family's farm."

"You're a ways from home," Wade said.

"Looking for work," she said.

"Well, your husband found some," Wade said. "I've got to go." He could see the men swinging the gates so the trucks could get out on the highway. He stuck out his hand, impulsively. "It's been nice talking to you. The name's Wade, Joe Wade."

The woman smiled wanly, shifted the baby, shook his hand. "Lisa Baines," she said. "This here's Jeremy."

On the trucks, the men huddled closer, shielding themselves as best they could from the rain. The woman's husband had removed his cap and waved it in the air. "Excuse me," Wade said, ending as he'd begun.

He walked hurriedly to the Bronco, let himself behind the wheel. The trucks were laboring forward now; they groaned onto the highway, turned south toward Garvey's. Wade followed, watching the men sway in the rain, like trees buffeted by wind.

· 13 ·

The rain stopped awhile after dawn; Tom didn't know exactly when. For Garvey his watch had lost most of its meaning, no longer regulated waking or sleeping, eating or drinking. As long as the rain fell, there was only the work that needed doing.

He'd stayed with the levee until long into the previous evening. He and the others had driven their dozers and tractors up the banks of the levee, pushing the piles of slag and debris heaped every twenty yards or so. While the men had done that, the women and children had shoveled sand into bags, an additional barricade to add to the levee's bulk. Hundreds were already in place.

Judy Birkin moved through the rain with hot cups of coffee, the steam a white fog like the breath issuing from their mouths in short harsh breaths. Mae thumped the top of the levee with a thick pole, checking for spots where the water was washing the dirt away. Lewis probed with a curved stick to find erosion, or hollow pockets. And everywhere Garvey turned, the bright yellows and oranges of their raingear looked like victory flags in the waning light.

Though the rain had been heavy all afternoon, the river hadn't overflowed. Almost eleven feet, it sent waves splashing at the boots of those who worked on the narrow path. Water sloshed under them, spilling in ragged sheets down the levee's side. The river's surface was white with froth from the pounding drops. They'd hooked up a diesel pump, and the overflow was being pumped back into the river. Together, the farmers and their families were holding it.

Near dusk, when Garvey saw Wade's Bronco drive slowly, turn, and speed back north toward Millrock, he didn't know what to think. What was the man up to? What was he doing sticking his nose where it didn't belong? What right did he have to come down and see what trouble the river was making, after all the trouble he'd made? But there was too much else to worry about; when Wade left, Garvey turned his attention back to the levee, the sandbags, the dozers, the water. Finally he sent all his neighbors, and Mae, Lewis, and Beth back to their kitchens and stoves and beds.

The river stayed steady at eleven feet, lapping at his boots, gently spilling over the edge. He walked the levee as though his presence alone could keep the water down. He remembered the story of the Dutch boy who saved Holland, wondered for how many years and in how many countries men had waged a battle with water. Around midnight, he thought, the invisible crux between one day and another, he finally gave up and plodded to the house. Maybe while he slept the levee would go. There wasn't anything he could do.

He was up before the first light, and soon the trucks and cars of his neighbors arrived again, back for another day. It steeled his resolve, buttressed his hope.

They'd all come. Rod Tessley and Dave Birkin, Earl Smoot, Youngdall, their families. And neighbors Tom hardly knew: people coming to help, knowing how little they could actually do. The only good news they could share with one another was simple: the river had stayed steady at eleven feet all night. Their work had meant something; the levee had held.

Tom had jumped down from the slick seat of his dozer, had taken a moment to stand with Rod Tessley, watching the sandbags fill. At first, he heard it, as though talk in a movie theatre had stopped when the lights began to dim.

or the ceaseless wind which swept the land in November had veered toward a different compass point. And then he felt it, the soft pounding his body had taken for days released into the kindness of air. Tom raised his hands, palms flat, not believing what he felt. He looked at Tessley and Tessley's face was turned up toward the sky, not believing it either. "It stopped," Tessley said. "My God."

"The rain's stopped," Garvey yelled, looking for Mae. He found her standing in mud to his left, and she floundered through it toward him, just as he made his way toward her. She hugged him tight, and he kissed her cheek, and all up and down the levee people were yelling, throwing their hats into the air, grabbing their children, their husbands and wives.

When Tom heard the shouting cease, a stony silence taking its place, he turned toward the road. A convoy of trucks, with Joe Wade's Bronco in the lead, pulled off and moved toward the levee. Garvey turned to his son, who had run up as soon as the trucks appeared.

"Dad?" Lewis said.

"Go get my shotgun," Garvey said. "Hurry." He watched as Lewis, without another word, sprinted toward the house, splashing across the field. The trucks pulled up some distance from the levee. Harve Stanley jumped from the back of one of the trucks and opened the tailgate holding the men in. They poured down, carrying picks and shovels, and huddled together, staring from under their hats at Garvey, Tessley, Birkin, all of them moving together now into a solid group. Wade's men looked uncertain, mean. Wade, who hadn't left the safety of his Bronco, drove slowly behind them, yelling at them from his open window. Birkin, Smoot, Youngdall walked to the dozers, started them, and turned their blades toward the men.

"Go on, get over there," Harve Stanley shouted. He carried the dynamite under his poncho, tried not to notice the hard round points of the sticks in his stomach. He'd argued and argued with Wade; he didn't like this at all. Why couldn't these men they'd hired just knock the fucking thing down? Why the dynamite? But Wade had been steady and firm; there was no other way, he'd said. The dynamite was the answer; the men were just a diversion. Wade drove alongside now, as he pushed at the air with his hands, trying to turn the men away from the farmers they stared at, toward the levee itself. Wade stopped the Bronco, and Stanley moved uncertainly over. "Harve," Wade said, and smiled. "You know what to do. I'm counting on you." Stanley swallowed, tried to smile. He nodded once; he'd do it, but he didn't like it at all. "Go on, get over there," he said to the men, then slipped away from the main group, behind the Bronco, into a stand of alders near the bank. He hunched down behind a slim trunk, looked out at the two groups forming, then crawled along the riverbank out of sight.

Lewis's blood was pounding crazily in his neck where the poncho was tight. He ran as hard as he could, through the water and mud, toward the farmhouse, reciting the steps he'd take when he got there: he didn't have time to waste. The house loomed larger as he ran, and then he wrenched the kitchen door open and rattled inside, not worrying about his boots, the mud, the water. He left a slurred track on the linoleum. The door blew open and slammed against the side of the house. The L. C. Smith twelve-gauge was in the closet, next to the deer rifle, right where it should have been. He grabbed the shotgun, broke it open to make sure it was empty, clicked it shut again. He grabbed a pocketful of shells, then slipped the shotgun under his poncho and slammed back outside. His foot splashed in a puddle beyond the back door, and he was running again, full tilt, toward where the certain confrontation shaped up.

"Raise them!" Garvey yelled, and the farmers hit their hydraulics, and the bulldozer blades rose like shields. Diesel smoke curled and billowed over their heads; they pushed the gas pedals, and the motors roared in warning. Wade had stepped from the Bronco and was yelling at the men he'd brought with him. To Tom, they looked shockingly familiar; then he realized where he'd seen them. Everywhere. These were the men he'd worked with in Birmingham, the ones who were camped outside the Harkness Ironworks, the drifters who milled before the old Woolworth's in Millrock; they were the homeless, the hungry, the unemployed. They were on the cover of national news magazines, and on the television screens, and for all their familiarity, they were totally anonymous. They stood uncertainly, edging toward the levee as Wade yelled at them to move.

When he heard his son's voice, coming closer, he turned and Lewis ran up through the mud and water. He was breathing hard, gasping, the air rasping in this throat. But he thrust the shotgun into Tom's hands and then fumbled in his poncho, brought out a fistful of shotgun shells and put them into his father's pocket. Tom grinned at the boy.

"Wade," he yelled. Joe Wade turned from the men he was screaming at and faced Tom. In short fast motions, so Wade could watch, Tom broke open the shotgun, put a shell in each barrel, and slammed the breech shut. "I'll give you ten to get off my land," he yelled. "I'm not fooling."

The motors of the dozers rumbled low, barely enough to keep the gas flowing. The entire tableau was frozen, everyone waiting to see what would happen next. It was Wade's move. He cupped his hands around his mouth and shouted. "I don't want any violence," he said. "I've been trying to deal peacefully with you morons all summer. I'll give you all one last chance. Ten thousand more to each of you. You can harvest your crops. I'll give you what you contracted for. But then you gotta clear out." No one moved. "I want your answers now," Wade shouted.

Garvey looked at Rod Tessley standing with his wife and children, waiting to see who would cave in first. It was a good offer, the best they could have ever expected, and he knew some of them were tired of this life. Even Mae, he knew, was ready to go. She held his arm, pressed hard. No one moved. No one said a word. They all stood staring at Wade as though he were something they'd never seen before, the aftermath of a terrible accident.

"Okay, boys," Wade said to the men who milled behind him. "Tear it down." They moved in a mass and began to climb the levee. No one else stirred, the farmers standing still; Garvey followed the drifters' path with the shotgun. "Get off that levee!" he shouted. One of them pulled a sandbag away from the top and the river started to spill. "That's your last move," Garvey yelled. "Put it back." The man grabbed another sandbag, and Garvey fired. A blast of buckshot whooshed through the alders over their heads. The crowd of men ducked, and some began to retreat.

"You don't get a nickel if you back away," Wade shouted. "He's not going to shoot anybody."

That did it: in answer, Tom Garvey whirled, taking in man after man with the swivel of the shotgun barrel, and fired the second shell. The blast hit the Bronco's radiator and blew it apart. A tire went, too, and the Bronco settled in the mud. All around the vehicle men dove for cover, though Wade, more steady than Garvey had thought, stayed where he was. "I said tear it down," Wade said.

The men looked uncertainly at one another, and one of them yelled, "Let's go!" He ran toward the levee and started to climb, reaching up to pull at the sandbags to widen the small breach the other man had made. Garvey reloaded the shotgun carefully, one barrel, two. He was breathing steadily, quietly, he had reached that point of solid peace, ready to act extraordinarily as though it were nothing strange at all. He raised the shotgun again, settled it against his shoulder, sighted on the man at the top of the levee. There was a calmness to his voice, dead level, when he said, "Get down."

Everything stopped. Wade said, "Mae, don't let him," but Tom knew that nothing his wife said, his children said or thought, nothing at all could dissuade him. All his life had been churning toward this moment. If he needed to shoot another man to show how strongly he believed in what was his, he would, without another moment's thought. Around him everyone waited, and then the man at the top of the levee turned and faced Tom Garvey.

Though the face was far away, Tom knew immediately who it was: that pinched and hurtful face, that carroty hair, that look of defiant disregard. He was instantly back in the factory, listening to Baines talk about his wife, the baby on the way, the death of his father, the bank's position on the farm. He was walking again down the gauntlet, spit dripping from his cheek. Still, he didn't lower the shotgun.

His voice was tired when he spoke. "Baines, you sonofabitch. I damn near killed you."

"They took my farm," Baines yelled, as though that explained why he stood there, one hand on a sandbag.

"I don't want to shoot you but I will," Garvey said. "You're on the wrong side. We've been on the wrong side before. Tell them." He motioned with the barrel toward the other drifters. Baines didn't move. He stood where he was, not speaking, not knowing what to do.

"Why are you doing his dirty work?" Garvey yelled.

Baines stood now, relinquishing the sandbag. "I'm hungry," he yelled. "My wife's hungry."

"We're all hungry," another drifter shouted.

"Go on, goddammit. Do what I'm paying you for," Wade screamed. He grabbed two of the men near him and flung them toward the levee; they stumbled and fell in the mud.

Garvey pointed the barrel of the gun directly at Wade. "He says we don't count," Garvey yelled. "We take care of the land and he wants to drown it. He wants to cover all this with a lake. Don't let him. All I've got is what's growing in these fields."

Tom saw the man running down the path on top of the levee before he knew who he was, or what he was doing. The figure seemed to materialize out of nowhere, out of the ground fog itself, moving as fast as it could. The explosion happened a second or two later, first the noise and then the tongue of flame leaping into the air, splitting the fog. The levee burst open, sandbags, firebrick, concrete, dirtclods flying into the air, and as the smoke cleared Garvey stared in disbelief as the river poured through the indentation in the levee's edge, down into the fields.

The man who'd come running, who dove to the ground as the dynamite blew, stood now: Harve Stanley put his hands on his hips and looked directly at Garvey, as though he'd been waiting ever since he'd been decked for this moment. But Garvey had other things to attend to before that score was settled. He threw down the shotgun and rushed toward the bank, stooping as he ran, grabbing two sandbags and jerking them to his shoulders. He stumbled under their load toward the flood.

He turned, and Mae was beside him, dragging a sandbag. And then the farmers and their wives joined them. But as Tom threw the bags in front of the onrush of water, he watched the river's force tumble the bags away as fast as he laid them down. This was it, as it had been last spring: once the water opened a hole for itself, there was little you could do before its voracious appetite. He thought of flinging himself into the flood, holding on, spreading his arms wide enough to pull the edges together, knit them, cause the hole to heal itself.

And then he heard the truck. It was a Leutzcorp truck, and Baines was driving. The engine roared as Baines put it in first and floored it; it churned a few feet through the mud and spun its wheels. Almost without thinking, it seemed, the men with Baines moved behind the truck and began to push. They bent and grunted, mud spraying back, covering their faces and clothes, but with their help, the wheels stuck again and the truck stuttered forward and up the bank, the men straining behind it, until the cab with Baines behind the wheel had driven into the hole in the levee, an enormous plug.

Baines jumped from the cab and grabbed a sandbag, wedging it where water still flowed. And following his example, the other drifters joined the farmers, grabbed more sandbags and piled them into the gap.

They formed a chain. They filled more bags and passed them up the line, bag after bag filling with sand, passing on to the next set of hands and the next, and then with a suddenness much like its starting the floodwaters stopped.

The ones at the top of the chain were the first to know, and they yelled in celebration, turning to relay the news until the whole crowd was yelling, waving their arms in the air. Mae whooped and ran to hug Garvey, and as he had done with his daughter when he first came home, he spun her around in his joy. All up and down the levee the alliance of farmers and drifters went wild.

Joe Wade watched the celebration, as always amazed at how quickly the current of power could shift, how one minute things flowed one way and the next, everything moved in the other direction. This was his final defeat, he knew; they'd won this round, would get to farm another year.

He watched as Harve Stanley stumbled down the levee, tried to escape; he watched as the farmers blocked his way. They formed a circle around him, drew tighter. He saw Stanley get slapped around a bit, poked at and punched, and then they raised him up, over their heads, and flung him in the river. When they turned on him, Joe Wade was ready.

It was partly that he simply didn't believe they'd do it, and partly the air of authority he managed to exude, but they stopped before they could surround him, and he knew once again the power had shifted: they'd leave him alone now.

He turned to Tom Garvey, who stood now with his arm around Mae. They were wet and cold; Mae's lips were blue, and her freckles stood out strongly against her skin, no longer tan. They looked like they belonged together, both of them cold and smeared with mud, both of them defiant, sure of themselves, smug. He'd get them yet; not this year, maybe, but next.

"Sooner or later," he said, "there's going to be too much rain. Too much drought. Too much corn. The Russians won't want it, or we won't. And the price will go down below what you can raise it for. Then you'll be finished. You want another year, Garvey? You got it. I can wait. But I'll be back, and you know it. I'm a patient man."

He nodded his head to Mae. "Mrs. Garvey," he said. He started to turn away, and noticed a trickle of water pouring through a small hole, one last remaining leak in the pile of sandbags. It streamed down the levee, nothing much, nothing that needed attention. But it struck him as a final gesture that would save his sense of himself, and leave them with a dignified image. He was Joe Wade, and his father-in-law owned Leutzcorp, and soon this would all be his.

He bent over, picked up a sandbag and moved to the levee. No one said a word as he tossed the bag on the hole and watched with satisfaction as the trickle stopped. Then he brushed his hands on his pants, and moved away. He'd have to get to a telephone, have the Bronco towed back to Millrock. He'd be back.

· 14 ·

The end of October was glorious, dry, clear—cool crisp nights and warm wind-swept days. The fields dried up a week after the rain had stopped, and the harvest was as good as Tom had hoped. Even the combine's belches of smoke couldn't mar the cloudless skies. Tom and Mae rode the combine together as it chugged like a steamboat through waves of corn, ripping the ears from their stalks. Behind them, like ducks hoping for hand-flung treats, their children followed.

Lewis was happy: it was Saturday, his parents were smiling and hugging again, football had started, and here they were, walking across their fields, the corn piling high, money in the bank.

His sister walked beside him, staring in her odd way at the hawk drifting overhead, at the stubble the combine left. "Lewis, are we gonna be rich now?" The combine had stopped and his father and mother had let themselves down, stood against it, looking out at the corn still to be picked.

"Don't be dumb," Lewis said.

"Who's dumb?" Beth said in indignation. "I bet we get a million dollars."

That cracked Lewis up. He knew they'd get a lot of money for the corn, but a million dollars? God, he couldn't believe his sister sometimes.

He shouted to his father, "Dad, Beth thinks we're gonna get a million dollars for all this corn."

They had reached their parents now, and his mother was laughing. "What would you do if you had a million dollars?" she said to his father, and poked him in the ribs.

His father took off his John Deere cap and wiped his forehead with his forearm; he scratched the back of his head. He looked at the sky.

"What would I do?" he asked. "I'd farm it 'til it was gone. What did you think I'd say? Buy a Bronco? Take a trip to the Bahamas?"

"No," Mae said. "That's what I thought you'd say."

And then his father grinned, and his mother grinned and shook her head, and Beth started laughing, and Lewis thought that, crazy as they were, they were his family, the best people on earth.

He forged a glittering dynasty out of the South African wilderness

CAROLYN TERRY

There was something masculine and enticing about Matthew Harcourt-Bright, something which the society ladies of Victorian England found dangerously seductive. At sixteen, he had a countess for his mistress; at nineteen, he was poised to marry a duke's daughter.

But then there was scandal, and the doors of the great houses were slammed in his face. Vowing vengeance, he fled to the untamed hinterlands of South Africa, there to make his fortunes among the diamond fields. Still the women pursued him – Alida, the tragic Boer girl; Lady Anne, a member of the aristocracy that had once spurned him; Katherine, the scheming temptress who tried to win his heart.

Some he loved, others he exploited as ruthlessly as he did his diamond mines. But nothing mattered more to him than his desire for revenge on English society – until he met the one woman who would not be dominated by his wealth and charisma, who could finally free him from the torment that wracked his soul . . .

GENERAL FICTION 0 7221 84042 £2.50

In those unquiet waters lay a mystery, threatening the future of a family empire . . .

ALAN SCHOLEFIELD

Bestselling author of THE STONE FLOWER

The naked body of a young woman is washed into a rock pool on a wild stretch of African coastline. A young immigrant from Edinburgh, Kate Buchanan, is drawn inexorably into the half-mad world of her employer, Augusta Preller, a Viennese who lives in the great decaying mansion 'Saxenburg', perched above the reefs of the Indian Ocean. But what does Mrs. Preller know about the drowned girl? And what secrets from the past have contributed to her brutal murder?

At once a family saga, a love story and a riveting murder mystery, THE SEA CAVE will grip the reader from the first page to the last.

'Alan Scholefield certainly knows how to keep his plot moving . . . fascinating.' *Daily Telegraph.*

'Very good.' Marghanita Laski, *The Listener.*

Also by Alan Scholefield in Sphere Books:

THE STONE FLOWER
GREAT ELEPHANT
THE EAGLES OF MALICE

FICTION 0 7221 7732 1 £2.25

Time is running out for the savage splendour of Imperial China . . .

MANDARIN

Robert Elegant

Creator of DYNASTY and MANCHU

After the First Opium War of 1840, China is in turmoil. In the South, insurrection threatens; in Shanghai, 'barbaric' Western influence is spreading – and on all sides, the dazzling old world of the Orient faces the onslaught of the new . . .

Against the gorgeous and turbulent panorama of Imperial China under the Great Pure Dynasty of the Manchus, MANDARIN unfolds an epic adventure of revolution and romance, peopled by a glorious cast of characters – warriors and lovers, concubines and courtiers, seekers of fortune in war and in trade . . . the merchant Saul Haleevie, bidding for power alongside the great European trading houses; Fronah his daughter, torn between love and virtue; and the unscrupulous Yehenala, whose destiny would one day be inextricably linked with that of China itself.

MANDARIN magnificently recreates China at a momentous turning point in its colourful history: a sweeping, spectacular drama – vast yet intimately human – of an exotic world that was to vanish forever.

'A huge tale . . . full of romance, exoticism and danger.' *Good Housekeeping.*

FICTION/GENERAL 0 7221 3275 1 £2.95